ISLE OF THE DEAD

A DCI Bone Scottish Crime Thriller

(Book 5)

T G Reid

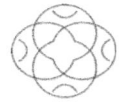

Glass Work Press

COPYRIGHT

ISLE OF THE DEAD

Published Worldwide by Glass Work Press.
This edition published in 2023.
Copyright © 2022 by TG Reid. The right of all named persons, to be identified as the author of this work, has been asserted in accordance with the Copyright, Design and Patents Act 1988. All rights reserved. No part of this book may be reproduced in any form or by any electronic or mechanical means, including information storage and retrieval systems, without written permission from the author, except for the use of brief quotations in a book review.

The story, all names, characters, and incidents portrayed in this book are fictitious. No identification with actual persons (living or deceased), places, buildings, and products is intended or should be inferred.

Editors: Emmy Ellis, Hanna Elizabeth
Cover Design: Andrew Dobell (creativeedgestudios.co.uk)
Original Photo Art: John Farnan (johnfarnan.co.uk)
Typesetting: Emmy Ellis

© tgreid.com 2023

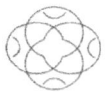

GLASS WORK PRESS

To Kath Middleton – he elucidated humbly.

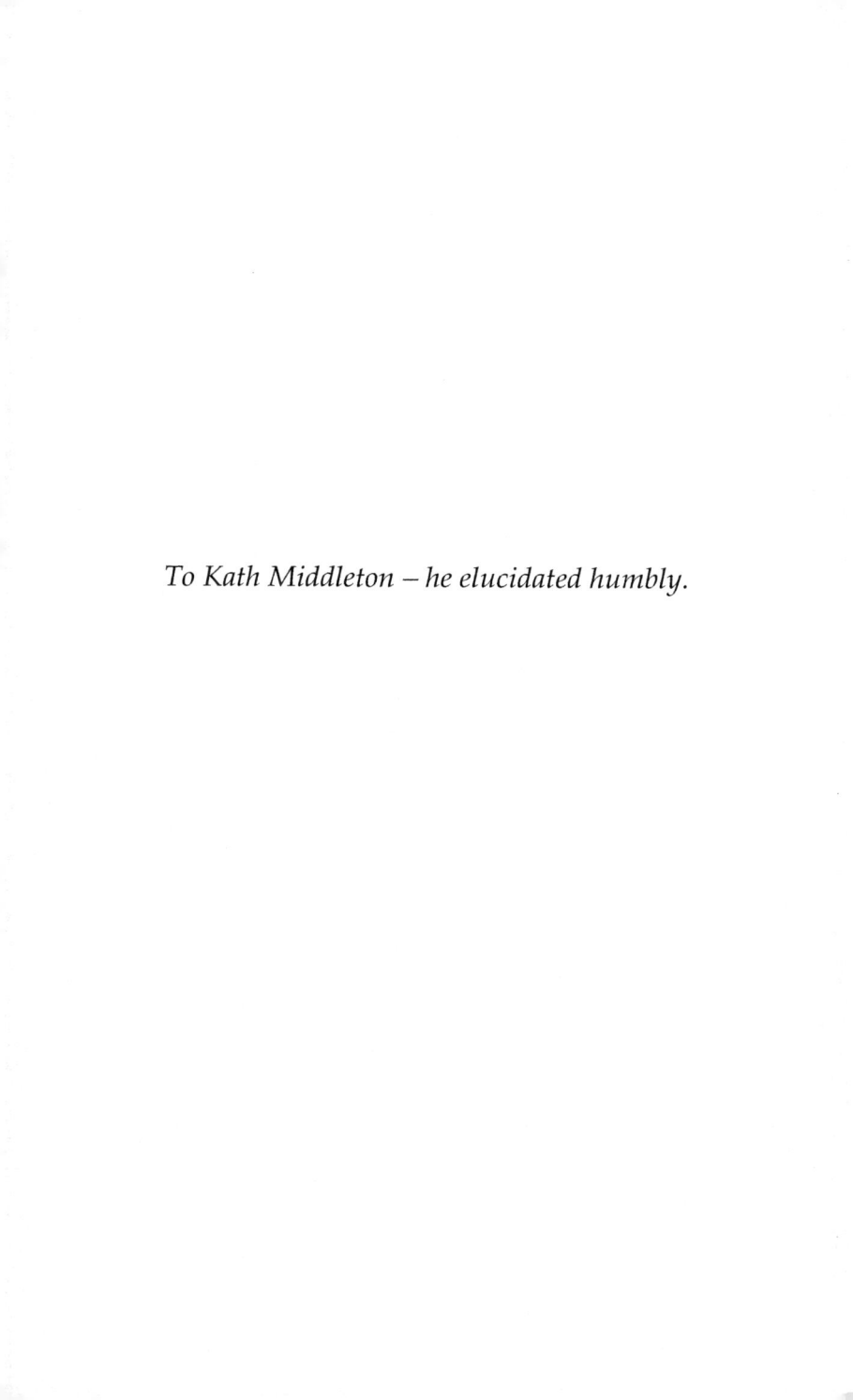

ONE

DCI Duncan Bone stopped swimming towards Loch Gillan's tiny harbour wall and glanced up at the sky. Since he'd set off from the narrow lochside beach, clouds had rolled in, obscuring a full moon, and a cold northerly wind was whipping up the freezing spring water around him. He about-turned and headed back to the shore, the conditions too dangerous to continue.

Clambering onto dry land, he snatched up his towel and cut through the trees to his cabin. By the time he reached the patio doors, the wind had picked up strength. He fumbled with numb hands to open the door, and a gust caught it. The handle wrenched from his grip, slamming against the wall; he rushed in and forced the door closed.

"Bloody hell," he muttered, dashing to the shower to warm himself up.

Forty minutes later, with his core temperature back to normal and his microwaved meal consumed, he headed out to the village hotel for a pint and to find out what was going on with the weather.

Bone entered the cosy and inviting lounge bar, and Gordon Urquhart, the hotel's cheery manager, greeted him from beside the roaring fire at the rear of the room.

"Evening, Duncan. I see you braved the storm."

"This wasn't forecast, was it?" Bone asked.

He approached the bar where a couple of life-worn locals were propped up on stools, one helping the other with a newspaper crossword spread out in front of them.

"An unexpected late delight from Lapland," the first said.

"Evening, Clem, Gaz. I see it hasn't put you off your pints," Bone replied.

The two old codgers nodded.

"Nuclear holocaust wouldn't deter those two from their Half And Halfs," Gordon interrupted and shovelled another heap of coal into the smouldering embers.

"The weather guy on the telly said we should expect significant snowfall over the next two to three days," Gaz, the older and more frail-looking of the two friends, added.

"Best place to be then." Bone rolled his eyes.

"Cheers." Clem raised his glass of whisky and downed it in one.

The manager returned to the pumps and poured Bone a pint of 80 Shilling.

"I reckon you'll be working from home tomorrow, Duncan," Urquhart said and handed Bone his drink.

"You think it's going to be that bad?" Bone sipped at the frothy top.

Urquhart shrugged. "Freak conditions at this time of year usually are."

"Cheers," Clem repeated and gulped his beer

"You take it easy, Clem. The last thing I want to be doing is hauling your drunken arse back to your house in a bloody snowstorm," Urquhart warned. "You weren't out swimming in that, were you, Duncan?"

"When I set off it was idyllic, not a cloud or wisp of wind, but I had to abandon ship, sharpish."

"Idyllic is not a word I'd use," Clem said. "Wearing my gonads for tonsils is not my idea of paradise."

"Hey, here's one for you, Duncan," Gaz piped up from his crossword. "An investigation hits cold ground with hard, painful consequences." He glanced over at Bone.

"My life?" Bone smiled.

"Disnae fit. Five letters, first one P," Gaz said, fiddling with his pencil in anticipation.

Bone rubbed at the scar on his temple for a second.

"It *is* my life, Gaz – Piles," Bone said, finally.

"Aye, right enough, cheers," Gaz said and filled in the blanks with gusto.

Just then, the door flew open and a wind-ravaged wreck of a man stumbled into the lounge bar.

"I wondered who it was that was missing," Urquhart said. "Good evening, Junior. Glad you could join us."

"Fuckin' tornado oot there, thought ah wiz gonnae end up in fuckin' Oz."

"Well, think of the hotel bar as your very own land of make-believe. Oh, wait, you usually do." The manager smiled. He leaned over the counter. "What's with the waders?" he asked, staring at Junior's clobber. "If you've been out poaching again, you could at least try and make it less obvious."

"Don't be stupit. I gave up poachin' years ago. Learnt ma lesson the hard way there." Junior shot Bone a guilty look. "I've run out of troosers, and these were all I had lyin' aboot."

"You mean you're in the scud under there?" Urquhart grimaced, and the patrons let out a collective moan.

"Naw!" Junior baulked. "I've ma boxers oan." He dropped one of the straps to reveal a pair of washed-out, greyish-blue baggy shorts, the worn fabric barely touching the sides of his pallid skeletal limbs, with the fly approaching a perilous state of openness.

More collective groans.

"And to think those legs win the annual fell race year on year." Urquhart shook his head. "Okay, put those away or it'll be bloody Narnia I'll be sending you to."

Junior yanked up his rubbers.

"How the hell do you win year after year, Junior?" Bone asked.

Junior tapped his temple and winked. "Every wee nook and cranny of they hills is in here."

It was then Bone noticed the soaked, limp roll-up still clinging to Junior's lower lip. "Do you want a light for that?" He pointed and smiled.

"Ach, Jesus Christ. That's where it went," Junior growled and plucked the drowned tobacco paper from his chin and deposited it in his equally drenched Crombie pocket.

"Anyhow, if you weren't poaching, why are you so wet?"

"I tripped on that bloody path of yours again and fell in the burn."

"Good job you're wearing those waders then," Urquhart cut in.

"The hotel path not on the fell race route then, Junior?" Clem said with a cynical smile.

"Fuck off," Junior retorted.

Gordon handed him a pint. "Behave, okay?" The bar manager gave him a long, hard stare.

Junior shrugged and took a mouthful of beer.

Bone retreated to an armchair by the fire. A gust of wind rattled the adjacent window and he peered out. Conditions outside had deteriorated significantly, and a blizzard was blowing sideways across the car park. He wiped the condensation from the pane and leaned in closer. He could just make out his old Saab parked up on the far side, its bonnet and roof already layered up with snow. "Good God, it's going nuts out there."

Urquhart came over for a look. "Yup, that's the morning delivery knackered, then. I'd better call Ross and warn him that he might have to rethink the full Scottish on his menu."

"As long as you've plenty of beer in the cellar, it can snow as long as it bloody well likes," Clem said.

"Aye, and I might no' make it back to the wife the night," Gaz added, his eyes widening.

"For God's sake, you only live across the road," Urquhart interrupted.

"You could die out there in that." Junior winked and raised his glass.

"God help us," the manager huffed and returned to cleaning a row of steaming wine glasses fresh out of the dishwasher.

Bone found his mobile and called Alice, but it went straight to answerphone.

"It's me, listen. The weather is insane up here tonight. I'm not sure I'll be able to make it back to Kilwinnoch tomorrow." The lights flickered on and off. Bone glanced up.

"Oh no. Here we go," the landlord said.

"I'll call you again in the—"

The lights went out again. The men at the bar cheered.

"Hello?" Bone said, flicking at the screen. "I've lost the signal as well."

"Looks like the whole kit and kaboodle's down," Gordon replied. "I'll go check the fuse box."

Bone peered through the window again, and the village streetlights were out. All he could see were flakes of snow fluttering onto the windowsill. The fire at his side roared and hissed as a gust blew down the chimney.

"It's coming for us," Junior proclaimed.

"What are you, a *Hammer Horror* extra or something?" Clem said. "Anyone would think you've never seen a bit of snow before."

The lights stuttered on again, and the men booed. Gordon returned from the back.

"I've switched on the emergency generator, but we're low on fuel. I don't think there's more than a few hours left, so I'm going to have to save it for the morning. You know what that means, don't you?"

"Oh no, come on, Gordon," Clem grumbled.

"I'm afraid the bar is now closed."

"But I'm only halfway through this, and worse still, Gena will still be up."

"Sorry, lads. I'm afraid you'll have to finish your drinks and bugger off, so I can turn that thing off."

Bone tried his phone again, but the signal was still down. "Right, I accept defeat. If there's no power by morning, I'll see you for whatever you have left for breakfast." He put on his coat and buttoned it up to the neck. "Does anyone need a police officer to accompany them home?"

"Like old times, eh, Junior," Clem said.

Junior pulled a face and downed his pint.

"Come on, let's all go together, and hopefully one of us will survive to tell the tale," Bone insisted.

ISLE OF THE DEAD

After a few minutes of fluster and bluster, the group ventured out into the wilds.

TWO

The storm continued to rage against the cabin walls and windows. Bone tossed and turned in bed until he couldn't stand it any longer. With a frustrating yawn, he creaked out of bed and checked his phone: 1:32 a.m. and still no signal.

Fumbling his way through the dark to the living room, he switched on the gas fire and the faint blue flame partially illuminated his surroundings. A blast of wind thumped the patio doors, and he went for a look at the chaos engulfing his home. The blizzard was still in full swing, with thick sheets of snow billowing and blasting against the cabin.

Shivering, he snatched up his dressing gown from the sofa and wrapped the belt tight around his waist. Thankfully, he'd just replaced the gas bottles outside, but if the temperature dropped any further the pipes could freeze, and then he would have to retreat to the hotel for the foreseeable.

In the kitchen, he uncorked a bottle of Macallan, poured himself a generous double, and topped it up with the remains of an open can of Irn Bru. With his customary apologetic nod to his favourite distillery for ruining their premium product, he slowly savoured his drink. Throwing open the patio curtains, he pulled a chair over to the doors and set his drink down on the floor.

"This calls for some Billie." He opened a side cabinet, turned on the light on his mobile and, searching a rack of LPs, he plucked out the album, *Lady Sings the Blues*, his go-to record in times of greatest need, which of late seemed to be most of the time. He carefully removed the record and placed it on the turntable of his beloved Dansette resting on top of the chest.

He reached for the 'on' button. "Ah, bollocks," he cursed and slumped back down in the armchair, defeated. "If you can't beat it, join it," he muttered and, reaching for his drink, he watched the snow spiral, race, and finally settle on the narrow jetty outside.

***

A loud thud woke him from a deep sleep. Coming around, it took him a few moments to work out where he was. A clunk sounded near his left side, and he spun around, kicking over the glass at his feet and spilling the remains over the new oak floor.

"Shite." He jumped up and fetched a cloth from the kitchen sink. Halfway back, he stopped. The cabin was silent. The low-pitched, ominous groan of the raging storm had vanished. He wiped up the spill and looked through the doors. The snow had stopped, and all was calm, at least for now, and a moonlit, starry sky had returned.

He unlocked the French doors, pushed at a substantial drift piled up against it, and stuck his head out. The air was cold and brittle and stole his first breath. The soft light from a resurgent full moon illuminated the line of snow-covered trees that ran alongside the cabin, the wide expanse of the loch visible beyond and the water now eerily still. He shut the door and sat back down to take in the spectacle. A glint of light caught his eye. And then a second flicker farther out towards the loch's horizon line. The faint, narrow beam flashed one way and then the other, then it disappeared again.

"What the hell is that?" He snatched up his boots and coat and shoved one of the doors further open. Clearing the snow as best he could, he carefully negotiated his way to the edge of the cabin's jetty for a less obscured view of the loch. He studied the dark edges of the horizon line again, and moments later, the juddering light reappeared, this time moving along the line, on and off, and on again. The pulse continued for a few minutes more, then disappeared completely. Bone stared into the dark, then followed the line of the moon's reflection outwards towards the area the light appeared.

"Balhuish Island," he said. "The Isle of the Dead. Who the fuck is on there tonight?" He peered into the gloom, and the faint silhouetted outline of the island appeared, like the backbone of a sea beast emerging from the deep. "Strange." Bone shivered and retreated to the warmth of his cabin.

Back in bed, he couldn't stop his mind from racing through scenarios of who might be on the island, from shipwrecked souls to drug dealers, thieves, and pirates, until finally, as he dropped into sleep, he dreamt of Celtic warriors burying treasures alongside their fallen kings.

THREE

At first light, the storm returned and the howling winds shook Bone to life again. Phone and power were still out, so he had no way of knowing if Alice had received his call. After a quick wash, he got dressed in his warmest and most waterproof clothes and headed over to the hotel. He thumped the snow from his boots on the top step of the entrance, and Ross, the hotel's chef, opened the internal door for him. The wind raced in, blowing brochures and tourist leaflets from the reception desk, and he quickly leapt in and slammed the door shut behind him.

"Did you see the four horsemen out there on your way over?" Ross asked with a wide grin.

"I thought we'd seen the end of it last night," Bone replied.

"That would have been the eye of the bastard." The chef winced. "Total nightmare this morning. We're down to our last serving of black pudding, and if you're here for a Lorne sausage, then you can swing for it."

"No Lorne sausage? It's definitely the end of the world," Bone huffed. "Hey, by the way, did you see those lights on Balhuish Island last night?"

"Lights? Are you having a laugh? The only lights I saw were the ones when I hit my bloody head on that bloody scaffolding at the Gormley's wreck of a house on my way home last night." Ross replied. "We have eggs and bacon, and some bread that will be stale tomorrow, just saying."

"You're all right, but thanks for thinking of me." Bone winked.

"In a few days, it'll be survival of the fittest, so that could be a bad decision," Ross joked.

"Aye, I'm thinking you should feed Junior. The last thing we need is to make him hungry and even more miserable."

They laughed, and Ross returned to his kitchen. Bone removed his boots, the snow now two puddles at his feet, and continued to the lounge. The public bar was deserted.

"Gordon, hullo?" Bone called. No reply. He leaned over the counter and squinted through the door to the office. "Gordon?"

Sidling around the bar, he went in search of the manager. The pokey office under the rear stairway was also empty, but a VHF radio transmitter resting on the desk hissed loudly. He cut back along the corridor to the entrance lobby. Fiona, the young receptionist, had just arrived and was shaking the last of the snow from her hair.

"You haven't seen Gordon, have you?" Bone asked.

"It's taken me nearly half an hour to get from my house to the hotel," Fiona complained. "It's totally horrendous out there." She hung up her coat on the stand next to the entrance.

A loud clatter sounded, and Bone turned. Doreen, the hotel's die-hard cleaner, was on the stairs, battling to bring an ancient vacuum cleaner under control. A couple were waiting patiently to pass.

"Morning." Bone nodded.

"What's good about it?" Doreen replied, the vacuum hose thrashing around like an angry anaconda.

The couple leaned back in unison to avoid contact.

"No heating, no telly, and my Pilates class has been cancelled."

"I'm sure Gordon would let you sit in the lounge to keep warm and watch TV after your shift, Mrs Docherty."

"Are you deliberately trying to wind me up?" Mrs Docherty grumbled.

The couple looked on, transfixed by the performance before them.

"Do you want a hand with that?" Bone asked, changing the topic.

"Oh no, I'm fine. I've always fancied a few months on the stroke ward." She rolled her eyes.

Bone rushed over to help her get the ancient contraption under control.

"Good morning," the man behind said with an upbeat American twang, finally stepping down into the lobby. "I'm Carl Ellis, and this is my wife, Clarisse. We arrived last night, and by gosh, we weren't expecting this."

"None of us were," Bone replied. "Are you from the States?"

"Ah, that obvious, huh?" Mr Ellis said, his grin threatening to spill off either side of his face. "Yup, Key West, Florida. So, as you can imagine, we are simply flabbergasted by the sight of all that wonderful snow."

"You won't be saying that when we run out of toilet paper," Doreen muttered.

"Your Highlands are so beautiful," Clarisse added with a friendly smile.

"Yes, it's like *The Shining* out there this morning," Bone teased.

The couple's grins narrowed, and their brows dropped.

"Duncan?" Urquhart appeared from the dining room.

"Just the man I want to see," Bone said. He turned back to the befuddled couple. "Have a great holiday, and I hope you manage to get out of here before—"

"This way, Duncan," Urquhart urged.

Bone followed the manager to his office.

"Please don't take the piss out of my guests, Duncan."

"Sorry, couldn't resist."

"Well, resist, if you don't mind. Our bookings are way down, and the last thing we need is a review comparing the hotel to a bloody horror film."

"Might not be so bad." Bone stifled a laugh. "Sorry, I must be going stir-crazy already. I promise I'll behave."

"You wanted me for something?"

"Aye, did you see those lights last night?"

"Lights? Are you trying to be ironic or something? I was down in the basement all bloody night repairing the generator. She packed up shortly after you left."

"The power's on now, so I'm assuming you've fixed it?"

"Aye, for now, but it could go at any minute, and if that happens again, we are well and truly fucked, for want of a better expression."

"I'd say 'well and truly fucked' covers it. I was hoping the freak weather show would have been over by now."

"Two to three days, they're talking. I mean, it's April, for God's sake. Aff its bloody heid." Urquhart looked up. "Anyways, what are you on about again?"

"I couldn't sleep for the wind knocking seven bells out of the cabin. At one point, I thought the cabin was heading for the loch, with me in it. I was up getting an Irn Bru about one, when I spotted lights on Balhuish Island."

"Ah, we can't see the island from here. The point obscures the view."

"Shit, of course."

"It was stupid wild out there last night. Only a nutjob would take a boat out in that."

"There's nobody living on the island, is there?"

"Aside from Robinson Crusoe and Man Friday, you mean?" Urquhart joked.

"Like travellers or homeless, or even walkers camping on it?"

"If anyone was out camping last night, I don't think they'll have anywhere to sleep tonight. Have you been on that island? It's always blowing a gale over there, even in a heat wave, and it's bloody weird with all those Celtic graves. Gives me the willies."

"That's what I mean. Maybe some dafties went out there on a dare and they got caught in the storm. It blew in pretty sharpish." The radio clicked and hissed again. "That's working then?"

"Aye, I keep that on for mountain rescue or medical emergencies, or in case a guest or villager needs urgent medical attention."

"What about the doc?" Bone asked. "He lives nearby, doesn't he?

"Are you serious? He's fine for grazed shins or mouth ulcers, but anything beyond that and we're talking certain death."

"You've not had any word of lost climbers or boats, anyone missing?"

"Nothing, no. I spoke to Charlie at the Mountain Rescue Centre earlier to check if any roads were passable."

"And?" Bone pressed.

"They're stuck up there as well. So short answer, no, not until a snow plough can make it through, and judging by current conditions, that could be some time yet."

"It's just a bit worrying, you know?"

"Are you sure you weren't seeing things? I mean, it was blowing a hoolie, and visibility was down to a few feet."

"No, it was in that five minutes of calm or whatever it was. The moon came out, and I had a clear view of the island. There were definitely people wandering about on it."

"No clue." Urquhart shrugged.

"Do you think any of the fishermen or boat owners might take me over there?"

"You're like a dog with a bone, if you pardon the expression."

"Occupational hazard. My professional gut is telling me something isn't right."

"I could radio inshore rescue and see if they'd send their vessel over?"

"I don't want to waste anyone's time here unnecessarily, and it's a long haul for them. Aren't they based up at the mouth, near Drumgoil?"

"Aye, and they're probably stranded as well." Urquhart scratched his head. "You could try Lonnie Kilpatrick. He owns a couple of boats and might be the only one willing to risk life and limb. But are you sure about this? It sounds like a harebrained hiding to nothing, and it's bloody treacherous out there. I don't want it on my conscience if you two end up at the bottom of the loch."

"I have an itch that needs scratching, Gordon. And I'm already bored off my face."

Urquhart rolled his eyes. "I'm sure I have a cream for that somewhere. Right, okay, you win, but if you're not back by lunchtime, I'm having your ration of bacon."

"Cheers," Bone said and returned to the foyer to retrieve his boots.

FOUR

Lonnie Kilpatrick was possibly the hairiest human being Bone had ever met. The Chewbacca lookalike greeted him at the door with a hefty handshake that nearly dislocated his shoulder.

"Morning, Lonnie. Have you got a minute?"

"Aye, no bother, come away in out the cold," said Kilpatrick, rubbing at the forest of thick black fur circumnavigating his head.

On their way down a narrow, dim-lit corridor, Kilpatrick leaned at an angle to fit his enormous frame between the walls on either side.

"You need a bigger house, Lonnie."

"I need a bigger everything, except myself." He stopped and smiled; a flash of white teeth emerging from the fur momentarily. "I'd offer you a coffee, but the bloody electrics are out and dafty here doesn't have a gas cooker."

"No bother, Lonnie," Bone replied when they reached Kilpatrick's inconceivably small galley kitchen. "I wanted to ask you if you could take me out to Balhuish Island."

"When all this blows away, you mean?" Lonnie rummaged in one of the kitchen drawers and removed a large butcher's knife.

Bone stepped back. "No, I was thinking—"

Lonnie produced a dead rabbit from a hessian sack and, laying it out on the kitchen table, he raised the butcher's knife and brought the blade down with considerable force on the rabbit's neck. Its head shot off the side of the table and skittered across the kitchen floor, leaving a bloody trail in its wake.

"Sorry, don't mind me. This has to be eaten today, so I thought I'd start prepping the casserole."

"Aye, fine, whatever." Bone leaned over to check where the rabbit's severed head had gone. "I thought you said you didn't have any power?"

"Ah, trying to catch me out, I see, Inspector Bone." Kilpatrick brandished the butcher's knife playfully. "I'm going to stick him on the fire next door. Slow cook for three hours. You're more than welcome to join me later."

"That's very kind, but I have stuff that needs to be eaten as well. You know, before it goes off." Bone squinted under the table again.

"So, when are you thinking of going fishing? I can book you in now," Lonnie said. He leaned over, and with a groan, picked up the skull and tossed it in the bin by the door, the skull clattering against the metal side.

"Not fishing. I want to go and check something out on the island. I was thinking today... Well, now, if that's possible?"

Kilpatrick put the knife down. "In this?"

"Yes, I know it's nuts out there but—"

"I'm not sure that's such a great idea."

"Gordon said you might be up for it, but I totally understand if you'd rather not."

Kilpatrick stared at Bone for a moment. "All right, aye. Let's go."

"What, now?"

"No time like the present to die." Kilpatrick sneered.

"Okay, right. What about your casserole?"

"Ach, that can wait. Is it like a police thing?"

"I saw some lights on the island last night and I'm worried people might be stuck out there."

"Oh Jesus, bet they're having a whale of a time." Kilpatrick grabbed his coat and boots from the cupboard. "So am I officially a detective as well, then?"

"Let's start with getting there and back in one piece." Bone was beginning to regret asking him.

As they trudged with difficulty through the driving snow towards the harbourside, Bone peered at the line of boats getting battered about in the wind and hoped that Kilpatrick would carry on past the coffin-sized death traps to the bigger vessels farther along. Unfortunately, he stopped at one of the smallest. A tiny wooden effort, barely big enough to be called a dinghy. A short mast at the front sported a pirate flag that flapped wildly in the wind.

"Here she is." Kilpatrick cleared the snow from around the ladder down to the boat.

"Seriously?" Bone said, spotting its name in faded letters along its paint-flaked hull. "*Sunshine Supernova*? It doesn't even have a bloody cabin."

"Ach, we'll be fine. I have a bigger boat, but I don't want to risk running her aground in this weather. Come on." Kilpatrick clambered down and jumped in.

The boat pitched alarmingly to the side. Bone glanced back at the hotel on the far side of the harbour, the warm glow of its sign above the entrance beckoning him to return to safety. Shaking his head, he followed Kilpatrick onto the dinghy and, tripping over the mooring, he snatched at the mast to avoid tumbling over the other side.

"Right, off we go," Lonnie said enthusiastically, and started up the engine. A tiny chimney at the back of the boat rattled, and a plume of thick, black, sooty smoke coughed out of the top.

"Life jacket?" Bone asked.

"No point in this weather," Kilpatrick replied. "If we sink, we sink."

Bone grimaced, trying to understand the boatman's logic.

"But there's a couple in the house. I could go back for them if you want."

Bone held up his hand. "Never mind. Let's just get this nightmare over with."

"We've got this, though." Kilpatrick pulled out a box from under a bench. "VHF radio. Lucky for you, I replaced the batteries last week, and I'm sure inshore rescue will be more than delighted to come out in this weather and rescue us."

"Hopefully not." Bone grimaced.

"Can you untie us?" Kilpatrick called out.

Reluctantly, Bone unwound the rope, and the boat set off. When they cleared the jetty, the storm hit the side of the boat, and it rocked violently, the top of the hull almost touching the waves. Bone grabbed the mast again and hung on for dear life.

"It'll settle down once we're out a bit," Kilpatrick promised.

But Bone was unconvinced. The boat puffed and spluttered slowly along the side of the jetty and out into the loch, the blizzard pummelling Bone's face and hands with ice-cold bullets of frozen snow.

Kilpatrick steered close to the shore, and the dark, ominous mountains loomed over them like giants, threatening to crush them. There was a sudden grinding noise.

"Oops," Kilpatrick said. "I'm a wee bit too close to the shore." He steered the boat further into the loch. "Wouldn't want to sink her without the life jackets." He grinned and shook some of the accumulating snow from his hair and beard.

"No, please don't!" Bone cried back.

As they headed further into the loch, the wind intensified, and icy spray lashed across the bow.

"There!" Kilpatrick pointed ahead. Through the gloom, the dark outline of Balhuish Island emerged. "Not far now."

The boat puffed, creaked, and moaned its way across the loch, almost capsizing a couple of times, and as it approached the island, Kilpatrick turned the bow into the wind and headed away from the shore.

"Where are you going?" Bone hollered.

"It's too dangerous to land here. I'll bring her in on the other side."

"Oh, Jesus," Bone complained and grabbed hold of anything he could, in readiness for even stronger winds.

They circled the tiny island, sailing close to a cliff edge that gave way to a line of trees and then a narrow strip of beach. A break in the trees revealed the silhouettes of gravestones and Celtic crosses peeking out above a white blanket of snow. At last, Kilpatrick steered for the shore and towards a tiny jetty barely visible through the relentless blizzard.

The boat chugged up to the jetty, and a gust of wind rammed it against the side with force.

Kilpatrick stumbled to the front. He climbed onto the jetty and tied up the boat.

"We can't stay for long. This wind'll take her apart," he said.

Bone clambered after him. "A quick look, okay?"

They set off along the jetty, careful not to slip over the side, and jumped down onto the rocky beach.

"Where do you want to go first?" Kilpatrick asked.

"The lights were in the middle and then over on the other side, I think." Bone tightened the straps on his hood.

"If I remember right, there's a path up to the graves through the trees over there."

"Is that the only landing spot on the island?" Bone followed Kilpatrick onto the narrow pathway.

"There's another jetty on the far side, but in this weather, we really would be chancing our luck."

Climbing a set of wooden steps, they carried on to the line of trees. The wind suddenly dropped, and the blizzard ceased. They stopped for a moment.

Bone pulled at his hood and wiped the snow from his face. "Bloody hell, that's a relief."

The tall conifers around them creaked and hissed as the storm raged far overhead. There was a sudden loud crack, and a broken branch tumbled down through the thick overgrowth, landing with a crash behind them.

"Jesus!" Kilpatrick cried out in fright, stumbling backwards along the path.

"It's bloody wild up there," Bone said.

Kilpatrick stared wide-eyed into the dark of the woods beyond. "This island gives me the creeps." He shivered.

"Come on," Bone said.

Climbing a steep slope, Kilpatrick helped Bone up, and they pushed on out of the cover of trees into a clearing. The howling tempest returned, and Bone quickly flipped his hood back up. They trudged across an exposed stretch of grass, with the first of the gravestones visible at the far side. Bone bowed his head into the wind as it whipped across the exposed top of the island. Reaching the first grave—a tall Celtic cross, one side blasted with snow—he ducked down beside it for shelter.

"It's mental up here," Kilpatrick yelled, the wind obliterating his voice.

"You check that way, and I'll meet you on the other side," Bone called back.

Kilpatrick nodded and ploughed through deep drifts to the line of crosses at the farthest edge of the field. Bone continued to the centre of the graveyard, slowly weaving between lopsided granite stones and carved crosses, some lying flat and buried under the snow.

Through the murk, he spotted two gravestones leaning into each other. Something was sticking out from behind one. He glanced back but couldn't see Kilpatrick. He carried on and, circling around the first stone, he staggered back in horror at the sight before him.

Two bodies were propped up against the stones, a young man and a woman. The man was wearing a morning suit, a bow tie twisted sideways around his neck, and the woman was in a wedding dress, the snow piled up in the creases and folds. They were frozen, hand in hand, their features blue and partially obscured by layers of ice and snow.

Pulling himself together, he knelt beside them. "Can you hear me?"

He nudged the man, and he toppled sideways into the snow, exposing a frozen pool of dark crimson beneath him. One side of his suit jacket was shredded, exposing bare flesh that was sliced and torn.

"Oh fuck! Lonnie, help!" Bone hollered, and he checked the man's neck for a pulse, but the flesh was frozen solid.

"Help!"

He turned to the woman, and leaning in, he searched for signs of life, but the howling wind and his numb fingers made it difficult to feel or find anything. He looked down at her body slumped over against the stone. There were multiple tears in the fabric of her dress as well, with more signs of frozen blood underneath.

Kilpatrick staggered over. "What the fuck is this?" he hollered.

Bone blew into his hands and tried again, pressing his finger against the woman's icy skin. He felt the faintest of heartbeats. He shifted position, and the slow, indistinct pulse continued.

"She's still alive!" Bone yelled. "We need to get help."

"How? On here? In this?" Kilpatrick sputtered in shock.

Bone frantically searched his coat for his phone. "No fucking signal!" He hit the 999 button and hoped the emergency line would connect. Removing his coat, he wrapped it around the woman's icy, lifeless shoulders and zipped it up.

"Is he dead?" Kilpatrick stared open-mouthed at the man lying on his side in the snow.

"This isn't connecting." Bone thumped the front with his fist. "What about yours?"

Kilpatrick continued to stare at the body.

"Lonnie!"

He frantically searched for his mobile, fumbled it out of his pocket, and dropped it in the snow.

"Come on!" Bone snapped.

"Nothing," Kilpatrick finally replied, picking it up and flicking at the screen.

"What about your VHF?"

"I think the battery should be okay, and there are flares in the supply box."

"Go!"

Kilpatrick started back.

"Wait. Give me your coat."

"What? It's fucking freezing."

"Give me your coat!" Bone ordered again.

Kilpatrick complied.

"Hurry," Bone added and tucked Lonnie's massive, quilted tent around the woman.

He checked for life again. He squeezed in closer to her and wrapped his arms around her shoulders, hugging her tight, to transfer as much warmth as he could.

He waited, counting the seconds and then the minutes. "Come on, come on," he muttered, scanning the sky for any sign of a flare. But still nothing.

"Where the hell is he?" Bone tucked the coat tighter around the woman, clambered to his feet, and rushed back across the field, through the trees, and down to the jetty.

Kilpatrick was nowhere to be seen. Bone called for him, but there was no reply. Skidding and sliding along the jetty, he checked the boat. The radio was laying upside down on the deck, smashed to pieces. Climbing aboard, he uprighted the broken mess and tried to turn it on, but it was completely destroyed.

"Lonnie!" He squinted through the snow to the beach. "Bollocks!" he cursed and, frantically searching the boat, he located a metal box containing a set of rocket and hand flares. He removed the rocket flare from its plastic bag, and turning against the wind, pulled the pin. It hissed into the sky, the bright-yellow light illuminating the driving snow. He fired the second and then set off a hand flare that belched out thick, red smoke.

A faint cry had him turning. Peering through the murk, he spotted a figure, slumped over on the far side of the shore by a cluster of rocks.

"Lonnie!" he hollered.

Kilpatrick half-raised his arm.

Clambering back onto the jetty, Bone rushed along the beach. "What happened?"

"Bastard clocked me." Kilpatrick rubbed the back of his head.

"Are you okay?"

"Sore head, but I'll be fine. Get the bastard." Kilpatrick moaned. "That way." He pointed along the beach.

"Help will be here soon now," Bone said and clambered over the rocks, trying not to tumble into the angry water hissing and gurgling beneath and around his feet.

He glanced back at Kilpatrick, who gestured to keep going. Bone stumbled on. He reached a dead end where the loch met the sheer side of a cliff. He cleared snow and spray from his eyes and spotted a set of narrow steps cut into the rockface. Clambering up onto a boulder, he leapt over a deep pool and skidded onto the first step, frantically snatching at an overhanging tree.

He continued up the steps, and when he reached the top, the wind was so strong it almost blew him over the edge. Ahead, there were two paths, one heading directly over the cliff, and the other into the trees beyond. He searched for footprints in the snow, but the covering was pristine. He moved towards the precipice, and kneeling, he leaned over.

The waves below roared and pounded against the smooth granite, but there was no sign of life or death. He about-turned and followed the path into the woods. But a few steps in, he was already lost in the dense, dark tangle of overgrowth. He fought on, pushing, pulling, unsnagging and breaking branches to clear a way through. A huge drift of snow tumbled down through the canopy onto the forest floor, crashing directly in front of him. Battling on, he finally emerged on the opposite side of the clearing.

There was a line of boot prints running across the snow towards the dead and dying couple. He dashed across, scanning left and right, readying himself for a fight, but halfway, the trail stopped. He scoured the pristine white covering around him.

Did they turn back?

With another glance at the woods behind him, he carried on to the victims. Kilpatrick's coat was lying in a bundle by her side, smothered in snowfall.

"What is going on?" Bone howled into the wind, and he checked her vitals again. "Hang in there. Don't fucking die on me."

With a second frantic look around the graveyard, he shook the snow from Lonnie's coat and, squeezing in next to her, wrapped layers around them both, praying his body heat might keep her alive until the rescue team arrived. He shivered and hunkered down, his senses on high alert for the first signs of hypothermia.

FIVE

"Inspector Bone," a voice shook him from semi-consciousness.

Bone opened his eyes. Bright white light hit the backs of his retinas, and he winced. The blizzard had stopped, and the sun's rays were streaming through the line of trees surrounding the graves.

"Are you all right?" the voice continued.

Bone refocused on the silhouette looming over him. He squinted again, and a figure in a lurid yellow Puffa jacket and matching hat emerged from his mental fog.

"Are you injured?" The bearded man's features formed.

"Yeah, I mean no." Bone shook his head. Then he remembered and turned. "Is she still alive?"

"So no injuries?" the man asked.

"No, just the cold. I need to warm up. But she's in a bad way, and the other one is already gone."

"Yes, let's get you up and out of the way." The man helped Bone disentangle himself from Kilpatrick's coat and get to his feet.

"I think you might be stage one hypothermic. Put this on." The man guided Bone's arms into a heated jacket. "Drink this, and then we'll get you back to shore." He unscrewed a flask and poured a cupful of steaming hot chocolate.

"I'm a wild swimmer, so I know what this is. I'm not shivering. I'll be all right once I move and get my core temperature back up."

Two members of the rescue crew pushed past him. One checked the deceased, now almost entirely lost in a small drift of snow, while the other attended to the woman.

Bone looked up. "The guy who did this might still be on the island."

"Drink, please," the man insisted.

Bone took the cup. "Okay, but I'm telling you. You need to search the island. See the prints over there? And someone was back at these two when I was down at Lonnie's boat raising the alarm. How many of you are there?"

The man glanced over the field. "I don't think anyone else is here, Inspector. Are you sure those aren't yours or Lonnie's footprints? You're probably disorientated."

"No, I'm not bloody disorientated." Bone stopped. "Hold on, who are you, and how do you know who I am?"

"Danny Matheson, inshore rescue. We radioed the hotel on our way here. Gordon told me you and Lonnie had set off this morning, and I can't imagine there would be many tourists or pleasure boats out in this nightmare."

"Did you see Lonnie by the jetty? He's been attacked."

"Yes, one of our paramedics is looking after him back at our boat."

"That's why you need to search the island. We're wasting time talking." Bone glanced back at the paramedics who had moved the woman onto a stretcher and were administering a line into her arm. "Is she going to make it?"

"We're waiting for the rescue helicopter to arrive and airlift her out, if this break in the weather holds. We'll take you back to the cottage hospital in Balhuish to make sure you're okay."

"Right, so I need some of your people to help me search the island before the bastard escapes. Do you have any police officers in your crew?"

"Aye, sir, Special Constable Matheson."

"Is he around?"

"You're looking at him."

"I thought you were inshore rescue?"

"I am, as well as occasional shifts at the Balhuish hotel bar. We tend to double up on jobs round here." He smiled.

"Right, I need you to check the area of woods on the far side of the graveyard."

"I really think you should be out of this cold and—"

"Just do as I say." Bone glanced up at the surprised constable. "I mean, please. See, I'm drinking." He smiled and took a couple of sips from the cup.

"Well, if the person who did this is still here, and those are his tracks, the gap in the trees just beyond is a shortcut down to the second jetty on the other side of the island."

"What are we waiting for, then?" Bone said.

Constable Matheson turned to the paramedics. "Is it okay to leave you?"

One of the crew members nodded.

Matheson whistled to a fourth member who was carrying a backpack about the same size as her. "Wait with the medics and give them a hand if they need it."

"Okay," the out-of-breath woman puffed.

Matheson helped her remove the hefty equipment from her back, and she sighed with relief.

"Right, let's go. This way."

"Isn't that in the opposite direction?" Bone queried.

"I know this island well, and there are shortcuts all over the place. Come on."

Bone took a final slurp of his drink and handed the cup to the female crew member.

"Thanks. Do you want me to wash it as well?" She shirked.

"Can you take some photos of the crime scene before they move them?" Bone asked the rescue officer.

"Aye." The woman nodded and fished her phone out of her pocket.

Bone followed the young constable across the graveyard and back into the trees. A well-worn track in the woods made the going easier than before.

"Is this the tourist route you're taking me?" Bone asked.

"Sheep," Matheson replied.

"What? Where?"

"The laird ships them over three times a year to keep the overgrowth down."

In under a minute, they emerged out the other side, with panoramic views of the loch reaching all the way from Balhuish Harbour in the mid-distance, to the mouth on the horizon.

"Down here," Matheson pointed to another set of steep steps.

Bone puffed. "Not again."

They descended slowly, careful not to slip on the snow-smothered surface.

"You think they'd install handrails in these bloody things." Bone slid off a step and was saved by Matheson's back. "Sorry."

Finally at the bottom, Matheson edged along the side of the cliff.

"Why the hell did they make it so difficult to reach?" Bone complained again.

"Probably a smuggler's thing or Bonnie Prince Charlie hiding from the English. You know he was supposed to have taken sanctuary here." He glanced over at Bone. "Are you okay, sir?"

"It's this bloody heated jacket. I'm on fire under here. How long do the heat packs last?"

Matheson stifled a grin. "I thought you were looking a little flush-faced." He choked out a guffaw on the last syllable. "Sorry, sir. It's a nerves thing. I get like this when there's a lot of stress around."

"Aye, it is horrific." Bone unzipped the jacket and wafted the sides back and forth. "And then there's me going from hypothermic to heat stroke in under ten minutes."

They both laughed, and it seemed to release the tension between them.

The pair squeezed around an outcrop of rock.

"Over there!" Matheson pointed at a twelve-foot, cream-coloured motorboat tied up to a rickety wooden jetty jutting out into the loch.

Matheson stepped up onto the half-rotten, creaking construction, teetering precariously above the choppy waters. Bone followed behind.

"I'm sure this belongs to the laird's estate," Matheson said, and kneeling, he grabbed the side of the vessel and attempted to control its movement as it bobbed around in the swell.

"Yup, thought so. See the nameplate here?" Matheson scraped the frozen snow from a brass plate screwed onto the stern. "Property of Loch Gillan Estate. I think he has a few of these that come with his holiday lodges he built a couple of years or so ago." He got up and walked to the end of the pier. "If you lean out here, you can just about see them on the mainland."

Bone carefully negotiated the slippery decking and stuck his head out.

"I've got you," Matheson grabbed a hold of Bone's coat.

Bone pushed out further.

"There was a lot of local opposition as they cleared a vast swathe of forest from the lochside to make way for them."

"It's some scar, isn't it?" Bone said. "I hope my cabin didn't cause similar anger."

"Yours has been there for years, in one form or other, so no, but these were a whole different can of piranhas, and many of the locals still haven't forgiven him."

They returned to the boat. Matheson climbed aboard and held up two life jackets, discarded on the deck.

"Anything else?" Bone asked.

Matheson checked under the narrow benches running along the length of the vessel. "Nope. Hold on." He crouched and retrieved a champagne glass.

"How has that survived the storms?" Bone asked.

Matheson tapped the side. "Plastic."

From his rucksack, Bone removed an evidence bag.

Matheson climbed back onto the jetty and dropped the glass in. "The lodges have proved very popular for romantic getaways."

"Unlucky honeymooners?"

"Well, yes."

"So, post-wedding romantic boat trip? Photo opportunities?" Bone pondered. He knelt by the mooring on the opposite side.

"Does that look fresh to you?" He picked at a damaged section of wood on one of the planks.

"Something's battered into it?" Matheson replied.

"Maybe the honeymooners tried to moor on this side first, but it was too rough?"

"It's a fibreglass boat. Whatever did that would punch a hole in the side of this." He checked the hull. "No, there's no sign. To me, that looks more like the damage a wooden boat makes."

Bone removed his phone and snapped a couple of pictures. "But if our attacker escaped on this boat, wouldn't you guys have seen it on your way here?"

"Not necessarily. Visibility was shocking, and we approached from the other side. If you sailed round the point there, you could land it on the mainland. I'll show you."

They returned to the shore and continued on the path around the outcrop.

"See?" Matheson said, pointing to the mainland a few hundred yards away.

"God, I had no idea it was so close. So, is there somewhere to land over there?"

"In theory, aye, there's another half-wrecked jetty like this one, but that wee strait may look narrow and a quick hop across, but the currents are bloody treacherous, especially in this weather. All sorts of death traps lurking under that dark water, plus there's no road out, just a farm track, and like this, I'd say it's impassable. Only a fool would try it."

"Or a desperate killer on the run, and if the bastard made it across, then they won't have gone too far."

"I'm more inclined to think it's likely the attacker headed further along the coast where it's safer to land, assuming we now believe he has actually left the isle?" Matheson squinted at Bone.

"Who the hell knows? I saw a light on the island about 1:00 this morning. The attacker might have been on the same boat, and the damage to the jetty is something else. Then once they'd done the deed, the blizzard took hold."

"So either they're still stranded on the isle or escaped in a second boat?"

Bone nodded. "You've got it in one. All options are open here. We need to secure the island as best we can and radio for support with the search. Do you have any more volunteers you can call on?"

"Mountain rescue's your best bet. There's also the yacht club which has experienced sailors who can deal with this weather, but they're unlikely to risk taking their pride and joys out."

"How many are in the mountain rescue team?"

"Six, including myself."

"What? That, too?"

"'Fraid so. It's either that or stay at home and eat my own body weight in Cheetos." Matheson smiled.

"And you can radio from the rescue boat?"

"Of course, aye."

"We'll need more people searching the woods and all the nooks and crannies along the shoreline, and we also need to get over there to the other jetty, asap."

"Out of the question," Matheson replied. "As I said, it's just way too dangerous at this time of year, or any time, to be honest. Maybe in a flat-bottom boat or canoe on a glorious summer's day, but now, it's a bloody death trap."

Bone blew out his cheeks in frustration. "Any other way in? I mean, from the mainland?"

"It's a hike and half, but it can be done, and probably easier from the Loch Gillan side."

"So if they did manage to land over there, could they escape on foot?"

"Aside from the farm, unlikely unless he or she has specialist knowledge of the route out. In this weather, you'd be a goner in a couple of hours, either hypothermia or a tumble off a cliff."

"And is there any way to contact the laird's estate?"

"With phone and roads down, it'll be difficult. The hotel and estate offices are even more remote than Loch Gillan."

"Christ," Bone cursed. "What about your VHF radio?"

"If they have any problems with their guests on the water, they dial nine-nine-nine, and we pick it up."

"Could you get me over to those lodges in the rescue boat?"

"Aye, we can certainly ask, but we only have one boat available, and I'm sure the skipper will insist on prioritising the emergency here. She's already complaining about being overstretched. And even when you get over there, it's another couple of miles or so to the main estate, along a forest road that I assume will be pretty much impassable as well."

"Okay, let's deal with the here and now and work that one out later. This weather is turning into a bloody accomplice."

"We should have it done for perverting the course of justice," Matheson added.

They returned to the steps, and with a sigh and another waft of his heated jacket, Bone started the long climb to the top.

At the rescue boat, the two paramedics were still attending to the woman, strapped into a stretcher on the jetty.

"How is she doing now?" Bone asked.

"Still with us, just, but we need that rescue copter," the first paramedic said.

Bone followed Matheson onto the vessel. Lonnie was slumped over inside the tiny cabin, wrapped in tinfoil like a huge, hairy Christmas turkey.

"No sign?" he muttered.

"Not yet, but they can't have got very far."

Kilpatrick rubbed the back of his head. "Don't know what he hit me with, but if I get my hands on him, I'll find something bigger and harder to return the favour."

"We need to get you seen to."

"Ach, I'll be all right. I've had way worse hangovers. Nothing a hair of the dog won't cure."

Matheson picked up the radio handset and called the lifeboat station.

"Ask them to try and reach the nearest police station, or better still, the Rural Crime Unit at Kilwinnoch," Bone said.

Matheson nodded, but his call was interrupted by the rumble of an incoming helicopter.

The skipper jumped aboard. "Let's go before the downdraft is too strong," she said and started up the engine.

Matheson quickly finished his call and sat next to Bone and Kilpatrick.

"I've radioed the hotel and asked Gordon to go get Doctor Cropper," the skipper shouted, before reversing the boat away from the jetty. "And you two need to get out of the cold as well."

"The doc's called Cropper?" Bone asked. "I never knew that."

"As much use as a fart in a spacesuit, but at least he knows his malts," Kilpatrick replied and massaged his blood-matted crown.

Back at Loch Gillan Harbour, Bone helped Kilpatrick onto the quay. Urquhart was waiting quayside, flanked by a short man in a slightly oversized tweed coat and matching deerstalker.

"And you, Danny. You need to warm up and recharge," the skipper insisted.

Matheson got off, and the boat's engine roared.

"Where are you going?" Bone asked.

"Back to assist," the skipper said.

"Just be careful. The lunatic might still be over there."

"Oh, we can look after ourselves, don't you worry about that." The skipper smiled.

"She's a black belt, sir. I wouldn't mess with her." Matheson smiled at her.

She shook her head and turned the boat back out towards the isle.

"What the hell's going on over there, Duncan?" Urquhart approached the pair.

"Long story. Morning, Doc," Bone replied.

"I see you made it out of Balhuish then, Danny?" Urquhart said.

"Only just."

"And now he wishes he hadn't," Bone added.

"I was told we have some walking wounded to attend to," Doc said, squeezing the collar of his coat tighter around his neck.

"Aye, this one," Bone said.

Kilpatrick stepped forward.

"I'm fine," he protested.

"I'll be the judge of that," the doc insisted.

Kilpatrick looked over at Bone and mouthed the word *help*.

The doc attempted to take Kilpatrick's arm. "Come on, let's get you inside. And you two need to get warm as well."

Lonnie shrugged him off with a tut, and they headed back to the village.

"Ross is making his fry-up special. He's held back what's left of the bacon and eggs for you."

"That's very kind, but what about the Americans?"

"This morning they finished off the remainder of our porridge supply, so don't worry about them. They said they wanted the full Scottish experience, so Ross served them UHU made with water and salt. And they loved it." Urquhart pulled a face. "Or maybe they were just being polite. Anyhow, they've saved your bacon. See what I did there?"

Bone grimaced. "I think I'd rather have stage three hypothermia than listen to any more of those. Any sign of power or phone?"

"Nothing yet. Apparently, Scottish Energy are working on it. That'll be a first."

"Okay, I'm going to head back to the cabin for a shower and a change." Bone turned to Matheson. "I'll meet you at the hotel in about thirty minutes, Danny. Okay?"

Matheson nodded.

"You can use one of the bedrooms to shower and change, Danny. I'll lend you a change of clothes if you need any," Urquhart said.

"That's grand, thank you."

SIX

After going through the day's events with Matheson, making sure they hadn't missed any details, and then talking again with Kilpatrick, who still managed to sink a few pints despite a possible concussion, Bone returned, exhausted, to his cabin.

The snow had finally stopped, and there was talk of a thaw on the way. He was hopeful that power, phones, and access would return soon. The cabin was dark and icy cold, and he quickly lit the gas fire and turned on a couple of burners on the hob to warm the rooms. In the bedroom, he dragged the duvet through, lay down on the sofa, and switched on a small battery-powered torch lamp on the side. Fumbling his phone out of his pocket, he flicked through some of the images he'd snapped on the island, but a few flicks later, his phone died. With a weary sigh, he slid further under the duvet, closed his eyes, and within seconds was asleep.

A loud rap at the door woke him with a start. Clambering to his feet, he stumbled to the door, but spotting the burners on the stove still roaring away, he paused to turn them off. The door rattled again.

"Coming!"

The hotel receptionist was on his doorstep, shivering.

"God, Fiona, how long have you been out there? Come in."

"Gordon sent me over. Your colleague is on the radio thingy."

"DI Walker?"

"I don't know. He just said get over there before he loses the signal."

"Shit, okay." Bone grabbed his coat and, pushing on his sodden boots, followed the receptionist back through the snow to the hotel.

***

"I had her a minute ago," Urquhart said, turning the knobs on the radio set.

Matheson was by his side. The speaker whined. Urquhart held up the handset and tried again.

"Detective Walker, can you hear me?" The static sizzled.

"God's sake, you'd think we were in bloody Siberia. We're less than an hour from Kilwinnoch," Bone complained.

"Detective Walker?" Urquhart repeated.

"Yes. I can hear you again." Walker's familiar Western Isles lilt cut through the hiss.

"Ya belter." Urquhart thumped the desk. He handed the handset to Bone. "Press the button when you speak."

Bone rolled his eyes. "Aye, I know." He pressed the button. "Rhona, Duncan here, can you hear me?" he shouted.

"Just speak normally. She'll not hear you any better if you bellow at it," Urquhart instructed, stifling a giggle.

"Sir, are you okay?"

"We're fine," Bone replied at a more respectable volume. "What's it like with you?"

"It's horrendous. Everything's at a standstill."

"Same, but listen, we could lose this at any minute. I need you to check who's got married recently in the Loch Gillan and Balhuish area."

"What?"

"There's been a murder. A bride and groom. I won't waste time explaining now. Try and contact the Balhuish Estate and get recent booking information for their holiday lodges." The line hissed. "Are you still there?"

"Aye, Balhuish Estate, anything else?"

"Check wedding registers in this area. Who's got married recently. And as soon as we have access, we're going to need Cash's team up here, and local support. Ask Gallacher to—"

The box crackled, screamed, and went dead.

"Hello?" Bone barked into the mouthpiece. "Rhona, are you there?"

He looked around at Urquhart who took the handset and checked the unit again. He pushed and flicked switches up and down, but the tiny office filled with the smell of burning plastic. He pulled the mains plug from the wall.

"What's happened?" Bone asked.

"Bloody thing's blown a valve."

"You're kidding."

"It hasn't been used for ages."

"Valves? How old is it?"

"Pre-Logie Baird. I hardly ever use it. Might be the generator caused a surge or something."

"This just gets better and better. Can you fix it?"

"Oh, aye. All I need is another valve."

"Well, go and get it?"

"That would be Amazon."

"Oh, God." Bone ran his hand across the scar on his temple.

"At least she got the gist of it," Matheson said, trying to save the situation from the ditch.

Urquhart wafted his arms about. "Stinks to high heaven. Last thing we need is a bloody electrical fire."

Bone shrugged. "Right, all we can do is plough on." He turned to Matheson. "What time tomorrow morning?"

"I'd say we'll need to leave at first light, so six forty-five?"

"Where are you going?" Urquhart asked.

"Up and over Ben Beulach," Matheson replied.

"Rather you lot than me," Urquhart muttered. "I'll stick to cleaning out the beer pumps."

"Right, I'll see you in the morning then." Bone nodded and left.

SEVEN

Another loud rap at the door shook Bone from the strange dream involving Alice being trapped inside the frozen belly of a snowman. The door sounded again, and he jumped out of bed.

"It's ten to seven, sir." Matheson was on the step, suitably attired in full hiking gear.

"Oh shit! Overslept. Give me ten minutes," Bone apologised.

"We'll be outside the hotel entrance." The young constable retreated down the path.

Bone dashed back to the bedroom to get dressed.

Approaching the hotel, Bone spotted Matheson going through the kit. Junior was sitting on a tatty canvas rucksack, smoking a roll-up.

"Sorry about that," Bone said.

"Partying last night, were we?" Junior said. He took a long puff and blew a plume of smoke high into the air.

"Glad to see you've ditched the waders, Junior," Bone said, sizing up his more suitable waterproof walking trousers.

"No' many salmon where we're going," Junior croaked.

Urquhart appeared in the hotel doorway and ran across to greet them.

"Ross made up some egg baps for you." He handed them each a warm, tinfoil-wrapped parcel. "For the journey—"

He looked over, and Junior was already assaulting his. Egg yolk spurted out either side of his bundle and sprayed down his already filthy oil-skin coat. After a couple more bites, he took another drag of his cigarette and then continued to annihilate his bap. Urquhart shook his head.

"Right, I think we need to get going. It's quite a hike up and down." Matheson picked up his rucksack and swung it over his shoulder.

"How long?" Bone asked.

"Four hours there and back, maybe more depending on how bad the snow is, though the weather seems to have perked up." Matheson glanced at the cloudless blue sky.

"Sleet then rain set to move in tonight, apparently. It'll be bloody floods next," Urquhart complained.

Matheson turned back to Junior. "Are you ready? Come on."

The old barfly wiped his mouth, handed Urquhart his sodden ball of tinfoil, and picked up his ancient bag, the side pocket almost completely torn free.

"I've got a smaller version of that back in Kilwinnoch. Is yours nineteen fifties?"

"No clue. I found it in the bothy when I moved in ten years ago," Junior said.

They set off up the lane, over a stile and into the nearest field, heading towards a clump of trees. As they trudged, the snow deepened, slowing their progress.

"Christ, if it's like this all the way it'll be autumn by the time we get back," Bone grumbled.

"Ach, it'll thin out when we hit the mountain," Junior retorted, already snow-ploughing ahead with inexplicable expertise.

Once through the woods, they followed the Forestry Commission track until they came to another stile.

"We have to get up and over that bastard," Junior nodded at the vast tsunami of solid rock rearing up ahead of them.

"And there's no other way to get there?" Bone asked.

Junior laughed. "You could always swim it if you prefer."

"Don't worry, sir," Matheson cut in. "We have the human Exocet with us."

"That's what I'm worried about."

They climbed over and carried on up the incline.

After negotiating a series of treacherous ridges and gullies, they finally neared the top.

Matheson clambered over a large boulder. "Almost there."

Up ahead, Junior disappeared behind an outcrop, then emerged above and fist-pumped the sky.

"What is he on?" Bone wheezed and hauled himself over the rock.

"Whyte and Mackay mainly, I think." Matheson smiled.

He helped Bone up and over, and with a final push, they both clambered up to join Junior at the summit. Bone slumped down, breathing hard.

"Check that out," Junior said, gazing out across the panoramic view of Loch Gillan and the surrounding mountains. The sun was now in full flight, smothering the sky in a deep orange glow.

Matheson sat down next to Bone. "Never tire of that. So worth the effort, isn't it?"

"If you say so." Bone winced.

Matheson fished out his egg butty and a flask from his bag. "Coffee, anyone?"

"Can I marry you?" Bone asked with a grin.

Matheson poured him a cup of steaming black heaven. "Junior?"

"I'll stick to the kipper lung variety," he replied and lit another roll-up.

"That's Balhuish Island down there," Matheson said, leaning over the cliff.

Bone shuffled closer. "Looks so picturesque from up here. You could never imagine the horrors." He leaned over to take in the whole island. "What's that dark thing in the middle of the woods there?"

Matheson checked. "That's an old World War Two bunker,"

"The Home Guard used it to pick off Luftwaffe as they flew up the loch on their way to bomb the shit out of Clydebank."

"And you didn't think to mention it when we were there?"

"It's all sealed off. You'd need a JCB to get in. Anyway, I'm sure the crew checked it. Everybody knows about it."

"Clearly!" Bone replied sarcastically.

"Right, what goes up, must tumble back down," Junior said. He nipped the end of his roll-up and tucked it into his coat pocket.

Bone downed the rest of his coffee, and with a loud groan, he was back on his feet.

Forty minutes later, and with aching knee joints, the group reached the narrow hillwalkers' path at the foot of the mountain. Cutting down between another line of conifers, the loch opened out ahead of them.

"If we take the shore path, we can save ten minutes," Junior said.

They followed him along a narrow strip of snow sandwiched between solid rock and the water's edge.

"Watch your feet, it's lethal," he added, and then almost took a tumble. "See what I mean?"

Moments later, Bone skittered off to one side, and his boot plunged beneath into a near-frozen rock pool.

He yanked it out. "Fuck's sake," he cursed and carried on.

"Maybe the forest track would have been easier, Junior?" Matheson mocked, clinging to the rockface as he negotiated another huge wet boulder.

"Aye, but no' as much fun," Junior replied, bounding on.

Bone tried to keep up, his wet foot farting loudly inside his boot. "This guy is definitely a bloody goat."

At last, they returned to the track that led down to a tiny wooden jetty at the water's edge.

"Last stop, all change here for the pub," Junior said. He dropped his bag on the ground, flipped it open, and retrieved a can of Guinness.

"I'm not sure you should be—" Matheson started.

But Junior was already halfway through.

Bone stepped up onto the jetty, and walking to the end, he checked either side. "Nothing here."

Matheson jumped back onto the rocky beach running alongside. "See the isle's jetty over there?" He pointed to the island, only a few hundred yards away across the narrow strait. "Hold up." He disappeared behind an overhanging rock. Moments later, he called again.

"What is it?" Bone asked, approaching Matheson, who was on his hunkers at the water's edge.

"Look." He pointed at a nearly submerged motorboat just visible beneath the waves. Matheson opened his rucksack and found a neatly tied roll of climbing rope.

"What else have you go' in there, Mary Poppins?" Bone asked.

Winding the rope slowly around his hand, Matheson tied the end in a noose, and with a glance at his target, cast the rope. The lasso looped over a protruding mooring cleat. He yanked it tight and hauled at the vessel.

Bone clapped. "That was smart. Where did you learn to do that?"

"My old man was John Wayne," Matheson said.

"The builder," Junior added.

"Give us a hand then," Matheson puffed.

The three of them hauled at the sunken boat, and it edged slowly towards the shore. Once near enough, Junior waded in and dragged it closer.

"Your feet'll freeze," Matheson said.

"Ach, this is tropical," Junior baulked and with the strength of a rugby squad, he heaved the front of the boat up onto the beach.

"*Mirabel*," Bone said, reading its name written in gold lettering on the side of the wooden hull.

"That's Vincent Trough's boat," Matheson exclaimed. "He runs a boatyard in Balhuish."

"Rents boats as well," Junior added.

"Okay, now we might have a link." Bone leaned over the side and looked into the waterlogged interior. "I was about to ask if it had been scuttled, but there's a huge hole in the bottom there."

Matheson peered into the murky water. "Aye, she's run aground. Like I said, it's treacherous."

"So has the occupant drowned?" Bone asked.

Matheson rubbed his neck. "The current in the strait is very strong, so if anyone tried to sail over they could get sucked out all the way to—"

"New York," Junior interrupted.

"But its proximity suggests it may have landed first and then sank."

"Or it was sunk?" Bone proposed.

"Aye, that's possible, too, I suppose, if you happen to be carrying a sledgehammer in your rucksack."

"The boat could have sunk a while ago. I mean, before any of this shite happened. Have you thought of that, Inspectors Morse and Clouseau?" Junior cut in again.

Matheson shrugged. "I don't think it would still be hanging about here after those storms."

"So apart from the mountain and the loch, there's no other way out, is that right?" Bone asked.

Junior thought for a moment. "The Dulhoon's farm is about three miles due south of here, but you'd have to know that, as it's all fields and farm tracks to get there, and in this weather, the way there is probably totally cut off."

"They own this strip of river," Matheson added.

"About the only thing the laird disnae own," Junior snarled.

"So if it were you, you'd take shelter until the weather improves?"

"In the Loch Gillan Hotel bar, aye," Junior replied.

"There's an old fisherman's bothy on the other side of the point," Matheson said. "Might be worth a look."

Bone sighed. "Aww Christ, please tell me that's nearby."

"I thought you lot were supposed to be fit," Junior joked.

Bone patted his stomach. "I need to get on your 'roll-up and Irish stout' diet."

They left the beach and carried on along the shoreline path, and once around the point, cut back into a narrow estuary with a stream running into the loch.

"There it is." Matheson pointed at an old tumbledown shack teetering precariously on the edge of another jetty.

They jumped up onto a track which disappeared over the rise of a slope.

"Where does that go?" Bone asked.

Junior glanced ahead. "Up to one of Dulhoon's fields,"

"Okay, as quiet as we can."

They approached cautiously.

"You go round the other side," Bone said to Matheson. "Junior, you come with me."

"Oh, so we're fucking Starsky and Hutch now, then?" Junior grinned.

Bone held up his hand. "Quietly, I said."

He edged around the side of the ramshackle structure and squinted through a broken panel board in the wall. The interior was gloomy and too dark to see anything. They crept on, keeping low. At the door, which was half hanging from its hinges, Bone reached out to pull it open when Matheson appeared suddenly from around the other side.

"Jesus!" Bone mouthed.

Matheson shook his head, and together they pulled gently at the door. It creaked and cracked, then finally swung open with a loud wail, like an infant screaming in pain. The stench of mould and decay wafted out. Bone stepped in first and peered into the darkness. The interior appeared to be empty, but he couldn't see into the farthest corners. Matheson switched on his phone torch, illuminating the room in harsh white light.

"What's that?" Matheson said, pointing at an unidentifiable shape on the floor in the farthest corner.

"Police, stay where you are!" Bone cried out.

The mound didn't move.

Bone edged closer. "There's three of us and one of you, so don't even think about it."

Matheson adjusted his beam, and the light flickered across a filthy tarpaulin covering a pile of lobster creels.

"Jesus Christ." Bone sighed.

Matheson swung the beam around the hut again.

"Give me that a second." Bone took the phone and directed the beam to the back corner and went over.

"Spot something?" Matheson asked.

Bone picked up a cream-coloured thermal glove. He redirected the torchlight to examine it. It was adult-sized, the type of glove a professional climber or walker would wear. He turned it over. The palm and fingers were covered in some kind of dark fluid that glistened under the torchlight. He went out into the daylight for a closer examination.

"Does that look like frozen blood?" Bone asked.

Junior leaned over. "It fucking is." He shivered. "Fucking horror nightmare, this is."

Removing his rucksack, Bone unzipped a pocket and found a plastic evidence bag he'd remembered at the last minute to pack. He dropped the glove in and zipped up the bag.

"What have you found?"

Matheson's interruption had Bone spinning around again in surprise.

"Jesus, Danny. Can you stop doing that!"

"Sorry, sir," Matheson said.

"The first rule of policing is to never sneak up on your colleagues," Bone complained.

"Not sure that's the first rule. Or any rule I've heard of, to be honest," Matheson replied.

"Well, it's my bloody rule, okay?" Bone blew out his cheeks. "So, no sign?"

"Not a single print, but then it's not exactly Florida out here."

Bone turned around. "What about this farm, then?"

"I'm not sure how bad the snow will be," Matheson said.

"And you'd need to know the way," Junior added.

"But worth a look? I mean, unless he's taking his chances on the mountain, where else can he be heading?"

Isle of the Dead

They collected their gear and set off up the track.

EIGHT

When they reached the first of the Dulhoon's farm buildings, there was no sign of anyone around. A few sheep were rustling around in one of the barns, and a cat approached to greet them.

They entered the main yard.

"Where's the house?" Bone asked.

"Up ahead, see the chimney sticking up behind that hay barn?" Matheson gestured.

They continued on, and the cat followed behind, then raced ahead when they neared a side door in the farmhouse.

Bone rapped the knocker. The door swung open.

"Hello, anyone there?" he called through the gap. He gently nudged the door. "Hello?" Still no reply.

He shrugged and stepped inside, Matheson close behind. Junior lingered by the door.

"Mr Dulhoon, police," Bone called down a dark, narrow corridor.

He edged in further, passing a door on his right. He was about to try the handle when it opened suddenly and a man stepped out and walked straight into him.

"What the—?" the man exclaimed and instinctively shoved Bone away, then raised his fists in defence.

"Whoa there, Scottish Police." Bone unzipped his coat.

The man towered over him, his huge frame almost filling the hallway.

"Mr Dulhoon? I'm DCI Bone, and this is Special Constable Danny Matheson. I think you know him?"

Matheson stepped into the house and nodded.

"Where the hell did you come from?" Dulhoon said, smoothing back a shock of blond hair.

"We've walked over from Loch Gillan," Bone replied.

The farmer dropped his fists. "Jesus, in this weather? We've been stuck in here for two days with no power. Another couple of days and one of our sheep would be for the chop. What brings you all the way here?"

"So you haven't seen anyone else for a couple of days?"

"No, not a soul. Why?"

"Can we come in for a minute?" Bone asked.

"Looks like you already are, but aye, of course, come through." He turned to the door. "Is that Junior I see loitering out there?"

"It is, aye," Junior called from the yard.

"Well, you two can come in, but he stays outside."

"Oh, come on, Red. Forgive and forget and all that?"

"You accepted employment from that wanker even though you said you never would. In my book that's unforgivable."

"A man's got to eat, Jock."

"Unforgivable. Shut the door behind you, Danny."

"I've no idea what's going on between you two, Mr Dulhoon," Bone said, "but the man could do with a hot drink and a warm up. You wouldn't want him to go down with hypothermia now, would you?"

The farmer huffed. "Well, as long as he keeps his traitor trap shut and doesn't o much as look at me. But I'm not happy about it." He started down the hall. "This way, oh, and take off your boots. Karen will have your gonads for dinner if you trail muck across her clean floors."

They removed their footwear and followed Dulhoon into an expansive, warm and welcoming farmhouse kitchen. Mrs Dulhoon was propped up at the kitchen table, sorting through a box of rosettes.

"Karen, we have company," Dulhoon said.

His wife stood in surprise.

"I'm DCI Duncan Bone, and this is—"

"I know these two, but I wasn't expecting a police detective. What's happened? Is it to do with the snow? Has there been an accident?"

"We're looking for someone in connection with a serious incident," Bone said.

Isle of the Dead

Karen's eyes widened. "What sort of incident?"

"Karen, the men need a hot drink," Dulhoon said. "They've walked over the Ben to reach us."

"Oh, dear God. Let me get you some coffee."

"That would be grand." Bone smiled.

At a vast range cooker, Mrs Dulhoon set up a percolator. She turned. "Or would you prefer tea?"

"A quick coffee is fine for me." Bone nodded.

Matheson and Junior agreed.

"Surprised to see you here, Junior," Mrs Dulhoon said and glanced over at her husband.

"Temporary ceasefire, but he's not forgiven." Dulhoon shook his head. "Mr Bone asked if we'd seen anyone else in the last couple of days?"

"Oh God, no. The weather has been absolutely atrocious. Thank God we have the Aga, otherwise we'd have frozen to death." She wiped her hands on her apron. "It's been so bad I've resorted to sorting through all our winning rosettes and finally getting them up on the kitchen wall."

Bone glanced down at the array of brightly coloured awards. "Cattle?"

"Clydesdales," Mr Dulhoon replied. "We're one of the last few who still breeds them."

The percolator whistled, and Mrs Dulhoon poured the men their drinks. "Would you like something to eat? We've still got a few sausages left that I could fry up for you."

"Oh yes, please," Matheson enthused.

"No, we'll be fine," Bone interrupted.

Matheson frowned.

"We'll drink this, and if you don't mind, could we have a quick look round the farm?" Bone said.

"Aye, of course, but there's been no one else here," Mr Dulhoon said. "Even our son's away in Stirling."

"What's he doing there?" Bone asked.

"Studying agriculture. It's beyond me why he needs to go to a classroom to learn how to do that when it's all here for him, and a hell of a lot cheaper, too."

"Oh, Red, it's the twenty-first century. You need to move with the times. He wants to modernise the farm, and this is the best way."

"Modernise, my arse. Farms are farms."

Mrs Dulhoon shook her head at Bone. "You see what I have to put up with?"

"Right, drink up, lads. Thanks for that, Mrs Dulhoon."

"That was quick. Are you sure I can't tempt you with a sausage?"

"It's a very tempting offer, but we need to keep moving. Thank you anyway."

Mr Dulhoon stood. "I'll take you round the main farm, Inspector."

"Any news on when the roads and phones will be back on?" Mrs Dulhoon asked.

"As soon as this thaw starts to kick in; I'm sure it'll be back on soon." Bone gave her a reassuring nod.

"Aye, it'll be a relief when it finally buggers off. I've got to pick up a ram on Tuesday," Mr Dulhoon agreed.

"Oh, before I forget. You haven't recently been over at that old tumbledown fisherman's hut at the edge of your farm?"

"Through that permafrost? Are you having a laugh? It's been hard enough trying to get up to feed the sheep on the top field," Dulhoon replied.

"It's just I found a cream-coloured, expensive-looking thermal glove and thought it might be yours."

Dulhoon shrugged. "Not mine, and anyway, I keep that hut locked so that the poachers aren't tempted to do some night fishing. Was the lock broken?"

"Didn't see any lock. The door was open."

"Christ's sake, if it's no' farm equipment, it's having a go at our fish stocks. One of them must have dropped it."

They carried on out of the house, across the yard, and down a lane to an old pebbledash cottage that was surrounded by a barbed-wire fence.

"Thought we should double-check here first," Dulhoon said. "We've had a couple of break-ins, and the wee bastards ripped out one of the old fireplaces. Bloody antique, it was, too, and worth a bob. Hence the security."

"Do you have a lot of bother with robberies?" Bone pulled at the fence.

"You name it, we've had it nicked, unless it's bloody cemented down, and even then, they still have a go. Tractors, ploughs, sheep, lead from our roof, milking equipment. What they do with that is beyond me. You know, they've even stripped wood from the side of one of our barns. Bloody epidemic. If things weren't tough enough for us."

"Do you have CCTV or anything like that?"

"Used to, but that got nicked as well. No, a licenced shotgun is my deterrent of choice."

He opened the gate in the fence and went to check the doors and windows on the cottage, then returned.

"All fine," he said.

They went back to the yard.

"What was the cottage used for, then?" Bone asked.

"My uncle used to have a farmhand who lived in it with his wife, but with automation and all that now, the three of us can cope on our own—when my son is actually here, that is."

He took them over to the byre and checked the equipment, tried the locks on a storeroom door, and then went on to a second building adjacent to the main house. There were two tractors parked up. He jumped up on one and peered through the cab window, and then checked the second.

He shrugged. "As I said, there's been nobody here. That's the only good thing about this weather. It keeps the thieving wee toerags away from our stuff."

The splutter of an engine starting up sounded on the other side of the barn.

He turned. The engine roared again. "What's Karen doing with the quad?"

"The what?" Bone said.

But Dulhoon was already on his way out. As they dashed around the side of the barn, a quad bike tore past, narrowly missing all three of them. Matheson spun around and snatched at the driver's coattails, but the bike's momentum yanked him forward with such force he tumbled to the ground, and the bike screamed on and out of the farm gate.

"Aww, no! Not again!" Dulhoon yelled. "I'm going to kill the fucking—" He ran to a Land Rover parked up in the drive next to the house and jumped in.

Bone climbed in next to him. A shotgun that was laying across the seat jarred into his spine. Dulhoon whipped the weapon out from behind him, popped it open and, fishing cartridges out of the glove compartment, slotted them into the barrels. He loaded both barrels with cartridges.

Bone raised his arm. "Hold on, Mr Dulhoon. We don't want to be shooting anyone."

"The thieving bastard is on my land. I'm defending my property. I have every right."

"He's not a stray dog worrying sheep, Mr Dulhoon."

"You take it then and shoot him."

"It's Scotland, not the USA—"

Ignoring Bone, Dulhoon tried to start the vehicle, but the engine wouldn't turn over. "Bloody diesel's frozen." He cursed and slammed his fists against the steering wheel.

"Do you have another vehicle?" Bone asked.

"All diesel, except the quad!" He jumped out. "Fucking little shit." He kicked the ground in frustration.

Matheson clambered to his feet.

"Are you okay?" Bone asked.

"I nearly had him, but I did get this." He held up a torn shred of green fabric.

"Well, that's some exchange for a quad bike, Danny. I can see how I'll be able to attend to all my lambing ewes with that." Dulhoon growled.

"Where's Junior?" Bone asked.

"I knew it. It was him," Dulhoon said.

"I don't think this material matches Junior's choice of grubby attire," Matheson said, examining his catch.

"He always was and always will be a lying, thieving, two-faced—"

"The lying, two-faced thief is here," Junior interrupted, emerging from around the side of the hay barn.

"Where were you?"

"Right behind you, and I saw the guy take off in that thing across the field over there, so I ran after him, but the snow got deeper and deeper, and he disappeared down a gully."

"I don't believe you. Show me," Dulhoon said.

"Jock, come on, what use is a bloody quad bike to me?" Junior said.

"Money. That's all you're interested in."

Junior shook his head and took them to the field. The bike's tracks cut a deep pathway across it, disappearing down a steep slope, as Junior had described.

"Where does that go?" Bone said.

"A stream, and then there's the rear track we use to access the bottom field."

"Does that connect to a road or main access point?"

"Aye, but not when it's like this. The snow could be as deep as a house down there."

"And there's no way through on foot, Junior?"

"Impossible."

"Shit!" Bone said.

"Was that him?" Junior asked.

"Who?" Dulhoon asked.

"The person of interest we're trying to find," Bone replied. "Well, as you said, Mr Dulhoon, considering how difficult it was for us to get here, I can't see this being another opportunist out on the make, can you?" He turned back to the farmer. "The bike thief would need the keys. Where do you keep them?"

"On the rack in the utility room." He shot a look at the house.

They ran back.

"Karen!" Dulhoon called out and ran down the hall to the kitchen.

She wasn't there, but the rosettes were scattered all over the floor.

"Oh, Christ! Karen!" he bellowed.

He was about to check the living room when she appeared on the stairs landing.

"What's all the shouting about?"

"Are you okay?" he asked.

"Fine, you've only been gone for ten minutes. What's with the emotional welcome?"

"Somebody just stole the quad. The rosettes are all over the floor in there. I thought you'd been attacked."

"That's the bloody cat. She won't leave them alone."

"Did you see anyone in the house?"

"No, at least I hope not." She frowned.

Dulhoon marched through to the utility room and checked the key rack hanging on the back of the door. He picked one out. "This is it."

"You only have one key, you say?"

"Yes, just the one."

"What about the spare?" Mrs Dulhoon interrupted.

Dulhoon shrugged. "What spare?"

"When you bought it, you stuck a spare key to the bottom of one of the drawers in your workshop."

"Did I?"

"I swear the man has dementia, Inspector." She blew out her cheeks.

"Oh Christ, aye, that's right," Dulhoon said.

"Not very secure there," Bone interrupted.

They went back out, around the side, and into a shed rammed full of tools and machinery parts.

"This is my repair shop," Dulhoon said.

The drawers at the back of the shed were open, and two were lying upturned on the floor.

"Oh Christ, the key's gone," he said, kneeling by the chaotic mess of nuts, bolts, and screws. "I had all of this in order." He sighed and flipped over the drawer.

"How would the thief know about your spare key?" Bone asked.

"I don't know. The whole place has been ransacked. Maybe they just got lucky?"

"Did you tell anyone where it was?"

"I've no idea. I might have mentioned it to someone in the pub when I first bought the thing, but I'd totally forgotten I put it there."

"So just you, Karen, and your son were in the know?"

"I don't think even my son was aware." He stopped. "Hold on, my son is in Stirling. What's he got to do with this?"

"I'm just trying to work out how the thief knew where the key was. It's a pretty random discovery."

"Thinking about it, I employ temporary farm workers for a few weeks each year during the harvest. One or two of them have used the quad in the past."

"I'll need names and addresses," Bone said.

"There are definitely one or two regulars that I trust, but the others, I wouldn't know where to start. They were all cash in hand. They work all over the place."

"Start with the regulars, and anyone else you can remember. I'd like to speak to your son, too."

"I am at a total loss why you want to bother him with this. He'll only worry about his mum."

"I want to ask him if he knew where the key was and if he told anyone."

"Fine, but please play it down. Don't tell him you're after some kind of wanted man or anything."

"Of course."

"Sir, I think we'll need to start thinking about heading back soon as the day is wearing on," Matheson interrupted.

Bone nodded and turned back to Dulhoon. "And if the quad makes it over the stream and up the other side, where does it go?"

"You can either head straight up the corrie, but you'd only get so far that way, or take a left and head for the road, but that'll be horrendous."

"So there's no way out?"

"I doubt it, unless he knows the land better than I do, eh, Junior?"

"I haven't nicked your bloody quad, Red." Junior frowned.

"Okay, there's not a lot else we can do here for now. I suggest you keep all your doors and windows locked tonight until we can get some support over to you."

"Don't worry about us. We can look after ourselves." Dulhoon smiled.

"I don't doubt it, but heed what I say about your firearm."

Mrs Dulhoon appeared at the farmhouse door.

Bone went over.

"Has it been stolen?" she asked.

"For now, aye, but hopefully the thief won't get too far, and you might be able to recover it when the thaw sets in."

"You don't think they'll be back, do you?"

"I've told your husband to keep everything locked up tonight. Sit tight, and I'll try to get some officers over here in the morning. Try not to worry. I'm sure they're well gone after they saw us lot here."

"Thanks, Inspector."

"Sorry we can't do any more until we get rid of this bloody stuff." He kicked at a small drift creeping up the adjacent wall.

She handed Bone a bag. "A few sausage sandwiches. It's a long way back to Loch Gillan."

"Very kind, Mrs Dulhoon. Thanks."

Bone returned to the group and put his rucksack on, and with a wave, they set off towards the mountain.

"Robert Shaw in *From Russia with Love*, isn't it?" Bone nodded.

"Ah, you mean Jock Dulhoon's nickname. Folks think he's a dead ringer for the villain he played in the Bond film, but I've never seen it so I've no clue," Matheson said.

Bone recoiled. "You've never watched *From Russia with Love*? It's class. What is wrong with you?"

"Young, that's what's wrong with me."

"Touché," Bone replied.

They quickened their pace to catch up with Junior, who was practically running towards the hills.

When they reached the stile at the foot of the Ben, Junior stopped. "Can you hear that?"

Bone turned his head into the breeze. "Trees and a crow?"

"Engine," Junior replied.

"Aye, I can," Matheson said. "It's coming from over that ridge."

They climbed over the stile and took a right up a steep bank.

"Watch your footing. There's ice under the snow here," Junior said.

But Bone was already on his backside. He picked himself up and carried on, cursing under his breath. As they climbed, the depth of snow increased and the purring rumble of an engine intensified.

When Junior reached the top, he called back, "It's the quad bike."

He disappeared down the other side. Matheson followed, with Bone not so close behind.

The bike was on its side, the front embedded in a deep drift.

"Looks like the scally ran out of road," Junior said. He reached over the chassis and turned off the engine.

"There's a trail through the snow here," Matheson called from the other side. "He's headed up that way."

"Where we're going," Junior said.

Bone knelt to inspect a boot print. There were frozen droplets of blood scattered across the imprint. "Looks like he's sustained an injury." He stretched his hand. "What would you say, size nine?"

Matheson leaned in. "Ten maybe, difficult to tell, but clearly in a hurry.

"Can I borrow your phone a second?" Bone asked.

Matheson retrieved his mobile from his rucksack and switched it on. "Hold up I'll set it to stay on for you." He fumbled with the device and then handed it to Bone.

"He can't be too far away, can he?" Bone said, taking a couple of snaps of the prints.

"Depends how experienced he is at negotiating this terrain in these conditions. If it were you, Junior, you'd be back at the hotel bar by now, wouldn't you?"

"Fourth pint," Junior replied.

"Well, at least Robert Shaw'll get his quad back," Bone said. "Come on, let's find this heid the baw before he causes any more mayhem."

Re-joining their previous route, they followed the prints and tracks leading back to Loch Gillan. On the other side of the hill, Junior stopped again.

"I think your man's tracks have disappeared. These are just ours, look."

Bone leaned over. "You're right. Where's he gone?" He scanned the slopes above and below them.

"The cheeky bastard has stepped in our treads for a bit then veered off somewhere back there."

"Shit! Should we go back and see if we can pick up his route again?" Bone sighed at the prospect.

Matheson checked his watch. "I don't think we can risk any more time up here. The light is already fading, and we still have to negotiate Gillan Pass."

"Agreed," Junior said. "I mean, I'd be fine, but you two would end up in the soup down there." He peered over the side of the path.

"Where is he likely to go if he veered off?" Bone asked.

Matheson pointed skywards. "The only way is up because a few yards down that way it's a sheer drop into the loch."

"Hopefully, the arsehole will freeze up there and that will be that," Junior said.

"I'd say only an experienced hillwalker or climber would find their way off the top of the mountain from here," Matheson added. "But once it's dark, then…"

"Okay, come on then. Let's get back," Bone said.

They carried on.

"We need this to thaw so we can get more people to help us. We're chasing our tails here."

"What you're saying is we're going to need a bigger boat," Matheson replied.

Bone squinted at him, then laughed. "Very funny. I thought you said you were too much of a toddler to watch old films."

"There's old and then there's *Jaws*." Matheson started singing, 'Show Me the Way to Go Home,' and as dusk slowly descended on the trio, their discordant rendition echoed out across the loch.

NINE

Exhausted and frozen to the bone, the three men finally arrived back in Loch Gillan.

"Pint?" Junior asked.

"Hot shower and change first, but there's definitely a couple in there with my name on them." Bone nodded enthusiastically.

A loud rumble interrupted the peace. A towering snow plough rolled slowly into the village, its huge headlights flooding the car park with dazzling white light. Bone shielded his eyes and squinted at the oncoming beast. It stopped directly in front of them, and the plough on the front rose. The trio stepped back, fearing a deluge of snow falling from the enormous steel blades.

"Well, bigger boat it is then," Matheson said.

The engine cut, the cab door opened, and DC Harper jumped out.

"Jesus Christ, Will!" Bone said and rushed over to greet him.

"Thought you might be needing a bit of help, sir."

He smiled, and they shook hands.

"I've brought someone else with me," Harper said.

Walker appeared from behind the snow plough. "Evening, Inspector, fancy running into you here."

She approached, and Bone gave her a hug.

"Where did you come from? Did you walk all the way from Kilwinnoch behind this thing?"

"No, I followed in this," Walker replied.

Bone looked around the giant tractor at an all-weather police Land Rover.

"Complete with snow chains and anti-skid technology, but it still wasn't easy, even for a banshee from the Hebrides like me. And we needed the help of this monster to get here."

"I'm so pleased to see you both."

"Aye, it sounds like there's been a wee spot of bother."

"That's an understatement," Matheson said.

"Special Constable Danny Matheson, meet my colleagues, DI Rhona Walker and DC Will Harper."

"Pleasure," Walker said.

"I can't believe you're here," Bone repeated.

"I'm not sure we can either. We have to thank this guy," Harper said as the snow plough driver emerged from his cab.

"Thanks, pal," Bone said.

"Nay bother. I was just about to end my shift when I passed these two stuck on the Rest and be Thankful. I was going to leave them, but they promised me fish and chips and a pint."

"The least we could do. We were looking at a very long, cold night," Walker replied.

"Trapped together in a tiny Land Rover cabin with only a packet of cheese and onion crisps between us," Harper added.

Walker checked out the bedraggled walkers' clobber. "What are you three doing out here, anyway?"

"Long story, I'll fill you in shortly," Bone said. "How are things back at the station?"

"It's just about as bad as up here. We're running at around sixty percent, with officers who live in outlying areas unable to make it in."

"What about the team?"

"The Super is in, and Sheila's managed to skid and skitter her way to work."

"The usual dedication from DS Baxter." Bone nodded.

"But poor old Mark, he was due to start back on light office duties this week, and the weather has put paid to his glorious return. He's claiming we've cooked up the blizzard deliberately."

"Sounds like our Mr Mullens is back to his moany best. So, you have power and phones?"

"Sporadic supplies, and we're on the emergency generator most of the time, but the council's promising by the close of play today."

Bone shivered and turned to the snow plough driver. "I suggest you get yourself inside and warm yourself up and take advantage of the free food offer. Ross, our chef here, is magnificent."

The driver nodded.

"And thanks again for your efforts. I know it couldn't have been easy."

"Nae bother," the driver repeated, and headed to the hotel.

Bone turned to the team. "I'm afraid before we can get out of the cold, we need to run a quick sweep of the village. While we were over at the Dulhoon's farm, someone nicked the farmer's quad. But we found it abandoned on our way back, so it's possible the thief might have been heading here."

"Quad?" Harper asked.

"Bike, and we think this could well be our suspect and he may have sustained an injury in his tangle with the mountain." He glanced along the village. "Danny, can you take Will and start at the top end and work your way back to the hotel, and we'll check the loch side, and meet you here in ten minutes or so."

"Okay, should we check door-to-door and ask if anyone's seen anything or anyone suspicious creeping about?"

"Only if you absolutely need to. We don't want to freak anybody out."

Matheson and Harper carried on, and Bone and Walker set off towards the loch to check the harbour and office buildings.

A few minutes later, the thorough search of streets, back lanes, and isolated buildings having proved fruitless, and when they all gathered back at the hotel, Matheson raised his hands in defeat.

"They could be anywhere and nowhere. It's impossible to know."

"Thought you were breaking into a song there for a second," Walker said.

Matheson stifled a laugh.

"Sorry, sir, the cold is playing havoc with my sense of humour," she added.

"Apology denied," Bone said with a smile. He checked his watch.

"Right, a quick shower and change for me, and we regroup in the hotel restaurant in thirty minutes?"

The team nodded, and with collective sighs of relief and exhaustion, they staggered up the steps and into the inviting warmth of the hotel lobby. Bone stopped Walker before she went in.

"I'm just going to check on Lonnie Kilpatrick, the boatman who was attacked on the island, and see if he can remember any more while it's still relatively fresh in his mind."

"You need to get warm as well, sir," Walker said.

"I know, but it's sort of on the way, and it'll only take five minutes or so more. I just need to try and tie up a couple of loose ends."

"See you shortly then." Walker nodded and followed her colleagues up the steps.

***

Bone approached Kilpatrick's cottage. He was about to knock when he caught a glimpse of footprints on the doorstep that tracked all the way back to the harbour road. Remembering he still had Danny's phone, he fished it out of his pocket, turned on the torch and knelt to inspect the prints. There were a few droplets of blood splattered across the disturbed snow. He quickly took another photo and rattled the door, but there was no reply.

He peered through the adjacent window into the tiny living room. The curtains were open, but the room was empty. He stepped back to look for signs of life upstairs, but all the windows were dark. He tried again, with more force and, pushing the letterbox, he was about to squint through the gap when the door swung open.

Kilpatrick appeared in his dressing gown roughly tied around the waist, his hair dishevelled, his eyes barely open.

"Inspector Bone," he croaked and rubbed at his beard. "I was asleep."

"So sorry to wake you. Can I come in for a couple of minutes?"

"Yeah, sure, but I'm still a bit out of it."

Bone stepped over the prints on the doorstep and followed Kilpatrick into the gloomy living room.

"Let me find some light." He disappeared into the kitchen and returned with an oil lamp. He lit the wick, and the room filled with a dim orange glow. "Sit yourself down. Would you like a cup of coffee or something?"

"No, I won't keep you. How are you now?"

"Bloody exhausted. The doc said concussion can make you feel like that."

"So you have a concussion?"

"He wasn't sure. He never is about anything, the quack, but I don't feel a hundred percent. I've been in bed most of the day."

"So sorry you were attacked," Bone said.

"It was a split-second thing. If I'd turned round sooner I'd have spotted him coming at me, and then he'd have known all about it."

"I bet. So when he hit you, did you fall over immediately?"

"I think so, aye. I must have blacked out for a second or two because I can't remember hitting the ground. One minute I was making my way across the beach to the boat, and the next I was slumped on the rocks with a sore head."

"And you said you saw your attacker run off over the rocks, is that right?"

"I just caught a glimpse of a coat disappearing round the point, but my eyes were all skew-whiff with the blow." He pressed the large white plaster stuck to the back of his head. "Luckily no stitches, though. God, the thought of that alkie's shaking hands pushing a needle into my skull gives me the heebies."

"Can you remember what colour the coat was?"

"God, now you're asking. To be honest, the whole thing feels a bit like a dream, or a nightmare, to be more precise."

"So when did the assailant smash up the boat radio?"

"They must have done it just before I got back to the jetty."

"Not after then. I mean, could you have been out for longer than a few seconds?"

"I'm not sure, but it didn't feel like a long time."

"And you didn't hear or see anything?"

"Not a sausage. I was keeping my eyes on the snow and the icy boulders, trying not to take a tumble. But there was no one on the boat when I got there."

"And you have no idea who the people are on the island or who might have done this to them?"

"No clue. But it's one of the most terrifying things I've ever seen in my life. I mean, what kind of psycho would do something like that?" He sat. "Sorry, feeling a wee bit dizzy. How did you get on over there today?"

"Do you know Jock Dulhoon?" Bone asked. "Red?"

"The farmer?"

"That's right, yes."

"Aye, did you see him? Has something happened to them?"

"No, just while we called in to check, someone nicked his quad bike right from under our noses."

"Really? God's sake. Do you think it was the guy on the island?"

"We found a submerged boat near the jetty on the mainland and followed a trail in the snow to the Dulhoon's farm."

"Shit, where did the guy go on the quad?"

"We found it abandoned on our way back to Loch Gillan."

"This is a bloody worry, especially if that lunatic is hiding somewhere round here."

"I noticed some blood on your doorstep on my way in."

Kilpatrick looked up in surprise. "What?"

"There's blood and some footprints in the snow out there that go all the way back to the harbour road."

Kilpatrick stared at Bone for a second or two. "Oh, I know, sorry, my head's nipping. I was in the middle of changing my bandage, and the cat jumped out the window. I've been keeping her in as she's so daft she'd bloody freeze to death. So I had to chase after her. By the time I finally rounded her up, this thing opened up again. Head wounds bleed like fuck." He pressed his palm against the bandage.

"When was this?"

"A couple of hours ago."

"Where's your cat now?"

"Where do you think? Upstairs in my bed, where she always is, the fat lump."

"Do you know the Dulhoon's son?" Bone continued to press.

"Aye, me and Fergus were at school together."

"You see him much?"

"Not since he started his course. He's at Stirling Agricultural College. The lucky bastard managed to escape the loch."

"So when's the last time you saw him?"

"Hogmanay party in Balhuish, I think. He was back for the weekend, and we all went first footing, then went to the party in the village hall. God, I got so bloody drunk." He shook his head.

"Whoever stole the quad must have come off it pretty badly and could be nursing quite a serious injury."

"Shame he didn't break his fucking neck."

There was a loud thump on the ceiling.

"There you go, that's Pussyface falling off the bed again. She does that on a regular basis."

"Your cat's called Pussyface?"

"Aye, not the best idea I had, especially when you're out at night trying to get her back indoors. The locals are never done taking the piss out of me about it."

"Okay, thanks for your help. If you think of anything else in the meantime, I'm either at my cabin or the hotel, with my colleagues."

"You mean Danny Matheson?"

"Two of my team from Kilwinnoch nicked a snow plough and its driver and managed to get through, so we have some cavalry to catch the person who did this."

"And lamped me in the process."

"Thank you again for stepping up. That took courage."

They shook hands, and Bone gave him a quick hug.

"Ach, I didn't do anything except cause grief for the inshore rescue guys."

"Well, it's very much appreciated," Bone replied.

Kilpatrick showed him out.

TEN

When Bone returned to the hotel, refreshed and starving, Urquhart had opened up one of the hotel's function rooms for Walker, Harper, and Matheson to set up a temporary incident room.

"Bloody hell, that was quick," Bone said, walking into a room designed for weddings and funerals.

His colleagues had moved the ostentatious furniture around and set up a couple of laptops on desks at the far end. Gordon appeared behind him, grappling with a flip chart stand.

"Coming through," he warned.

Bone stepped out of the way. "Good God, where did you find that?"

"In the basement store. Believe it or not, I once had ambitions to make the hotel a conference centre, but the few companies that we managed to snag complained that all their employees wanted to do was get pissed and go mackerel fishing."

"Can't see the problem there," Bone said.

The manager stopped halfway in. "Where do you want this?" he asked Walker, who was setting up a printer in the corner.

Walker looked up from a printer she was trying to connect. "Just by the wall where you are is fine. Are you sure you don't mind us commandeering hotel equipment?"

"As long as Police Scotland pays for the lot, it doesn't bother me. Happy to help as best I can." He turned to Bone. "Speaking of which, I'm assuming you'll all be wanting fed."

"What have you got left?"

"Fresh fried mackerel and chips?"

"Sounds splendid, thanks."

"Well, I say fresh, I mean frozen—just."

"As long as you don't kill us, we'll eat it," Bone replied.

Urquhart left.

"So what's been going on, then?" Walker asked, dropping a cable and approaching her boss. "When I radioed in, all I caught was a bride and groom had been murdered and to check recent weddings in the vicinity?"

"You might want to make some notes, Will," Bone said.

Harper opened one of the laptops and pulled his chair in.

"Two nights ago, in the middle of the blizzard, I spotted lights over on the Isle of the Dead."

"Is that what you're calling it now, or is that its actual name?" Harper asked.

"Its reputation precedes it, I'm afraid. Early the next morning, I went over to investigate and discovered a bride and groom, in full wedding regalia, propped up in a tiny graveyard. The groom was already deceased, stabbed and as frozen as a fish finger, his bride the same but showing signs of life."

"How macabre," Harper said, pushing the rim of his specs up his nose.

"I think in my head at that point I was pondering the idea that it might have been a domestic between the two of them. The couple were hand in hand."

"At that point?" Walker asked.

"I stayed with the woman to try to keep her alive. I sent the boatman, Kilpatrick, to raise the alarm, but when he didn't return, I went to check and found he'd been attacked and was out of it on the beach, and his assailant had smashed the radio, I presume to try and stall a rescue."

"So no domestic, and the killer was still on the island?" Walker asked.

"The weather was so bad, we thought it likely they'd got stranded, but after I discovered my injured boatman, I returned to the victims to find someone had been back at them. At least that's what I thought. But my coat had been thrown to one side and some fresh prints were in the snow. But then an initial search found no one, so I'm not sure. There was, however, a jetty on the mainland a few hundred yards from the island, but Danny," —Bone nodded to the constable— "warned that the narrow strait was treacherous."

Matheson nodded. "Aye, that's right. I suggested we walk over from Loch Gillan and see if we could find where this psycho was hiding out."

"So at first light, Danny, Junior, and I set off over the mountain to track down our person of interest. At the jetty, we found a submerged boat, either scuttled or run aground but with no sign of the occupant. But I did find a bloodstained glove." He searched around his feet. "Shit, it's still in my rucksack back at the cabin."

"You don't think the attacker might have drowned?" Walker asked.

"We did speculate on that, but we decided to carry on to a farm owned by a Mr Jock Dulhoon, about three miles farther up a track. And to cut a long story short, while we were talking to the farmer and his wife, someone nicked a quad bike from one of his outhouses and escaped right from under our noses."

"Did you ID the thief?" Walker asked.

"No, but Danny managed to tear a strip off him, literally."

Matheson held up an evidence bag. "I nicked a bit of his coat, army-green Barbour."

"But then on the way back, we found the bike overturned with blood in the snow indicating that the thief has probably sustained an injury of some kind with the trail leading back towards Loch Gillan."

"That explains the search, but do you think they would come back here with all of us swarming around?"

"It seemed like it, but the tracks disappeared at the foot of the mountain, and to be honest, they might have wandered off and got lost, and if that's the case, then they would most certainly be dead by now, so I'm fifty-fifty on that at the moment."

"How is the bride doing now, do we know?" Harper asked.

"She was airlifted out when the weather broke. The last we heard, she was fighting for her life at Stirling Royal."

"Danny and I took a load of photos of the victims and crime scenes," Bone said. "I figured it was going to be a wee while before forensics would be able to get on the sites." He found his phone and handed it to Harper. "Could you charge that and stick them up on the laptop and also maybe print some out? Matheson's too."

"Aye, sure," Harper replied, collecting the phones. "I've brought a bag of cables."

"As you do in a blizzard." Walker smiled.

"The password is—" Matheson started.

"You're okay, I'm already in," Harper interrupted.

Matheson shrugged. "Huh?"

"Don't ask, Danny, something to do with Will's placement at MI5. If he told you what he did, he'd have to brain wipe you, or something like that," Walker said.

"He does that most days to me anyway," Bone interrupted and smiled at his young colleague.

Harper pulled a face. "You must be missing Mark, that sounds like one of his insults."

"The Dulhoons have a son at College in Stirling," Bone carried on. "But the thing I found a little odd was the thief managed to locate the spare key to the quad, which was hidden at the back of a drawer in the farmer's workshop."

"That's lucky," Walker said.

"No such thing in our game. The only people they said who knew about the spare were the two of them and their son, but they insisted he was still in Stirling at the Agricultural College there."

"Did you believe them?" Walker asked.

"Why would they lie? Did you, Danny?"

"They seemed pretty shocked by the whole thing," Matheson said. "They didn't come across as people trying to cover up anything. I mean, they openly told you about the spare key, so if they were protecting or shielding their son, why would they do that?"

"Why indeed. The perennial question." Bone rubbed at the scar on his forehead.

"Though if you're suggesting that Fergus is involved or even responsible for the attacks, then I'm not sure that holds water. I haven't seen him for a couple of years, but I knew him pretty well when we were growing up and kicking around at school together. Fergus is kind-hearted and sensitive, at least when I knew him, so unless something dire has happened to him to twist his personality, I don't think he's capable of doing something as heinous as this."

"And to bring us all up to speed, I called in on Lonnie Kilpatrick earlier to double-check his story,"

Harper looked up. "Who's that again? Sorry, I'm trying to multitask here, and my brain's still a bit frozen."

"The injured boatman," Bone replied. "He restated more or less everything he'd said before with not a lot that might help us."

"Did you get an ID of his attacker?"

"No, just the flash of a coat. He was knocked unconscious for a bit, so his memory is a little hazy."

"I hear a 'but' coming on," Walker cut in.

"There were some bloodstains in the snow with footprints leading towards the main road out of the village. When I asked about them, he claimed his cat escaped earlier and he'd chased after it, and that the blood was his, from the wound he sustained in the attack."

"Credible?"

"I'm not sure. He seemed a little surprised when I asked him."

"One to keep an eye on then?"

"He's also mates with the farmer's son and told me they'd been out at a Hogmanay do together but hadn't seen him since."

"Sir, to be fair, everybody is either family, mates, or sworn enemies round here. Aside from you lot, there's no such thing as a stranger."

"Aye, I know, but it all suddenly feels a little incestuous and tangled."

"Welcome to my world, sir," Matheson replied. "*Emmerdale's* got nothing on this place."

The printer clacked.

"Got it," Harper exclaimed, as the machine spewed out paper.

"And that's where we are now," Bone resumed. "Two unidentified, mutilated newlyweds, and the killer on the loose injured, trapped, possibly close by and desperate to escape."

"Or dead on the mountain?" Walker interrupted.

"Aye, or that, too." Bone's phone pinged, followed by a barrage of hoots, hums, whistles, rings, and tings from all the other devices in the room.

Harper picked up the nearest on his desk.

"ET has phoned home," he said and handed Bone his mobile.

Bone snatched it up.

"It's working. Are yours?"

"Yes, I'm on," Walker said.

Matheson nodded.

"Right, ring through to the station and request forensics and a support team up here asap. Also, ask Sheila to try and make contact with this Fergus Dulhoon and find out where the hell he is."

"On it, but whether they can get through is another matter altogether," Walker said.

"I also need the Super to clear our investigations up here with HQ. We'll need formal permissions and collaboration from the local force as we are just outside our jurisdiction."

"Okay, it's ringing now."

"I'll shut up now." Bone checked through his messages. There were eight or nine texts and over a dozen calls from his wife.

"Back in two minutes," he said and stepped out into the corridor.

Urquhart came running down to meet him. "The phones are back on."

"Yup, but for how long?" Bone hit the call button, and within a couple of rings, his wife answered.

"Alice!" he yelled, unable to control his relief at finally getting through.

"Duncan, oh, thank God. Are you okay?"

"We're all fine here."

"I was so worried about you. I couldn't get through, and the weather has just been apocalyptic."

"It's okay, I'm okay. The phones have just come back on, but everything else is down."

"You must be freezing to death up there in that cabin."

"I still have gas, and the hotel has a generator and enough mackerel and tatties to keep us going to the next millennium, so don't worry. I was worried that you and Michael might have set off and got caught in it. It came in so fast."

"We were just about to leave when my neighbour warned me, and then when I tried to call you, the call wouldn't go through."

"Well, we're all fine, thank God, and it looks as though a thaw is coming, so hopefully I'll be able to get the hell out of here and back to you both in a couple of days."

"Michael wants to say hello," Alice said, and the speaker clicked.

"Hello, Dad," his son said.

"Michael, it's good to hear from you, son. Are you enjoying the snow?"

"Aye, it's great. I've been off school for two days."

Alice shouted in the background.

"Mum thinks it's a nightmare." Michael giggled. "Are you still snowed in?"

"Stuck in the hotel bar. The absolute pits."

Michael giggled again. "How deep are the drifts?"

"Put it this way, the Saab has completely disappeared."

"That's a good thing, though, isn't it?" Michael joked.

"Aww, not you as well?"

"I'll hand you back now."

"Okay, see you soon, son."

"So I take it you're going stir crazy yourself then?" he asked Alice when she returned.

"There's only so many times you can go sledging with Michael's school friends and their weird parents. Come home as soon as you can, please, Duncan?"

"Try and bloody stop me."

"I went down to the station to find out if they'd heard from you. They said Rhona and your DC—"

"Will."

"Aye, they were on their way up to join you. I couldn't believe it. Are they mad?"

"Yes, pretty much. They actually made it, but they had to commandeer a snow plough."

"But why would they risk it? Is there something going on up there?"

"Oh, there's been a spate of robberies. They offered to help me out, and I foolishly said yes." Bone didn't want to worry her but felt bad for lying.

"As long as you're okay."

"Everything is totally fine, love. I'll be home very soon. Listen, I've got to go. There's a fried fish with my name on it waiting to throw itself into my hungry gob."

The line went dead.

"Hello?" he said. He redialled, but the signal failed. "Oh bugger, not again." He tried one more time, then returned to the incident room.

"Signal's gone," Harper said.

"I know. Did you manage to speak to Sheila?"

"I called her at home, and she's on it. She said she'll get back with more first thing in the morning, so hopefully this is a temporary blip and they are working on it."

"Hopefully indeed," Bone agreed. "Did everyone else manage to get through?"

"I called Maddie after Sheila, but we got cut off about three sentences in. I did manage to tell her I'm okay, though," Walker said.

Bone frowned. "Sorry, Rhona."

"It's not your fault."

"I should have let you call your partner first."

"Ach, don't worry. She's fine."

"How about you two?"

"Yes, I had a brief conversation with Catriona," Harper said.

"Danny?"

"I called the mountain rescue centre and asked for more support."

"Did you have time to call a loved one?"

"Who would that be?" Matheson said with a wink.

Urquhart appeared at the door.

"Dinner is served, ladies and lady," he said.

"Let's adjourn for the evening and continue with fresh minds in the morning," Bone said.

And without a second's hesitation, there was a polite stampede to the dining room.

ELEVEN

Back at the cabin, Bone slumped down, exhausted, on top of the duvet. The day's events rattled around in his head for a few minutes, but his limbs were so worn out he couldn't halt the inevitable tumble into a deep and restless sleep.

A loud clatter in the living room woke him with a start. He sat up and listened, staring into the impenetrable dark engulfing the bedroom. A second thud. He got up, quietly slid over to the door, and put his ear to the wood. Then came the faint sound of breathing and the scrape and groan of furniture being moved. He silently counted to three and was about to burst through when the alarm on his phone sounded.

"Bugger."

He yanked open the door. The room was empty, but the French doors were swinging back and forth on their hinges. He ran across and out onto the decking. He spotted a shadow on the path adjacent, heading for the beach path. Running back inside, he pulled on his boots, and with laces undone, he gave chase.

The figure disappeared behind some trees ahead. Bone skittered on, trying to stay upright in the snow. At the trees, he peered into the dark but couldn't see anything. A loud crack to his right sounded. The figure was making for the beach. Bone raced on, but the going was treacherous, and at the end of the path, he slid backwards and skidded down, arse-first, onto the pebbled shore.

"Fucking hell!" he cursed, and jumped back to his feet.

The figure had vanished again. He clambered across the snow to the water's edge so he could catch a glimpse of the harbour. The figure re-emerged from the gloom farther up.

"Stop! Police!" he hollered, but the figure carried on. "Oh, just stop, for fuck's sake." Bone gasped.

He approached the harbour wall, and a motorboat engine started up. Climbing the wall ladder onto the quay, he scanned the cluster of small boats moored on the other side. But it was too dark to see much of anything. He was about to run back around the quay when one of the boats emerged from the flotilla and accelerated along the side of the harbour wall.

Bone turned back and ran, slid, and stumbled along the quay in pursuit of the intruder. The boat's engine roared again, and the craft sped out towards the open loch. Bone chased on, now almost alongside the craft, but the end of the pier was fast approaching. He contemplated a wild, desperate leap onto the deck, but he was spared certain injury when the boat made a sharp turn at the end of the quay and escaped across the loch. Careening towards the edge, Bone just managed to stop himself from tumbling over. He bent over and took a few long, deep breaths and watched the vessel disappear into the night.

"Bastard!" he wheezed and set off as fast as he could back to the centre.

At Kilpatrick's cottage, he hammered on the door again. "Off out are we?" he cried out, and moments later, the next-door neighbour's light went on. Bone thumped the door again. "Oh, I wonder why."

The neighbour's window opened. An elderly woman with a shock of wild grey hair stuck her head out. "What in God's name are you doing?"

"Sorry to disturb, but I wanted to have a word with your neighbour." Bone panted.

"At this hour? What are you, a bloody vampire?" she moaned, then more lights went on along the lane.

"Oh, Jesus," Bone mumbled. "It's a police matter."

"Oh, right. Then can you conduct your police matter a bit quieter as it's the middle of the night for us mortals?"

The neighbour's neighbour appeared at his bedroom window.

"Is that you making all that bloody racket, Pauline?" he said, leaning out.

"No, it's Dracula down there."

"Duncan?"

"Aye, evening, Gaz," Bone replied.

"If you're after some food or anything like that, then you're on a hiding."

"Aye, he's after some blood." His neighbour sneered.

"Quit it, you, with the ghosty ghoulies rubbish. I'll no' sleep now."

"Don't blame me, blame Vincent Price doon there roaring his head off."

Bone was about to apologise again when Kilpatrick's door opened.

"Inspector, you're back," he said through a yawn. "This is getting to be a habit." He peered out into the dark.

"What time is it?"

"Have you been out at all this evening?"

"When?"

"About ten minutes ago?" Bone continued.

"Oh aye, I've been up the corrie, doing a bit of paragliding."

"Sorry, it's just that someone broke into my cabin and has taken off in a powerboat."

"And you thought that was me? Do I look like James bloody Bond?" Kilpatrick replied, his anger rising.

"The intruder had a white bandage on the back of his head, like yours."

Kilpatrick turned around. "Gone. I took it off earlier this evening. It was pressing into the wound when I lay down."

"So you've been in bed the whole night?"

"And most of the day. I've just been feeling crap."

"Well, maybe you need to speak to the doc again about it."

"Much as I love standing here freezing my nuts off talking to you, is there anything else I can help you with? If not, I'm going back to bed."

"Sorry to disturb you," Bone said.

"And us," the neighbour called down.

"Good night, all." Bone waved and made his escape.

"That's him away back to his coffin before the sun comes up."

"Pauline!" Gaz complained and slammed his window shut.

Back in the cabin, Bone searched the chaos the intruder had made of his living room. Luckily, nothing was broken, especially his beloved Dansette, but drawers had been ransacked, cushions and storage cupboards emptied onto the carpet, and coats strewn across the room. He searched for his rucksack, but it was missing.

"The glove," he said, and on the decking, he peered over the side of the terrace into the water. On the other side, he spotted the rucksack lying upside down on the gravel next to his son's canoe. He jumped down and reached inside. It was empty. "The thieving get!"

He returned to the cabin, locked up, and made himself a hot drink. There was nothing he could do about it until the morning.

Isle of the Dead

TWELVE

Walker called for him just before seven, and for once he was already up.

"When was this?" Walker asked, stepping into the cabin, trying to process what her boss had just told her.

"About 2 a.m. He took the glove."

"Loaded with DNA," Walker replied. "Definitely a 'he' then?"

"Most definitely. I ran after him, but he made off in a motorboat."

"Made off where?"

"Across the loch, heading towards Balhuish and the island."

"We need to get over there, then?"

"Ach, they'll be long gone by now. They're not going to return to a crime scene."

"Unless that's what they think we'll be assuming and double bluff us."

"What?" Bone pulled a face.

"You need some breakfast."

"If it helps decipher your drivel, I'm in." Bone smiled.

"Did you get a make on the intruder?"

"I caught a flash of white on the back of his head, so I thought it was Lonnie Kilpatrick. The guy looked big enough to be him."

"And?"

"When he gave me the slip, I went straight to his house."

"And?"

"He was in and not too pleased about me waking him, and that goes for his neighbours as well. I was a bit wired and may have been a tad loud."

"Okay, let's get some grub and work out a plan," Walker said.

"Aye aye, Captain Birdseye." Bone winked.

"Sorry, sir. Am I taking over again?"

"No, it's all fine. I'm just pulling your chain. All hands to the pump."

In the hotel, the team had gathered in the bar where Ross was serving up some poached mackerel on toast.

"More fish?" Bone winced.

"We're getting down to the bottom of the freezer now," Ross said.

"No bacon left?" Harper asked.

"Ha, not unless you're hiding a pig in your room." The chef looked up. "Sorry, that didn't sound quite right. I didn't mean—"

The team laughed.

"On so many levels," Bone replied. "Have you brought your Taser, DI Walker?"

Ross set down a bundle of cutlery and plates. "If the worst comes to the worst, we still have three kegs of Guinness. In Ireland, they call it liquid avocado. We all might be totally hammered, but we won't starve to death. Help yourselves. Enjoy."

"I hope everyone slept well, unlike me," Bone said when he'd gone.

"What happened to you?" Harper asked, spooning one of the fish onto his plate.

"I had a break-in. Long story short, at approximately 2 a.m. the intruder stole a key piece of evidence and escaped in a boat across the loch."

"The glove?" Matheson asked.

"The very one."

"Oh, shit. We still have the ripped pocket; at least that's something."

"If you're thinking of becoming a detective, you're going to have to turn down that optimistic tone, Danny."

"If this was the killer, then I suppose the good news for Loch Gillan is that they are no longer hiding out here," Harper said.

"Aye, and the bad news is they could be bloody anywhere now," Bone replied.

"Any updates on phones and power?"

"Not a thing as yet," Walker said.

"The thaw is set for tonight apparently, but with freezing rain first, so it could get worse before it gets better." Matheson added.

Bone rolled his eyes. "Brilliant."

"I still think my double bluff theory has legs," Walker said. "The killer or whoever it was who reclaimed their glove would probably know that the area will be in lockdown for at least another twenty-four hours, so why not make a stop there, safe as anywhere else?"

"Or he could have doubled back later in the night and he's back with us, and might even show up for a pint this evening, in this very room."

"There is that, too."

"The first thing we need to do is find out if there's a boat missing and whose it is. Then I think we're going to have to bite the bullet and start door-to-door enquiries. Between us, it won't take long to get round the village."

"What about the panic you mentioned yesterday?" Matheson asked through a mouthful of fish.

"I'm sure everybody probably knows what's been going on by now, and the people of Loch Gillan are not exactly shrinking violets. We run with the line that we are looking for a person of interest in connection with an incident on the island and they should keep an eye out for strangers or anyone acting suspicious."

"That's us caught then," Harper joked.

"And three-quarters of the population of Loch Gillan and Balhuish," Matheson added.

"Danny, do you know who the harbour master is again? I've forgotten," Bone asked.

"Harbour master? That's funny. Where do you think we are, Ardrossan?" Matheson laughed. "One of the laird's lackeys mans the harbour hut once a week to collect mooring fees and check everything is okay."

"Will they be there today?"

"In this, I seriously doubt it, but I can have a look."

"Finish your breakfast first," Bone said.

"There's only so many mackerel one can eat in a twenty-four-hour period." He grabbed his coat.

Bone turned back to his plate of white fillets drowning in a thin milky sauce.

"Hold up, I'll come with you," he said and followed Matheson out.

The harbour hut was locked up, and a makeshift sign in the hatch window read: *Closed due to bad weather.*

"Can't say I'd noticed," Bone joked, then clocked a local down on his hunkers near the end of the quay. He approached.

"Morning."

The bearded man who was securing the moorings on one of the boats below, turned in surprise.

"Morning, Harry," Matheson said. "Your boat's still in one piece, then?"

"Aye, just about." He continued to loop a thick mossy rope around the metal post.

"Are you familiar with all the boats here in the harbour?" Bone asked.

Harry stopped what he was doing, stood, and wiped the muck from his hands. "Aye, are you after a boat hire or something?"

"No, late last night someone took off in a motorboat, and I was wondering if it might have been nicked."

"What sort of motorboat? There's plenty to choose from."

"Light coloured with a weird pointy sort of back to it."

"Are those nautical terms you're using?" Harry grinned. "That sounds like Vinnie's boat. He usually moors it over in Balhuish, but I noticed it here a couple of days ago."

"Vinnie?"

"Vincent Trough."

"That name again," Bone said to Matheson. "Where is it?"

"I think it's over on the other side." Harry returned to his rope, tied a quick knot, and shuffled across the quay. "Watch yourselves there, some frozen water," he said, stepping around a solid smooth puddle sunk into the snow. "Well, that's odd. It was definitely here a couple of days ago." He leaned over the side and checked the length of the quay. "Nope, gone."

"So was the owner stuck in Loch Gillan or something?"

"I've not seen Vinnie over here for months."

"Did you not think it a bit odd that his boat would be here without him?"

"Not at all. He's back and forth in it all the time, and sometimes his boats are there for weeks if he's got a lift back to Balhuish with one of his mates after a late session in the hotel bar."

"Who might have taken it last night, do you think?" Matheson asked.

"No idea. Everything's gone haywire. I've been eating out of tins for two days."

"And you didn't see or hear anyone take the boat last night?" Bone continued.

"I live at the back of the village, so not a thing, no. But it's worrying if some clown's nicked it. Bloody parasites. I heard there's been some kind of assault on Balhuish Island, is that right?"

"We're trying to get to the bottom of an incident over there, yes."

"And you think Vinnie's boat might be connected?"

"As I said, it's early days, but if you think of anything else, however small or trivial, or through the grapevine—"

"Like what?" Harry interrupted.

"If someone else spotted something suspicious or has concerns but might not think it worth speaking to us, let us know anyway."

"Like Huggy Bear, you mean?" Harry said.

"Who?" Matheson replied.

"You know, like the guy in Starsky and Hutch."

"What is it with you lot and that bloody programme?" Matheson said.

"What?" Harry frowned.

"We're just trying to sort this out as quickly as we can," Bone said.

"Ach, I'm only joking, no bother," Harry said. "But if it turns out to be a family thing, then you might struggle to get anyone to talk to you about it."

"Why would you say that?"

"Trouble round here usually involves some family squabble or feud. Everybody is either related, wants to be related, used to be related, or shouldn't be related, if you know what I mean."

"Yup," Matheson agreed.

"Are there any families in particular you have in mind?" Bone asked.

"Ach, I'd be better making you a list of those who don't squabble, and that's usually because most of them are deid and they're down to the last relative."

"Okay. Thanks, Huggy." Bone nodded.

Walker joined the group. "Here comes the cavalry again." She pointed to the inshore rescue boat fast approaching the village.

Gliding in alongside the quay, a crew member jumped off and tied up the mooring rope, followed by a woman in a white combat parka, matching waterproof trousers, and mirrored shades.

"Oh my God," Walker went over to greet her and they embraced.

"What the hell are you doing here?" the woman asked, removing her sunglasses.

"Working, and you?"

"Same." The woman smiled. "But I thought you were up in Inverness."

"I thought you were in Stranraer?"

"Reassigned," they both said together and roared with laughter.

"Morning," Bone said.

"Sir, this is Lesley Buchan, a former classmate at the Police Academy. Lesley, this is DCI Bone."

"Duncan," Bone added.

"I knew you were living up here now, so it's good to finally meet you, sir. I've heard only good things about you," Buchan said.

"That'll be a first," Bone replied.

"And hello to you, too, Officer Matheson."

"Ma'am,"

"Oh, 'ma'am' it is now. I take it you're on duty as well, then?"

"I'm doubling up again." Matheson winked.

"I heard there's been a serious assault and death over on Balhuish Island."

"You heard correct." Bone glanced over at Harry, who was pretending not to be listening in. "Thanks again for your help, Harry."

"No bother," Harry replied, still lingering with his ear on the conversation.

"We'll crack on then." Bone nodded.

Harry stood for a moment, staring at the detectives. "Oh right, aye." He returned to his boat.

"Last time I saw you, Danny, you were belting out 'I Will Survive' on the karaoke machine at the Balhuish New Year's party," Buchan continued.

"Don't remind me, though to be fair, I seem to remember you murdering 'Wonderwall.'"

"How did you make it over from Drumgoil?" Bone asked.

"Inshore got a message through to us, and I managed to get the four-by-four over to Balhuish. Well, I say that, I actually got stuck about five miles out, and mountain rescue had to come a pull me out, but here I am."

"What are you now then, Les?" Walker asked.

"Detective Inspector, for my sins."

"Snap," Walker replied.

"That's hilarious. Look at us, bloody high flyers. Who would have thought it when we were messing about at the academy? Hey, do you remember Vicky Grogan?"

"Egg-gate, oh God, I haven't thought of that for years." Walker giggled and turned to Bone. "Silly cow claimed she could eat one hundred and fifty hard-boiled eggs in one go."

"How many did she manage in the end?"

"Thirty-eight. It was the soft-boiled one that finally made her throw up," Lesley grimaced. "She blew up like a bloody barrage balloon."

Walker snorted. "Thank Christ, we weren't in the same dorm as her."

"Thank you for making it over. I'm not familiar with Drumgoil station. How many detectives are based there?" Bone cut in.

"Just the one, and I work between the Drumgoil and Lomond stations. My boss, DCI Harris, is over at Lomond office, and I haven't managed to get through to them for a few days. This white crap has its advantages."

"You don't get on?" Bone asked.

"It's not my place to say, but if there was a competition to find the country's most irritating man—" She looked up. "Sorry, that was unprofessional of me."

Bone smiled. "Don't worry. Your secret's safe with us."

"Good job Mullens isn't here then," Walker added.

"Who?" Buchan asked.

Walker shook her head. "You don't want to know."

"So in a nutshell, we have one dead, one critical on Balhuish Island, another victim on the mainland, Kilpatrick with a sore head, and the killer on the loose somewhere in the vicinity," Bone continued.

Buchan's eyes widened. "Good God, that's serious crime. We're more used to poaching, farm thefts, and domestics, with the odd bag of dodgy powder washing up from time to time." She turned to the skipper. "Thanks for dropping me over, skipper."

"Inshore Taxis, no job too big," the skipper joked.

"Any more updates on the female victim?" Bone asked.

"Last I heard, she's still fighting. Doctors are a little more confident than yesterday, apparently."

"Do you know if she's conscious yet or said anything about the attack?"

"Don't know. My conversation with the air ambulance crew was cut off when they got called out."

"I need to get over to Balhuish to speak to Vincent Trough, do you know him?"

"You mean Vinnie, who runs the boat repairs yard?" Buchan asked.

"Everybody knows Vinnie," the skipper added. "He's part of the Balhuish DNA. His family boatyard has been there since the Dark Ages. You don't think he's connected to this, do you?"

"The intruder who broke into my cabin last night took off in his boat."

Buchan looked over at Walker. "You RCU lot don't do things by half, do you?"

"Can you take me over?" Bone repeated.

"Of course, aye," the skipper said.

"And then on the way back, can we stop at the isle again? I need to check something out."

"We're supposed to be patrolling the mouth of the loch this afternoon, and if anything happened down there, we're too far away to respond. But we could stop on the way over to Balhuish as long as you're fairly sharpish."

"Great." Bone turned back to his colleagues. "Okay, I'll go and speak to Mr Trough."

"Would you like me to come with you?" Walker asked.

"No, you three stay here. You can fill DI Buchan in on events to date and carry on with the house-to-house. I'll only be an hour or so."

"Okay." Walker nodded. "Why are you going back to the isle?"

"Something's bugging me. I'll tell you when I get back."

The officers returned to the village, and Bone followed the skipper onto the boat. A second crew member handed Bone a life jacket and untied the mooring rope.

"A bit calmer than our last visit," Bone said.

The skipper nodded and the boat set off for the isle.

At the island's jetty, Bone jumped off. "The World War Two bunker is on the other side of the graveyard, is that right?"

"Yes, through the trees, bear right when you get to the graveyard, and at the topside, you'll see another narrow gap in the trees. The bunker is about a hundred feet in."

"Thanks."

"But I'm sure one of our team has already checked it," the skipper added.

"Professional curiosity, bear with me. I won't be long," Bone said.

The skipper glanced at her watch. "Twenty minutes tops, okay?"

"I'll be as quick as I can," he said and set off up the slope, following a well-trodden path in the snow to the trees.

He entered the graveyard. The breeze dropped, and an eerie silence surrounded him. He weaved through the first few gravestones and stopped close to where he'd discovered the bride and groom. A crow sounded above him, and he followed its flight across the sky and into the woods beyond. A hooded figure appeared at the farthest edge of the clearing.

"Hey!" he called out.

It turned and disappeared behind a tall Celtic cross. He ran towards it, almost toppling over a flattened tombstone lost under the snow. Bone recovered. The figure was before him. It was the creature, the grotesque manifestation of his bomb-injured mind.

Peek-a-boo.

"You!" Bone exclaimed.

The ghoul's rotting, charred skull emerged from under the hood, an eyeless socket oozing black, tar-like fluid.

The creature raised a fleshless skeletal hand to its gaping toothless orifice.

"Blood," a faint whisper hissed in Bone's ears.

"What do you mean?" Bone asked, no longer frightened by the antics of his unwanted apparition.

The creature lowered its arm and dropped its head.

"Look, you can't just turn up like this uninvited and not explain what you mean. It's getting very tiresome."

Bone moved towards it, but with every step, the creature slid farther from him.

The crow suddenly returned, and with a loud, ear-piercing scream, its wings flapped past his face, and he stumbled backwards, colliding with a cross directly behind him. He clambered back to his feet, but the creature was gone.

"Typical," he moaned. "I suppose the crow was your idea?" he called out across the graveyard.

Brushing off the snow, and locating the gap in the trees, he carried on. A hundred feet or so in, the canopy cleared, and he spotted a thin line of concrete peeking out from a high mound of snow. He approached.

The bunker was partially buried in the ground, and a deep drift of snow on top had almost buried it completely. Bone slid down a slope, and the bunker reared up above him. He cleared the snow with his boots and searched for a window or door in the solid, circular-shaped structure. The incline increased again, and he stumbled down a set of three hidden steps and thumped against the side of a small rusting metal door.

There were deep scratch marks in the metal around a fist-sized, heavy-duty padlock. Leaning in, he examined the marks, then, gripping the lock in both hands, he yanked it with as much force as he could muster. The shackle sprang open, and he fell backwards into a drift, still clutching the broken mechanism in his hands. The door swung open in front of him, and a dank, musty stench escaped.

He peered inside, but the darkness was impenetrable. Finding his phone, he turned on the torch, and the beam filled the circular space with light. The bunker was empty.

Cautiously, he stepped in, and the temperature rose slightly. He flashed his torch along the walls. The snow above had blocked narrow windows that were cut into the concrete and running around the circumference of the bunker. Directly above his head, the snowfall had covered a rusty grille in the ceiling. The dome shape made the bunker feel like he was in some kind of decaying alien spacecraft.

He shivered and turned the beam back to the muddy, wet floor. A flash of silver on the far side caught his eye. Stepping over a semi-frozen puddle in the centre, he directed his torch to the object ahead. He leaned over and picked up a thin strip of foil. He turned it over, then sniffed at it.

"Wrigley's," he muttered.

From his rucksack, he removed an evidence bag and dropped the wrapper in. To his right, he spotted a bundle of tissues piled up in the corner. Kneeling, he picked off a couple and exposed a half-frozen, neatly curled turd, resting proudly atop a small boulder.

"Oh, Jesus," he exclaimed and dropped the tissues.

The door slammed suddenly, and the structure boomed like an artillery cannon firing a live round. In a panic, Bone dashed over and pushed at it with force. It flew open, and he fell out into the light, ready to take on whoever was there. But aside from the wind rustling the surrounding trees, all was quiet. He glanced back into the bunker. A set of red eyes stared back at him from the deep, dark interior, and a hushed voice inside his head hissed again.

"Blood."

He slammed the door shut and returned the broken lock to its shackle.

***

"Thought you said your men had checked the bunker?" Bone said to the skipper when he returned to the boat.

"They said they did, why?"

"The lock had been jimmied and then crudely reattached with clear signs that someone had used the bunker as a shelter or hideout."

"Oh, shit. They must have overlooked that."

"Aye. I suppose at a glance the lock looked secure."

"Do you think they were there when we landed?"

"That I don't know, but they were there for a while. They left a little foul-smelling calling card."

"Oh, shit," the skipper repeated.

"Oh shit, indeed."

"Okay, Balhuish?"

"Yes, please, let's crack on."

Bone pulled over his life jacket and sat, still pondering what his PTSD partner was trying to tell him.

THIRTEEN

Vincent Trough loosened his grip on the rope and lowered himself down the side of the boat, a twenty-eight-foot clipper, one of the largest he'd restored for a long time. It was sitting at a forty-five-degree angle at the top of the ramp in the dry dock, making Trough's task of repainting the hull more difficult. He stretched for his brush and dipped it in a tin of black hull paint resting at the end of the harness bench. He worked the paint into the wood, stopping once or twice to scrape a barnacle or two from the surface.

When he'd finished a section, he balanced the brush on the side of the seat and adjusted the rope again. The top snagged on the side of a mooring hook and, picking up the pot, he shimmied his body sideways, freeing the rope. The harness dropped three or four feet, his legs slammed into the hull, and his brush toppled off onto the slipway runners beneath the boat.

"Ach, Jesus!" he cursed.

The restoration process had been nothing short of a nightmare with many more problems emerging than he'd anticipated or budgeted for. He was already two weeks overdue, and his clients—a wealthy couple from Edinburgh—were not happy. He yanked angrily at the rope. The pulley squeaked, and the harness lifted Trough back up towards the deck.

A loud clang sounded beneath him. He stopped pulling, and leaning over, tried to locate the source of the noise.

A second clang, and the boat juddered. He twisted the other way and caught a glimpse of someone moving around close to the slip.

A third was followed by a fourth boom, and the boat lurched forward.

"Get the fuck away from there!" Trough called out.

He pulled at the rope again, but before he reached the top, the boat took off down the slipway, sending him careering sideways and almost off the wooden seat. He frantically tried to unhook the safety line from the harness so he could jump free.

With a deafening roar, the clipper hit the water, its bow plunging deep under the surface, sending an immense surge across the loch.

Still attached to the harness, Trough was dragged under the hull. His body corkscrewed in the swell, and the violent movement pummelled the air out of his lungs.

Half-conscious, he fumbled again for the safety clip to set himself free from the assault, but he was already drowning, his lungs screaming for oxygen.

The boat sped on across the loch into deeper water. The harness line unfurled, and Trough slipped further under the stern, the rope tangling around the huge rudder. He grabbed it and tried to lever himself away, but the rope lashed and twisted around his back, squeezing his chest against the steel frame.

He gurgled in agony, and water rushed down his windpipe, saturating his lungs.

The boat slowed to a gentle drift. The wave receded and calmed.

Trough's final breath surfaced with a futile, pathetic pop.

FOURTEEN

When the rescue boat arrived at Balhuish harbour, the skipper attempted to explain where Trough's boatyard was, then decided it was easier to show Bone herself. They approached the entrance. The high, wrought-iron gate swung back and forth in the breeze. They walked through a metal arch with Trough's name written in gold lettering above.

"Just in case he forgets who he is?" Bone commented.

"Vinnie?" the skipper called. She turned back. "Let's check his office, over here."

"Vinnie?" she called again when they reached the door of a black corrugated iron workshop.

She went in, Bone following. Trough's coat was on the back of the chair, and his radio was blaring out some Gaelic folk song. There was a half-empty mug of coffee on the desk. Bone leaned over.

"It's still warm."

"He must be at one of the boats," the skipper replied.

They returned to the yard. On the far side, an open-sided barn was packed with partially dismantled boats, with various parts stacked up in the corner. A disembowelled motorboat engine lay in bits on a worktop. They carried on towards the dry dock area. There were three in total.

"God, I didn't realise it would be so big," Bone said.

"Aye, his skills are in demand from all over the country, the world even. He's what you call an old-school master craftsman."

The first dock was a smallish pit housing a twelve-foot dinghy with a gaping hole in the side of the hull.

"Ouch," Bone said. "Shark attack?"

"Loch Gillan's treacherous currents attack, I suspect," the skipper replied.

The second dry dock was empty, but there were a multitude of guide ropes laid out along the length of a slipway into the loch.

"Looks like he's just launched one," the skipper said.

"Is that it?" Bone pointed at a yacht floating adrift a few hundred yards out.

The skipper turned. "It could well be, but where's it going?"

The bow of the boat was facing the shore, and the stern was heading slowly towards the harbour wall.

"Is he on it?" Bone said.

"That boat's out of control. Shit, it's going to collide. Come on."

The skipper ran back through the yard and onto the road. Bone followed, trying as best he could to stay upright in the snow and slush. When they reached Balhuish's tiny picturesque main street, they cut down an alleyway that took them to the harbour. Running along the jetty, the skipper called for assistance, but there was no one around.

Ahead, the yacht careered into the jetty's wooden frame, smashing through deck boards and ripping a section off the end. It continued, its hull screeching and grinding slowly past. By the time the skipper reached the boat, it was too far out to attempt a jump on board and bring it under control.

Bone finally caught up with her. "Good God, look at the mess it's made."

"It's heading for the main wall. If it hits that at speed, it could sink it."

"What's that?" Bone gestured to a red object floating in the boat's wake.

The skipper stared at the water for a moment.

"Jesus Christ, it's Vinnie!" the skipper cried out.

Bone removed his coat and pulled at the laces of his boots.

"What are you doing?"

"He's drowning."

"You can't go in. The water's too cold."

"Trust me," he said, and before the skipper could stop him, he ran as far as he could to the end of the damaged jetty and dived in.

With three or four sharp breaths, his body adjusted to the temperature, and he set off for Trough's limp body. As he approached, the boat turned in the water, dragging Trough sideways and away from Bone, but he continued his pursuit, and when he reached him, he grabbed Trough's sodden boiler suit and yanked his dead weight towards him.

Finding an arm, he tried to flip his body over onto its back, but a tangle of ropes kept pulling him back. Bone searched around Trough's torso and chest and, locating the harness clip, he fumbled with the mechanism. The clip clicked, the safety rope whipped free, and Trough rolled over, his ashen face emerging from the water, his mouth gaping open, and his lifeless eyes bulging out of their sockets. Holding Trough's neck above the water, Bone lay on his back and kicked towards a pencil-thin beach adjacent to the dry dock. The skipper waded in and helped Bone haul Trough out, and immediately administered CPR.

Bone collapsed alongside, shivering and panting.

The skipper checked Trough for signs of life and resumed pumping at his chest.

"Do you have a defib?" Bone asked, shivering so much he was barely able to get his words out.

The skipper ignored him, and then, after a few more compressions, she stopped.

"Nope," she said, and her head dropped.

"He's dead?"

"Well gone." She turned to Bone. "You bloody fool. That could be you lying there as well. What the hell were you thinking?"

"I told you, my body is conditioned for these temperatures."

"But not when you're swimming around a dangerously adrift thirty-foot boat, with the weight of a corpse on top of you." She blew out her cheeks.

"There was no other way," Bone replied through chattering teeth.

"You need to get warm. Rescue boat. Now. Tell Gary to come."

Bone sat shivering a moment longer, staring at the drowned corpse he'd just dragged up the beach.

"Now!" the skipper ordered.

Bone stumbled to his feet and, putting his coat back on, he left the skipper to attend to the body and headed back to the rescue boat.

Crewmate, Gary, provided Bone with a change of clothes, a couple of oversized jumpers and baggy leggings, and took Bone up to the nearest hotel where the manager let Bone shower and warm up in one of the vacant bedrooms.

Once he'd recovered his core temperature, Bone caught up with the skipper and Gary in the hotel bar.

"Thanks for that," Bone said, handing the manager his wet towel.

"The least we could do after you jumped in after him like that. I can't believe it. Drowned, you say?" the burly manager said.

Bone looked around at the skipper. "You told him?"

"It'll be news soon enough."

"But it's Vinnie. Vinnie doesn't let a boat loose like that and then drown in the process. He's been at that game for too long to do something stupid like that," the manager cut in.

"Could I have a word?" the skipper said to Bone.

"I'll make you a hot drink, Inspector," the manager said. "Unless you want something stronger?"

"No, coffee will be fine, thanks."

"Shocking," the manager repeated. "Everyone's going to be devastated."

Bone and the skipper sat by the fire.

"Are you okay now?" she asked.

"Absolutely fine."

"I won't say any more on this, but please don't do anything stupid like that again."

"I think we'll have to agree to disagree on that one. What have you done with Trough's body?"

"We put him on a stretcher and carried him round to the rescue boat. Luckily, nobody saw us." She rubbed her forehead.

"Never mind me. Are you okay?"

"It's all a bit… you know?" She sighed.

"Aye, intense. So sorry. Do you think this was an accident?"

"That's what I wanted to talk to you about and why it's even more bloody shocking. The manager is right. There's no way the boat could have been released like that without some significant interference."

"What do you mean?"

"All the chocks that hold the boat in place were lying to one side, and the ropes have been cut."

"Trough was wearing a harness, and I had to unclip him from a tangle. That's why it took me so long to get him out."

"You see, a total death trap out there." She shook her head. "Anyhow, sounds like he was probably hanging off the side doing some renovations."

"But it looked like it had just happened!"

"Not long before we arrived, I'd say."

"How long?"

"A few minutes maybe, ten at the most?"

"That means if this wasn't an accident, then the culprit is here in the town." Bone stood. "We need to search the area." But his head spun, and he slumped back down.

"You're not searching anywhere," the skipper insisted.

"It's nothing, just a head rush from the shift in my core temperature." He rubbed at the scar on his temple. "This is getting crazy. We need to stop this lunatic. He clearly didn't want me to speak to Trough. Last night his boat was over at Loch Gillan, and the same bastard who broke into my house and stole vital evidence made off on Trough's boat and now seems to be on a clean-up mission."

"Well, it's a town of two thousand inhabitants. This monster could be hiding anywhere, and we don't have enough people on the ground to run any kind of effective search."

"This fucking weather!" Bone thumped the table. He looked up. "Onset hypothermia, obviously." He smiled and then sighed with frustration.

"At this rate, there won't be anyone left in the Loch Gillan area."

The manager approached with two cups of coffee and some biscuits.

"Cheers," Bone said and took a couple of sips, watching the manager retreat. "We need forensics and search teams up here right now. Where is this thaw?"

"We'll drop you back at Loch Gillan and take Mr Trough up to the cottage hospital," the skipper said. "They'll be wondering what the hell we're doing up here."

"What about his next of kin?" Bone asked.

The skipper called the manager back over.

"Does Vinnie have any next of kin nearby?" she asked.

The manager frowned and stared at the floor for a second. "He lived on his own in a wee cottage close to his yard. I seem to remember he was married a good few years ago now, but she ran off with some Aussie bush farmer or something."

"Brothers, sisters, parents?" Bone asked.

"Not that I know of. He was very much his own man. Quite a humble guy who lived simply, considering how much his yard raked in every year."

Bone stood again, his head behaving itself. "Where's his cottage?"

"There's a wee row on a narrow lane behind the yard. His is the one right on the end with views over the bay."

Bone grabbed the washed-out fleece Gary had given him and headed for the door.

"Hold up," the skipper said and followed him out. "I told you to take it easy."

"Aye, sure." Bone nodded and carried on.

Trough's cottage, a tiny pre-Victorian two-up two-down, butted up against a sheer drop into the harbour, and its higgledy-piggledy stonework made it appear as though it could topple in at any moment. He peered through the tiny window adjacent, but couldn't see beyond the dirt on the pane. He tried the door handle.

"What are you doing?"

"Police business," Bone replied.

The door swung open and thumped against something on the other side.

Bone checked the frame. "To me, that looks like someone's forced entry."

"Really?" The skipper couldn't see any marks. "People tend not to lock their doors round here."

But Bone was already inside. The matchbox-sized living room was ransacked, with furniture upturned and debris strewn all over the carpet.

The skipper hung back behind him. "Are you sure this is legit?"

"Suspicious death, yes."

"What are you looking for?"

"What were *they* looking for more like?" Bone nodded at the mess.

"Oh, God."

"Clearly, something that links Trough to the person who killed him," Bone added. "His phone or address book, laptop, photographs, anything like that."

"Where do you start with all this?" The skipper sighed.

Bone went through to a narrow galley kitchen at the rear of the living room. There was similar devastation, and he had to step over pots, pans, and smashed crockery on the stone floor.

"They've really gone to town," Bone called through.

The fridge door was hanging wide open, with its contents laying in a messy wet heap beneath. He retreated through the living room and up a steep, narrow staircase tucked between the two rooms. The first door led into a poky bathroom with an ancient, olive-green suite. The unit above the sink had been ransacked, and toiletries were spilled or smashed on the floor.

He carried on next door to an equally tiny bedroom, with a double bed that practically filled the entire space. An impossibly slim wardrobe was rammed into the far corner. He squeezed along the end of the bed. Clothes were hanging out and strewn on the floor. A waterproof coat lay discarded across the bed, its pockets turned out.

Kneeling as best he could in the narrow space, he picked up some of the dumped garments and laid them out next to the coat; there were a couple of moth-eaten jumpers, a few work shirts and trousers, heavily stained with paint and oil. He turned back to the wardrobe and removed the last remaining item dangling precariously from a hanger: a bright yellow, three-buttoned suit, complete with granddad shirt, waistcoat, and braces still attached to the trousers. He searched the pockets, not sure what he was looking for, and his hand jarred on something sharp.

"Ouch!" he said, dropping the suit and examining a bleeding puncture mark on his forefinger.

He tried again and carefully removed a Stanley knife. He turned it over. It was an antique model from the 1960s and was quite beautiful, with the company logo embossed in metal along its side.

A shaft of sunlight shot through the partially pulled curtains on a tiny window on the other side of the bed. The sun's ray hit the opposite wall, illuminating a ten-centimetre-high glass case. With a quick suck of his dripping finger, he squeezed around the bed for a closer look.

Inside was a display of a giant beetle around the size of a fist, its jet-black shell shiny enough to reflect Bone's surprised expression. A near-invisible pin, inserted between the beetle's neck and alarmingly large pincer claws was holding the creature in place. He noticed a latch on the case and slowly opened the front. He was about to reach in when his phone rang.

"Jesus!" he exclaimed in fright. "Hold on!" he said, checking one pocket then another.

"Rhona?"

"We're back in the twenty-first century," she replied. "Sir, power is back on—"

"No, listen. There's been another murder. The boat restorer has been drowned."

"Oh, Jesus."

"Hold on." A phone was still ringing downstairs. "Are you going to answer that?" he shouted down to the skipper.

It continued to ring, and Bone ran back downstairs.

"It's not mine," the skipper replied.

"It's coming from the kitchen," Bone said. He returned to his phone. "Hold the line a second." He dashed into the kitchen, and the ringing intensified. "Where is it?"

"The cupboard," the skipper said.

Clearing pots and pans blocking the door, Bone yanked it open, and a floor brush and mop fell out. An ancient, rusting top-loader washing machine was rammed into the space behind.

"It's coming from inside." He pulled at the lid. "How do you open these things?"

The skipper waded through the chaos to help. "The lever there, flick it back."

The lid sprang open. The machine was stuffed to the gunwales with damp, mouldy-smelling clothes. Reaching in, he yanked the bundle out, and a phone dropped out of a pocket of a pair of filthy, oil- and paint-stained overalls and clattered onto the floor. He snatched it up and hit the answer button. He gestured to the skipper to remain silent and held the handset to his ear. Faint breathing rasped on the other end. He pressed it closer. The breathing stopped, the phone clicked, and the line went dead.

"I think that was him," Bone said.

"How do you know?"

"Who calls someone then doesn't say a word?"

"A pervert?"

"Well, yes, there is that. I think he must have been looking for this, but with the phones out and it tucked away in ET's flight home, he was never going to find it."

"Do you think we spooked him then?" the skipper said.

"I think he'd already gone. There's no back door."

Bone's phone rang again. "Sorry, Rhona."

"What happened to Trough?" she asked.

"It looks like our killer got to him before me. He sent him down with one of the boats he was restoring."

"Oh, Christ. Now the phones are up, I'll call the station and find out how Sheila's getting on with the hunt at her end."

"Any joy with the door-to-door?" Bone asked.

"Nothing yet."

"Okay. Keep at it." Bone hung up.

They went back outside.

"We need to lock this door and keep the house sealed until forensics gets here, whenever the hell that'll be," he said.

"They're going to be busy when they do." The skipper leaned around, snibbed the lock, and slammed it shut.

"Is that rain?" Bone held up his hands.

"I think it is."

"Thank fuck for that." Bone nodded. "Let's have another look round the boatyard, and then could you drop me back in Loch Gillan?"

"Sure," the skipper said.

They set off to continue their search.

FIFTEEN

"We still have power and phones," Walker said when Bone entered the makeshift incident room.

"Great," Bone replied. "Is the coffee on?"

"My number one priority, boss." She turned and pointed to a coffee percolator bubbling away in the corner. "Courtesy of room eight." She glanced down at his improvised outfit. "Nice clobber. Are you moonlighting in a Happy Mondays tribute band?"

Bone pulled at his overstretched tracksuit bottoms. "Very funny."

"Shocking news from Balhuish," Buchan said. "Any more from over there?"

But Bone was over at a display of crime scene images arranged along the far wall. "You've been busy, Will."

"Seeing as the queen of the incident board isn't here."

Walker joined him.

"This one here is bugging me," she said, pointing to one of the photos.

"Aye, sorry that some of these are such poor quality. It was so cold, and we were lucky to get our phones working at all."

"No, it's not that."

"Sir," Harper interrupted, and nodded at the open door.

The American tourists were lingering in the entrance.

"Can I help you?" Bone approached.

Mrs Ellis gasped in awe. "Wow, this is so exciting! So this is where it all happens. Is this your actual incident room?" she added, her eyes as wide as flying saucers.

"That's what it says on the door, and it's private." Bone smiled, slammed the door shut, and returned to Walker.

"You said they were hand-in-hand when you found them," Walker said, pointing at the two bodies propped up against the tombstone, "but to me, that looks more like she's gripping his wrist, or am I imagining things and I need a holiday?"

The others came over.

"It's quite grainy, but I think you're right," Bone said. "Is she pulling or restraining him? So strange what the cold does to your brain. I have no recollection of that at all." He sighed. "Before we speculate any further, I need caffeine." He went over to the peculator and poured a mugful.

"What happened over at Balhuish?" Buchan asked.

"Someone sabotaged Trough's boat while he was busy working on it, and it ended up in the loch with him under it."

"Oh, Jeez," Harper said.

"Someone ransacked Trough's workshop and cottage. In his office at the shop, we found a laptop charger but no laptop, and this…" He reached into his rucksack and removed an evidence bag. Laying it on a table, he asked, "Got any gloves?"

Lesley fished a pair from a sports bag and handed them to him.

"It's a bookings ledger," Bone said, and slid the book out. "Unfortunately, the bastard has ripped out swathes of pages." He opened it up. "See here?" He ran his gloved finger along the tear.

"Killer's boat hire?" Buchan said.

"I suspect so. However, at Trough's house, we did find his mobile. With the phones down, our man clearly couldn't ring it, so he didn't find what he was looking for." He placed a second evidence bag containing the phone on the table. "Lucky for us, Trough must have forgotten to take it out of his overalls which were bundled into his washing machine. We only discovered it because it rang."

"Did you answer?" Harper asked.

"No, Will, I thought it was only polite to let Trough answer his own phone." He frowned at his young colleague.

"Sorry, sir." He put this mug of coffee down on his desk.

"Do you think it was him?" Walker asked.

"Well, unless it was a pervert, as the inshore skipper suggested, heavy-breathing down the line, I'd take a wild guess and say most definitely. So I have a number for you to check, Will, along with the rest of the phone."

"With pleasure." Harper's eyes lit up.

"But now the killer knows we have Trough's phone, so his desperation meter will be off the scale," Bone added.

"Not good," Buchan said.

"But the good news is we have power and comms and it's started raining."

"What?" Walker exclaimed.

"Yup."

"Thank fuck for that," Walker replied.

"That's exactly what I said." Bone grinned. "So, hopefully, we'll be able to move forensics in along with some urgent backup and nail this bastard before he inflicts any more tragedy."

Bone took another couple of sips of coffee.

Buchan moved forward. "Danny and I were talking about the Hogmanay party, and we remembered there was an altercation outside in the car park we had to break up. It was nothing serious, just a bit of drunken nonsense, but it involved a group of men who we think included Lonnie Kilpatrick and Fergus Dulhoon."

"How many people are we talking?" Bone asked.

"Three or four men."

"Were they fighting with each other or together?"

"It was more of a scuffle," Matheson replied. "It was difficult to say, as by the time we went out, it was more or less over. But Dulhoon had red marks on his face, so he'd definitely been on the receiving end of a fist or two."

"And you've just remembered this now?"

"Sorry, sir, but we were all very drunk, and as I said, it was something and nothing and everyone either went back in or went home."

"What happened after you went out?"

"I'm not sure," Matheson replied. "Can you remember?"

"I think Kilpatrick sang another song, but I don't remember seeing Dulhoon again," Buchan said.

"Okay, so we have two dead, a third critical, two boats, one owned by Trough and the other the laird, Trough's phone, a drunken scuffle in a car park—"

"And a partridge in a pear tree," Harper interrupted.

Bone glared at him.

"Sorry, sir, it's the coffee. I'm not used to it." Harper cowered and continued to fiddle with the mobile. "Bingo, we're in."

"You really are a nerd, aren't you?" Matheson said.

"Proudly." Harper beamed and pushed his glasses up his nose. He scrolled through Trough's texts and call records. "Looking at last week, the same number appears," —he scrolled for a moment— "eight times."

"Is it the same number that rang this morning?"

"It is, yes."

"Can you run a trace on it?"

"Not from here, but I can request a closed source check."

"Do it," Bone replied. "Anything else?"

"Just checking messages now. Same number, messaged four days ago.

Just a single exclamation mark. Then yesterday…" He scrolled some more. "Two exclamation marks."

"Code?" Buchan suggested. "Or a warning?"

"Good, keep going with that," Bone said. "Rhona, have you managed to contact Sheila?"

"I called her a few minutes ago. She's sent over a list of wedding ceremonies booked in a fifty-mile radius of here over the last month."

Harper glanced up from the phone. "I've got it."

"That's going to be very long, isn't it?" Bone asked.

Harper adjusted his glasses. "Yup."

"Okay, let's work through that together as fast as we can. What about the Dulhoon's son, Fergus?"

Walker checked her notebook. "He's currently in his second year at Agriculture College in Stirling, but the departmental secretary said his attendance has been very poor and he hadn't completed a number of assignments or paid his accommodation fees, so he's on an official warning."

"Is he there now, though?"

"Sheila also spoke to the warden at Dulhoon's hall of residence. They said they'd send someone round to check on him and get back. She's still waiting to hear but said she'd chase."

"Okay, and did she try the number his parents gave me?"

"Of course. No reply."

"Right, so we need to find him asap. Danny, do you think the road to the Balhuish country estate will be passable by now?"

"In the police Land Rover, it might be possible."

"I think we have to try. Are you up for it, Rhona?"

"No such thing as bad weather on Lewis, sir. Just bad clothes."

"Right, and while Rhona gets us stuck in the middle of bloody nowhere again—"

"Thanks for the vote of confidence, sir," Walker interrupted.

"Carry on working through the wedding list and keep an eye out for the elusive SOC team."

"I'll take this phone apart," Harper said.

"I'm sure you will, Will."

"Right, let's do this. Pray for us," Bone joked, and they left.

SIXTEEN

The Land Rover skidded to a halt in front of the estate's main house.

Walker released the steering wheel and let out a long sigh of relief.

"That was bloody hairy," she said. "I think the slush is even worse than snow to drive on."

"You did very well to keep us alive." Bone grinned.

"More off-road but upright at least." Walker flexed her hands.

Bone climbed out and stared up at the twin stone towers looming over them both.

"He owns a bloody castle," Walker said.

"Keeps the riffraff like us out," Bone replied.

Walker followed Bone up the steps, through a portcullis, and into the main reception. Inside, the vast space was furnished in authentic Scottish Tourist

Board clichés: roaring fire inside an inglenook the size of a garage door, tartan carpets, mounted stags' heads complete with oversized antlers, and walls festooned with ostentatiously framed portraits of kilted, flush-faced, redheaded aristocrats, clutching a plethora of weaponry or slaughtered game of various shapes and sizes.

"Hoots mon, Haggis?" Walker muttered.

The tartan-suited hotel receptionist jumped back in surprise when they approached the desk.

"Sorry, sir, I didn't see you come in." He tucked an errant red curl back into the nest balanced on top of his head. "Took me by surprise there, as we've been completely cut off for two days. Did you manage to drive here?"

"I'm Detective Chief Inspector Bone, and this is Detective Inspector Walker. We're from the Rural Crime Unit in Kilwinnoch, investigating an incident."

"Oh my goodness, you've come a long way. What sort of incident? Here?" the receptionist asked, a hint of panic in his voice.

"Could we speak with the laird or your general manager?"

"Sir John is unavailable at the moment, sir, but I can try and get a hold of Ms Temple, our general manager, for you."

"Why is the laird unavailable? It would be extremely helpful to talk directly with him," Bone pressed.

"I'm afraid Sir John spends the winter months abroad."

"I bet he does," Walker mumbled again.

"Where?"

"He has a number of residences. This year I believe he is residing at his property in the Seychelles Islands."

"All right for some, eh?" Walker added.

The receptionist attempted an uncomfortable smile. "Let me try Ms Temple now." He picked up the reception phone and dialled through. "I'm afraid there's no reply. I'll take you over to her office. It's possible she's on another line." He snatched up his tartan jacket and stepped around his desk.

"I reckon the Scottish army should redesign their uniforms in tartan," Walker said, following the receptionist across the foyer.

"How so, Inspector?" the receptionist asked politely.

"It's so effective. It's like you've completely disappeared into the carpet."

Bone stifled a laugh.

The receptionist carried on through a stone archway, up a flight of steps, along a mahogany-panelled corridor to a second wooden door. He knocked gently. There was no reply.

"I'm afraid I don't think—"

"Can I help you?" a voice called from the far end of the corridor.

The detectives spun around.

"Ah, Carol, these police officers are looking for you," the receptionist said.

"Police officers? Has there been an accident?"

"May we speak to you?" Bone said.

"Of course, I was just about to check our kitchen stocks with the head chef, but that can wait. Please, come into my office." She unlocked her door and turned. "That's fine, Rod, thank you."

The receptionist smiled curtly and left.

"Please take a seat. Excuse the mess. We've been fighting fires, or blizzards, I should say, over the last few days."

She cleared some papers from one of the chairs adjacent to her desk, and the detectives sat.

"How did you manage to get up here?" she asked. "I spoke to the groundsman this morning, and he said the main road into the drive was still blocked."

"I have my expert rally driver here." Bone nodded to his colleague.

"The thaw is improving things hour by hour now," Walker said.

"I'm DCI Bone and this is DI Walker. We're from the Rural Crime Unit in Kilwinnoch."

"DCI Bone, as in the wild swimmer who lives in Loch Gillan?"

"Yes, that's right."

"Your reputation precedes you, sir," Walker said, smirking.

The manager smiled. "Indeed, it does. I hear you've made quite a splash in the village, pardon the pun. I didn't realise your—what's it called, patch—covered the loch area as well?"

"The weather has skewed everything."

"Hasn't it just. We have eighteen guests in the hotel, and put it this way, our creative resources with the menu and indoor pursuits are being severely tested."

"There's been an incident on Balhuish Island," Bone said.

"What sort of incident?"

"Two victims of an assault, one dead, one critical. We have reason to believe that they may have been renting one of your lochside lodges."

"Oh my God. What?" the manager replied, her mouth falling open.

"Do you have booking records that we could check? We're still trying to identify who they are."

"Of course, of course. Hold on." She switched on her computer. "Okay, so let me just bring up the spreadsheet." She stopped for a moment. "Sorry, my hands are shaking." She tapped the keyboard for a few moments. "Yes, here it is. Only the one lodge is booked out this week to a Mr and Mrs McDermid."

"McDermid?"

"Yes, Laurence and Clare McDermid."

"Can I see that?" Bone stood.

The manager turned the monitor. "Booked our spring honeymoon special for one week from the 1st to the 8th of April, so they are still here with us."

"You hope," Walker interrupted.

"Oh my God, these aren't the two people who were found on Balhuish Island?"

"Possibly," Bone said. "One of your boats was recovered from the scene."

"No, this is awful."

"Are your lodges kitted out with boats for guests to use?"

"They are, but they are not available until the Easter weekend, which is next week, so I don't know how one of our boats, or indeed our guests, could have taken it over there."

"Are the lodges serviced?"

"Yes, they are cleaned daily, and the honeymoon special includes daily supplies of treats, such as champagne, flowers, and chocolates. But this sudden weather has thrown everything into chaos as the lodges are isolated and two miles from here along a forest road that is difficult to drive on at the best of times. It's the seclusion that our guests love the most and why the majority of lodge bookings are for romantic breaks. Let me check with the housekeeper and groundsman and find out what's going on."

"Thank you," Bone said.

"Just a quick question," Walker interrupted. "How did the guests pay for the booking?"

"I can check that now for you." The manager tapped at her keyboard again. "I'm sure it's probably—"

She stopped. "Oh, they paid in cash when they arrived. That's a surprise, as it's quite a substantial amount to bring with you."

"How much is substantial?" Bone asked.

"Our rate for the honeymoon special at this time of year is one thousand, eight hundred per lodge, per week."

"I see what you mean." Bone recoiled.

The manager picked up the phone sandwiched between two teetering towers of files on her desk. The receiver clipped the top of one, and files toppled over and onto the floor.

"Sorry, this is all rather upsetting," she said.

Bone leaned over, picked one up, and handed it back to her.

"Good morning, Fiona. Could you come to my office for a second?" the manager said. There was a pause. "Well, leave that for now and come down. This is urgent." She looked up, smiled nervously at the detectives, and hung up. She dialled again. "Just trying the head groundsman's office." She waited a moment or two and then tried the number again. "Sorry, he must be out and about."

A few moments later, the door rattled, and a flustered woman in a slightly dishevelled tartan uniform entered.

"You wished to see me?" She glanced down at the two detectives.

"Fiona, these are police officers. They wish to ask you a couple of questions about our lodge guests."

"Has there been some kind of complaint?"

"No, no, nothing like that, Fiona." Bone smiled. "When did you last service the lodges?"

"I told you, Carol, that we couldn't get down there."

"Don't worry, this is not about your work, Fiona," the manager said. "It's Mr and Mrs McDermid in number one lodge."

"Yes, there's only one occupied at the moment," the housekeeper replied. "The forest road has been blocked since Tuesday, and we haven't been able to get down there. But I believe when they arrived, they requested not to be disturbed, including daily cleaning."

"It's often the case with honeymooners," the manager added. She tapped at her keyboard again. "Yes, that's correct. The front of house logged that request on our system."

"So nobody has called in on them at all in the three days since they checked in?" Walker asked.

"What about their power?" Bone queried.

"The lodges are off the grid," the housekeeper clarified. "They run on biofuel generators. I rang them two days ago, and I spoke to the young woman. She said they were fine and had plenty to eat and drink for now."

"And do you know if the groundsman managed to get through the snow to them?" Bone continued.

"I spoke to him yesterday, and he confirmed lights were on, but he didn't knock as he didn't wish to disturb the young lovebirds. Those were his words."

Bone frowned. "I'm struggling a bit here to understand how you could leave a young couple alone in the middle of nowhere in this horrendous weather."

"We offered as much support as we could, but they didn't want any," the manager said. "Our guests' wishes are paramount, Inspector. We ensure there are plenty of supplies in each of the lodges as a contingency for such requests or weather events."

Bone turned around to the housekeeper again. "Do you know how Mr and Mrs McDermid may have taken their lodge boat over to Balhuish Island?"

"No." She looked over at the manager. "I thought the boats weren't available until the Easter holidays."

"Oh dear, let me try Peter again." The manager picked up the phone.

"It might be better if we talk to the groundsman face to face and then, if possible, try and get over to the lodge," Bone interrupted.

"Yes, er, of course. I don't know what has happened there."

"Is that all, Carol?" the housekeeper said.

"Yes, thank you for your help," Bone said.

"If you'd like to follow me, I'll take you over to Peter's office," the manager said.

They returned to the corridor, exited the building, and walked out across a snowy courtyard to the rear of the estate house.

"This way, mind your step on these slabs." The manager cut through a narrow passageway and headed towards a line of outbuildings. "These used to be the stables. The former laird once raced horses." She approached the nearest door, knocked, and pushed her head around. "I'm afraid he's not here."

"Can I help you?" A man emerged from the alleyway, clutching a roll of chicken wire.

"Ah, there he is," the manager said.

"You looking for me?" The groundsman deposited the wire at his feet. "I was down at the coops. Some hungry foxes tried to get in again."

"Peter, this is Inspectors Bone and Walker," the manager said.

"The AA? In this weather?" The groundsman pulled a face.

"No, police officers."

"Has there been more thefts? I haven't heard anything."

"Hello, sir," Bone interrupted. "We're investigating a serious incident that took place on Balhuish Island two days ago."

"Oh aye, what's happened?"

"Two people were seriously assaulted. One is critical, and the other has sadly passed away."

"Oh my God. That's terrible. How did they— I mean, the weather has been so atrocious. What the hell were they doing on Balhuish Island?" the groundsman stuttered.

"That's what we're trying to ascertain, sir. We found one of the estate boats tied up over there. What's your full name, sir?"

"Er, Peter Conroy. We're not talking about the guests in number one lodge, are we?"

"At this point, we have been unable to identify the victims. The female is still unconscious in Stirling Royal. When was the last time you checked on them?"

"It was day one when they arrived. I called in to make sure they had everything they needed and all the lodge's facilities were up and running."

"So before the storm hit?"

"Yes."

"And you haven't been back since?"

"They made it quite clear to me, and to the housekeepers, that they wanted to be left alone. Love's young dream and all that."

"The boats are out of bounds from October until the spring bank holiday," the manager interrupted. "Any idea how one of them got over there?"

"I'm not sure." Conroy frowned.

"Can you check, please?" The manager's tone sharpened.

"Aye, of course." He took the detectives into his office, and on the wall, he unlocked a metal box. "This is where I keep all master keys, including the pleasure boats." He ran his finger along a cluster of Yales and mortices large and small, and then stopped.

"Number one isn't here. I'm not sure—"

"You keep saying you're not sure, Peter. You should be sure. Our rules explicitly forbid the use of lodge boats until the Easter holiday, and then only when weather permits," the manager said angrily. "So sorry about this, Inspector."

"I've been so busy dealing with weather-related problems with extremely limited support. Half the staff couldn't make it in. It's been hellish," the groundsman complained.

"But it's important, especially if our guests somehow managed to get a hold of a boat key when they shouldn't have been anywhere near the water with the storm forecast."

"So how did they get the key?" Walker asked.

"I'm at a loss, sorry." Conroy glanced over at his boss.

"We need to have a look at the lodge," Bone said.

"I was out on the forest road earlier this morning, and it was pretty bad in places," Conroy said.

"I'm not asking," Bone insisted.

"Okay, we'll take the tractor. It has a shovel on the front in case we hit a drift."

"Is there room for three?" Walker asked.

"Aye, just."

They trudged across the yard into one of the outhouses and climbed aboard a tractor that had been reversed into the space. The detectives stood on either side, clinging onto the seat.

After a rough and bumpy ride along the forest track, Conroy parked up alongside a snowy pathway that skirted the edge of the trees. Walker and Bone jumped out.

"That was a Bone-shaking experience." Walker smiled.

Bone rubbed at his legs. "If it's isolation you're after, then they certainly tick that box."

"Down here," Conroy said. "Mind the steps under the snow."

At the end of the pathway through the trees, the wide expanse of the loch appeared ahead. The first of the lodges was directly below another set of buried steps down to the shore, a rustic wooden structure with a pitched roof and box windows at the rear.

"I was expecting something ultra-modern," Bone said.

"It was one of the conditions of the planning application that the lodges fit in with their surroundings," Conroy said. "I think the laird wanted something more Scandinavian, but between us, I'm glad the council put their foot down."

"Yes, I heard the lodges were controversial."

"I believe so. A lot of local opposition, but before my time."

"When did you start, then?"

"Two years ago. My wife and I moved up from Gretna. I was a groundsman at a hotel there."

"What made you change jobs?"

"The pay and conditions were better, and my wife has family in Perth. Here we are." Conroy stopped at the door and searched a bunch of master keys. "I'll ring first, just in case."

"Before you do, can you put these on?" Walker handed the groundsman and Bone pairs of rubber gloves.

"Oh God, really?" Conroy asked.

"I'm afraid this is a possible crime scene now, and we need to minimise contamination," Bone said.

Conroy wrestled to put on the gloves and then pressed the buzzer. It sounded on the other side. After a moment or two, he resumed his key search, picked one out, and opened it up.

"Hello?" he called into the narrow hallway, then stepped in.

Bone and Walker went in behind him.

"Anyone home?" he called again and pushed the internal door which led into an open-plan living space.

"Look at that view," Walker exclaimed, taking in the panoramic vista that opened out beyond a set of bi-folds, floor-to-ceiling, that extended the width of the room.

"I thought you said they were traditionally designed?" Bone said.

"Aye, with one compromise." Conroy nodded at the glass. "I'm still not sure how he got away with it. Mind you, they are all eco-friendly and zero carbon, so that's what probably swung it."

The interior of the living room was a classic alpine design, with plenty of soft furnishings and light-oak fixtures and fittings. There was a wood-fired stove in the centre with a vast steel chimney that disappeared through the ceiling.

Bone approached, and kneeling, touched the front of the stove. "Stone cold."

Walker checked the open-plan kitchen. "Wow, this is swanky," she said, opening a matching oak cupboard.

Inside there were a few boxes, jars, and tins of food. She pulled at a door beneath, a fridge stocked with milk and various other chilled products; two bottles of champagne and a couple of bottles of beer resting on the top rack. She opened the next door, the freezer. It was rammed with frozen ready meals prepared by the hotel.

"They weren't going to starve then," she said.

"The lodges come well-stocked," the groundsman replied.

"So they should at those prices," Bone muttered.

On the floor by the front door, he spotted two flute glasses and an opened bottle of champagne resting on a silver tray.

"Housekeeping usually collects all the waste every morning, but they didn't want anyone near," Conroy explained.

"Where's the bedroom?" Bone asked.

"Through here." Conroy took them along a short corridor to a master bedroom with another set of bi-folds, and beyond, a patio that reached down to a small jetty. The bed was unmade, with sheets and duvet pulled back, and clothes scattered on the floor. A pair of jeans were hanging upside down off the end of the bed, its pockets turned out.

Bone picked up a few garments and checked the pockets.

"What are you doing?" Conroy asked.

"Looking for anything that can help us with our investigation," Bone replied.

"But do you have permission to do that? I mean, it's private, isn't it?"

"The hotel has granted us access." Bone continued his search.

"What's through there?" Walker pointed at a sliding door.

"Walk-in wardrobe and en suite."

Bone picked out some coins from a jacket pocket and laid them out on the dressing table. "No phone or ID, just fluff. Where are their bags?"

"There's a utility room adjacent to the kitchen," Conroy said.

Bone followed the groundsman back to the kitchen, and he opened a narrow door at the rear. The space was rammed from floor to ceiling with white goods, and a drying line dangled from the ceiling. A row of women's fashion boots and shoes were lined up alongside. Bone picked up one of the high heels and checked the size.

"Four and a half. The woman in hospital was petite," he said, half to himself.

There were two small suitcases on the floor but they were both empty.

"Sir!" Walker called out.

Bone dashed back through to the bedroom. She was at the back of the wardrobe.

"More clothes in here, and I found this laying on the floor." She handed him an envelope.

Bone carefully opened the unglued flap and removed a slip of paper.

"It's a newspaper cutting." He unfolded it and turned it over. "It's an ad for this place. Romantic Getaway, look." He handed her the cutting and checked the envelope again. "Hold up, there's more." He pulled out a business card. "Jon Hoskins Photography. Have you heard of him?" he asked the groundsman.

"Yes, Jon's a local wedding photographer. He does a lot of work for the hotel, ceremony and reception packages, that sort of thing."

Bone checked through the few clothes that were hanging up. "That's not a lot of clothes for a week's trip. What's the bathroom like?"

"See for yourself, it's through there," Walker went back in and Bone followed.

"Nice roll top," Bone said, admiring the bath resting by a huge window with unrestricted views of the loch. He went over. There was a thin rim of soap on the inside surface. "I'd be in there all the time as well." There were a few toiletries lined up along a sink unit, and a shaver was lying on the side, still plugged into the mains. Bone shrugged. "It's still all a bit threadbare, isn't it? And no sign of bags or technology, phones, tablets, or laptops. Did they take it all with them?"

"That card suggests they could have been out attempting some kind of photo shoot over on the isle," Walker said. "That would explain their getup?"

Bone turned back to the groundsman, who was lingering at the door, looking increasingly uneasy.

"Is that something honeymooners do?" Bone asked.

"Possibly, but not that much. It's not exactly romantic with all those graves over there."

"Gothic-themed ceremonies, maybe?" Walker said.

"But why bother when the views from here are so spectacular?" Bone replied. "So, where is the boat moored?"

"Out the front." The groundsman took them back through the lodge, unlocked and opened the bi-folds, and stepped out onto a decked area.

"Where?" Bone scanned the empty jetty.

The groundsman rubbed at his face. "I'm sorry, Inspector."

"For what?"

"It's just—"

"Go on."

"I really can't afford to lose this job. We have a new baby, and our mortgage payments have gone up yet again."

"What is it?" Bone pressed.

"When I met them on day one, they were terribly disappointed that they couldn't take the boat out. They said that they'd paid a lot of money and were very angry about it. I explained that they should have booked for a few days later, but they were both quite distraught, Mr McDermid in particular. Anyway…" He grimaced.

"Spit it out," Bone exclaimed.

"He approached me on his own when I was leaving and offered me some money to release the boat key a few days early. I thought as we were only a week away and I didn't want to ruin their honeymoon, I took the money and dropped the key in later that day."

"How much did he pay you?"

"I'd rather not say."

"I'm afraid you have to,"

"Two hundred and fifty pounds. I'm so stupid. I should have said no, but I never dreamt in a million years something like this would happen."

"But weren't you concerned when the storm blew in that they might get themselves in trouble?" Walker interrupted.

"I assumed they knew and would be sensible about it. I'm such a bloody fool."

"Yes, I think you are, Mr Conroy," Bone said.

"Do you have to tell the manager and the hotel about this?"

"You think we can just forget about it?" Bone asked. "I'm sorry, but I'm afraid you'll have to face the consequences of your actions."

"Oh, Christ."

"We'll need the lodge completely sealed until forensics can get in to examine it."

Conroy fumbled with his keys again.

"Then take us back to the reception," Bone ordered, removing his gloves.

The groundsman pushed the door to confirm it was locked, and they returned to the tractor.

"Is that a police boat over at the isle?" Bone asked, squinting across the loch.

"It is, indeed," Walker confirmed.

Bone sighed. "At last. Hopefully, forensics will dig something out and move this bloody thing forward."

"Do you think we've ID'd the couple?"

"I can't see how it could possibly be anyone else. Could you ring Will and ask him to check if a Mr and Mrs McDermid are on Sheila's wedding list?" He turned on his phone.

"Are you calling the Super?"

"When we get back. Mark, first. I've something I want him to do."

SEVENTEEN

Mullens rang the bell of the care home, and a nurse came to open up for him.

"Hello, Mark, you made it here then?"

"Only just. It's like a slurry pit of slush and muck out there."

The nurse winced. "How are you today? How's the old ticker?"

"Ach, you know. Bored off my ti—" He looked up. "Very bored."

"How long have you been off work now?"

"Six weeks. Actually, I started working from home on Monday, but the buggers still haven't given me any work to do."

"Still, at least you're making good progress. No problems post-op?"

"No, the planet is going to have to put up with me a bit longer. Speaking of liabilities, where is the old codger?"

"Ah yes, you're just in time to join him in this morning's activity."

"Oh God, it's not that ventriloquist again? The last time he came, my da made him run through as many swear words as he could think of without making his mouth move."

"I know, I remember." The nurse rolled her eyes. "Fair play to the performer, he did try his best. Though, I do remember he wasn't very good at the ones beginning with B and F, and there seemed to be quite a lot of those. He wasn't so bad at the C ones." She laughed. "No, thankfully, today it's a little less rowdy. They're learning or trying to remember how to knit."

Mullens pulled a face. "Oh, dear God. You think that's a good idea?"

"Come see for yourself. In here." The nurse took Mullens through to the dayroom.

A group of residents were sitting around a large table. The young tutor was opposite, busy helping an elderly woman who was staring blankly at her set of wooden needles. As usual, Mullen's father was in the middle of the group, waving his knitting set around and hollering at the top of his lungs.

"You were saying?" Mullens said to the nurse.

"What's all this, George?" the nurse said, approaching the table.

"She's no' letting me make what I want," George complained.

"Look, George, your son's here," the nurse said, trying to distract him from his rant.

"Who?" George eyeballed Mullens. "Ach, him. I thought you meant somebody else."

"Who else? You only have one son, Da," Mullens replied.

"Aye, and don't I bloody know it."

"Well, good morning to you, too."

"Are you fucking joking? This clown wants me to knit." He complained and thrashed his needles around again.

"Steady, Da." Mullens grabbed his dad's arms and gently forced them back down onto the table.

"Haw, Victor, what are you making?" George elbowed his nearest neighbour.

Victor stared back and then returned to a tangled bundle of wool, squeezing it gently, over and over.

"Diana, this is George's son, Mark."

The flustered workshop tutor nodded. "Your father is quite a handful, isn't he?" She smiled nervously.

"I can think of other words to describe him."

"Hey, who are you talking about?" George interrupted.

"You, ya menace."

"Dennis, that's me, eh, lads?" George thumped the table.

One or two of his fellow residents looked up and smiled.

"Gnasher!" A man in a wheelchair opposite removed his false teeth and bounced the plate up and down on the table.

"You're going to need those at lunchtime, Harry." The nurse helped him reinstall his errant plates.

"Is it your first time at the care home?" Mullens asked.

"Aye," the young tutor said.

"Ah, good luck then." Mullens glanced back at the nurse. "What is it you want to knit, Da?"

"Oh, God," the tutor mumbled.

"G-string," George announced to the entire dayroom.

"I'm not sure that's suitable, Da. How about a scarf?"

"A scarf? Are you joking? It's forty degrees in here. Whit dae a need a scarf fur?"

"But what do you need a G-string for?"

"Spice up our sex life."

"Da," Mullens tried to stop him.

"Yer mother's always complaining that I'm useless in that department, so a wee bit of hanky-panky with these, and hey, presto. I'm a sex god."

"No, Da, listen. This is making me feel sick. Stop now."

"Oh, come on. It's a win-win-win. I knit a new pair of skegs, yer mother is happy in the sack, and there's no' as much tae knit." He picked up one of the balls of wool and lobbed it at the tutor.

"Right, that's enough, Da. Cool the beans."

George puffed out his cheeks.

"A scarf, okay?"

"Fine," George replied. "But you'll need to smuggle me in some viaduct."

"Some what?"

"Viaduct, you know, for the half mast." He gestured with his arm.

"Aye, and do you want me to bring a canal boat with that as well?"

"Whit?"

Mullens shook his head. He stepped back for a moment to speak to the nurse. "What's all that about?"

"It's just the dementia. His brain is triggering distant memories."

"That's what's bloody disturbing."

"The disease distorts everything. In an hour, he'll be on to some other bodily function."

"No, that's not dementia. That's his personality."

He returned to the table and helped his dad unfurl a line of wool, and together they followed the tutor's instructions. For once, George fell into silence as he engaged with the process. Half an hour in, the two of them had successfully completed three rows. Mullens' phone rang, interrupting the tutor's demonstration.

"Sorry," Mullens said.

"If that's yer maw, tell her I'm still at work." George winked.

Mullens stepped out into the corridor and answered the call.

"Well, well, well, if it isn't chief bottle washer himself. How's it hanging arshooz numero uno? I mean, er, good morning, boss."

"Got there in the end," Bone replied. "And good morning to you too, bawheid. How are you today?"

"Sadly for you, I'm still here, though I'm at my da's care home, and it makes me wonder if I should withdraw my undying thanks to Will for sucking my face off and saving my life."

"Listen, I can't speak, but I have a job for you, if you're up to it."

"Oh God, aye. Anything as long as it gets me out of the house. I'm going out of my mind with boredom. A few more days, and you'll be investigating the brutal assault and murder of your fellow officer at the hands of his raging wife."

"How's the weather with you now? Are the roads clear?"

"Aye, slush puppy abattoir, but roads are fine."

"I need you to drive over to Stirling Agricultural College and speak to a student called Fergus Dulhoon. He might be linked to a serious incident up here."

"Aye, Sheila filled me in. I bet the locals regret welcoming you into their midst."

"Just the usual RCU carnage. What's not to like?"

"*Aye, Sheila filled me in.*" One of the residents had sidled up behind him, mimicking his deep brogue.

"I know, you said that," Bone said.

"No, that wasn't me."

"*No, that wasn't me,*" the elderly woman repeated, her impression unsettlingly accurate.

Mullens looked around for help. "There's knitting in there," he said, trying to persuade her to leave.

"*There's knitting in there,*" she parroted.

A nurse appeared. "Mrs Dawson, come with me."

"*Come with me,*" the resident said, her voice rising a couple of octaves.

The nurse led her away, and at the door of the dayroom, the old woman turned and waved.

"Sorry, boss, it's like the bloody *Exorcist* in here today. You were saying?"

"The lad is a second-year student at the college. He has a room in their halls of residence."

"What's his connection with the shenanigans up there with you?"

"Not sure at this stage, but something's not sitting right in my head with this guy, or his family, for that matter."

"Are you sure that's not just your head that's not sitting right on your neck?"

"Well, there is that, too, but he's a local kid. His parents own a farm nearby, and quite close to the crime scene. If you manage to track him down, ask him where he was two days ago when the crime took place and if he borrowed his dad's quad bike. When we were talking to his parents at the farm, someone made off with it. If you need any more, Sheila has the lowdown."

"Okay, I'll see what I can find out. Thanks, boss."

"Oh my God, did you just thank me? Hold on and I'll record it on my phone."

"You see, I'm definitely losing my bloody mind stuck at home. Next thing you know, I'll stop fucking swearing."

"Don't exert yourself too much, though, okay? You are still recovering from a major heart operation, and technically, you're officially working from home."

"It's only Stirling in the car. Hardly a fifty-K endurance run."

"Later, Mark."

"Sir." Mullens hung up and returned to the dayroom.

He was surprised to find his father still thoroughly engrossed in the activity, along with the rest of the residents.

"Wow, good work," Mullens said to the tutor. "The only time he's this quiet is when he's asleep." He patted his da on the shoulder. "That's brilliant, Da, two more rows."

George glanced up at his son, his tongue sticking out in concentration, then he returned to the task in hand.

"He's really got the hang of it," the tutor said.

"That's going to be a fine scarf," Mullens continued.

"It's a cardigan for your mother. She loves her cardigans, so she does." George looked up again. "Do you think she'll like it?"

"She'll absolutely adore it, Da," Mullens replied and smiled at the tutor.

EIGHTEEN

When Bone and Walker arrived back in Loch Gillan village, the hotel car park was rammed full of police vehicles.

Chief Forensic Officer Frank Cash jumped out of one of the Land Rovers.

"Sight for sore eyes," Bone said, approaching his colleague. "What the hell kept you?"

"An act of God, blame him, or her," Cash replied. "It took us a wee while to negotiate our gear through the pass, but no lives lost, so all's fine. I heard you're up to your neck in stiffs again, Duncan."

"It's been bloody difficult, put it that way."

"We've been called in to assist the Lomond forensic team, who I believe is out there somewhere." Cash pointed to the loch. "Apparently, there are too many crime scenes for them to cope with alone. You don't do anything by halves, do you?"

"A couple of nights ago I discovered two victims on Balhuish Island—"

"The Isle of The Dead," Cash cut in. "Murder waiting to happen out there with a name like that. I got most of the lowdown from the Super. One dead, one critical, and another victim in Balhuish village?"

"Correct," Bone replied. "No ID on the victims as yet, but most probably out-of-towners."

"Newlyweds, is that right? DC Harper sent me over a rogue's gallery of images."

"Or dressed for anyway. We've just been over to Loch Gillan Estate Hotel. They have some waterside lodges over there, exclusive, isolated, popular for romantic getaways."

"And ideal for murder," Cash interrupted.

Buchan approached from the hotel.

"DI Buchan, meet our Chief Forensics Officer, Cash. Lesley is from Drumgoil station."

Cash nodded. "So he's roped you into one of his tangled webs, has he?"

"More knots by the hour, sir,"

Bone searched the car park. "Where's Danny, Lesley?"

"He's over on Balhuish helping the forensic team set up."

"We think the victims may have been staying at the estate and headed over in one of the boats that come with the lodge," Bone continued.

"At this time of year?" Cash frowned.

"A greedy groundsman took a bung and released the keys a week early. The lodge is sealed, so it's all yours."

"Okay, but I'll have to liaise with Forensic Officer Bennett. She's technically in charge, as it's her turf. I'll radio through and alert her we're here. It would be helpful to get over to the Isle of the Dead for a face-to-face, take a look at what we're dealing with and what assistance she requires. I love that name, Isle of the Dead." He dropped his voice into a hammy octave. "Why is it called that?"

"It's littered with graves of Celtic kings and rebel soldiers," Bone said.

Cash frowned. "Once noble, courageous and vital, now lost and forgotten. How sad." He looked out across the loch, and his frown deepened.

"The inshore rescue boat isn't here at the moment, but I can ask one of the local fishermen to take you over," Bone said, interrupting his inevitable descent into existential doldrums.

"No, don't worry. She'll hopefully send a boat to collect me. How far is it, anyway?"

"In one of their police boats at top speed, probably ten or fifteen minutes, tops."

"Excellent, I'll call her now."

"No need." Walker nodded at the incoming police boat.

It approached the harbour at speed, and the forensic officers gathered quayside stepped back in alarm. It turned quickly, slowed, and came to rest with expert accuracy against the side. A short, stout, ruddy-faced man clambered awkwardly off the boat and onto the quay, his overstretched lifejacket squeezing his frame like an angry fist strangling a plastic ketchup bottle. He turned back to the crew and seconds later let out a loud, bellowing laugh that echoed out across the bay.

"And there he is," Buchan said as he approached. "The DCI."

"Hardly effing Cunard, is it?" The DCI bellowed again at his own joke.

Bone twisted his head to try and shield his ears.

"DI Buchan, of all the whisky joints in all the world—" the DCI started.

"It's gin," Buchan interrupted.

The DCI pulled a face. "What?"

"Of all the gin joints, *Casablanca*."

"Thank you, Barry Norman. Oh, you're probably too young to remember him. What an effing old fart I am." The DCI laughed again.

Bone glanced over at Walker and winced. DI Buchan's earlier assessment of her boss was proving to be disturbingly accurate.

"I assume by your vacant look, you're DCI Bone?" The DCI sniggered.

"Sadly not. This is DCI Bone," Cash corrected.

"DCI Robert Harris from Lomond nick. My friends call me Hannibal, but you can call me Robert, ha ha ha." His chins dropped, and his whole body wobbled up and down.

"Wasn't it Thomas Harris who wrote those books?" Bone asked.

"I know, effing morons, eh? But that's what you get when you join the effing force." Harris guffawed, and a couple of seagulls resting on the hotel roof flew off in terror.

"I hope you don't mind that I jumped into this investigation," Bone said.

"Needs must. We were totally cut off over there. I couldn't even comm with the lovely DI Buchan. *Thank effing Christ for that*, I hear her cry."

"I couldn't possibly comment, sir." Buchan forced a smile.

"I've just come over on the vomit comet from the isle. Excuse me a second—" Harris unhooked his lifebelt, and the straps pinged and shot out like an uncontrollable man bra. "Ah, that's better. They make these things too small. I don't know how you ladies put up with such contraptions day and night." He stretched out his arms, and his belly pressed against the buttons on his coat. He looked back at Bone. "You're the wild swimmer from Kilwinnoch, aren't you?"

"Correct, yes."

"Well, hats off to you, but you must be off your effing head. As you can see, I prefer eating the fishes, rather than swimming with the effing buggers, preferably with chips." Harris rubbed at his bulging tummy. "Well, thank you for all you've done so far on the case. Now I'm here, I'm happy to take over as OIC."

"If that's what you wish, but I have been in the middle of this shitstorm for three days and might have a few insights, pardon my language," Bone fought to contain his frustration.

The DCI bellowed with laughter again. "Your face! Keep your lanyard on, DCI Bone. This is all a bit too effing 3D for me. I'm more of a behind my desk with a dram of whisky… I mean, coffee, kinda guy. As you should be, too. You are sullying the reputation of DCIs as lazy-arsed gets."

"Glad to be of service."

Walker stifled a laugh.

"I just thought I'd show my face and check you're happy to proceed on the ground, as it were, and I'll coordinate operations from my office. As far as I'm concerned, the sooner I'm out of all this horrifically beautiful scenery and fresh air, the better."

"That suits me, too."

"So joint OICs? You do all the work and I'll smoke the effing joint." Harris laughed so hard he choked on his own joke.

"Perhaps if we work separately on different parts of the investigation, then come together when necessary. That way we can save time," Bone agreed.

"Like a BOGOF deal," Buchan ventured.

"You see, I knew there was a sense of humour buried away behind that smacked-arse face of yours somewhere," Harris said.

"That's what the Lomond forensic team and I agreed on. Otherwise, we'll just get in the way of each other," Cash interrupted before things turned ugly.

"Good, yes. Okay, so let's say I'll deal with the isle and Balhuish bloodbath, and you focus on the carnage over here, how about that?" Harris suggested.

"Not exactly how I'd put it, but that sounds like a plan," Bone said.

"Not far enough," Buchan mumbled.

"Okay, but first, could you update me on the series of events so far?" Harris enquired.

Bone was about to land an excuse to escape such torment, when Harper came running down the hotel steps.

"Sorry to interrupt, sir. We've just had word from the hospital. The female victim is conscious."

"And talking?"

"They didn't say."

"Right, we need to get over there."

"Ahem, I need to sanction that decision," Harris said.

Bone spun around.

"Just kidding." Harris snorted. "No, go on, knock yourselves out. I'll get the rest of the lowdown from my colleague, Lesley, and your Joe 90 lookalike."

"DC Will Harper, sir," Harper replied.

"Does your mother know you're out?" Harris sniggered.

"My mother passed away a couple of years ago, sir, so no," Harper shot back.

"Oh, sorry to hear that. Though clearly, if you're her sprog, then she didn't die of old age." Harris continued digging the hole.

Walker shook her head.

"Terminal cancer." Harper frowned.

"Oh right. I'll shut the eff up now."

"Might be a good idea," Buchan said.

"How are the main roads now, do you know?" Bone asked, changing the subject.

"Improving. You should be okay, give or take the odd brush with certain death." Harris chuckled. He glanced over at the hotel entrance. "But first, I must empty the old bilge tanks. See you shortly." He marched off, pulling at the waistband of his trousers.

Bone turned back to the others. "Right. Will, can you alert the family liaison to meet us at the hospital? Lesley, I need you to go and interview Jon Hoskins at his photography studio over in Drumgoil and find out if the couple booked him for a shoot on Balhuish Island."

"Okay, will do. How will I get there?"

"Steal one of the support vehicles. I'm sure they won't mind." Bone smiled.

Buchan sighed. "I have to say it's such a relief to be working with your team rather than the David Brent impersonator I have to put up with."

"You wouldn't be saying that if Mullens was here," Walker joked.

"Rhona, shall we go?" Bone asked.

Walker rolled her eyes. "Thought you'd never ask." And leaning over to Buchan, she whispered, "Good luck."

"Les wasn't wrong," Bone said once they were across the car park.

"I don't know how his colleagues at Lomond haven't taken out a contract on him. I mean, either swear or don't fucking swear. What the hell is all that about? And those jokes, Jesus Christ!" Walker ranted.

Bone stifled a laugh. "Another effing eff and I was going to drop him. Right, do you want me to drive?"

"Are you out of your effing fucking mind?" Walker replied and imitated DCI Harris's bellowing laugh.

NINETEEN

Stirling Agricultural College was located about five miles out of the city in the foothills of the Ochils. The last stretch of road was a little more hazardous than Mullens would have liked, but the pool car that a PC had delivered to his door was more than adequate to cope with the weather conditions.

He followed his satnav down a lane banked up with melting drifts on either side, turned into the college entrance, and carried on along a windy drive, completely cleared of snow, until he reached the main building, which appeared to be a former country house, with all its associated grandeur. He parked up by the front door, in a space designated for the vice-chancellor, and had a sudden urge to dash out and scribble Miami on the plaque next to the title.

"Sorry, Detective Crocker, my needs come first." He slowly climbed out with a groan, and grabbing his coat and new iPad—a gift from his wife Sandra, who thought a new toy would keep him happy and out of her hair for at least a short while—he headed up the steps.

"I'm sorry, Officer. I'm afraid I can't just give out that sort of information to all and sundry." The college secretary glared at him over a pair of horn-rimmed spectacles. She was perched high behind a desk, like a mantis waiting to strike the first person who entered the foyer. "There's such a thing as data protection, you know."

"Please don't make me go all the way back to Kilwinnoch to hassle my extremely busy boss for his signature on a form, Ms—" He clocked her name badge. "Menzies."

"It's pronounced Ming-is," she corrected him.

"By name and nature," Mullens muttered.

"What?"

"Look, Ms Ming-is, we are investigating a very serious incident. You wouldn't want to slow down our inquiries, now would you, and risk further harm?"

"I'm sorry, Detective Mullens."

"It's Mullens," he replied sarcastically.

"Yes, that's what I said, Mullens," she snapped back. "I could lose my job, one that I am extremely fond of. I'm sorry, but until you have demonstrated to me that formal procedures have been followed, I'm afraid I can't help you. Now, if you'll excuse me, I have a lot of work to catch up on. This is my first day back after the storm." She disengaged her glare and returned to punching over-assertively at her keyboard.

"I can take this higher, if that's what you want," Mullens said, trying threats instead.

"That is your prerogative, but I'm sure the vice chancellor will agree with my position on this."

Mullens sighed. "Has anyone told you that you bear a remarkable likeness to the late Margaret Thatcher?"

"I beg your pardon?" the receptionist asked.

"As Arnie once said, *I'll be back*." Mullens sneered. "I am allowed to have a look around the campus, though, or is that in breach of data protection as well?"

"Be my guest." The receptionist huffed and continued her assault on the computer.

On his way out, he noticed a student who'd come in behind him and was waiting her turn to speak to the receptionist. She followed him out.

"I couldn't help overhearing what just happened there," she said, zipping her anorak back up.

"Oh, you mean me getting a roasting?"

"She's a total nightmare. Everybody's terrified of her."

"Add me to your list of traumatised victims."

"Who is it you're looking for? It's a small college."

"Fergus Dulhoon, do you know him?"

"Kind of, aye. His flat is in Block C. I can take you over there if you like?"

"That would be brilliant. Shall I just pop back in and let our friend know?"

"Are you kidding?"

"Yes, I am."

They laughed, and she took Mullens across the small campus and down a flight of steps between two modern blocks.

"Block C is at the end, by the fields."

They carried on along a path cleared of snow.

"What's your name?" he asked.

"Karen Maguire, but I prefer Kallie," the young student said.

"You said you know Fergus Dulhoon?"

"Not really. We went out for about three days."

"Love on the rocks?"

"I think he didn't like it when I told him he kissed like Hitler."

"Oh, that would do it."

"In my defence, I was totally hammered, but between us, it was probably worse than that."

"My wife tells me that regularly, and we're still together," Mullens joked. "So apart from having the snog action of a salted slug, what's he like?"

Kallie laughed. "You don't talk like a policeman."

"Damn, you've sussed me out." Mullens chuckled.

"He was nice enough. The quiet type, you know?"

"I bet you don't get many of them to a dozen here."

"Aye, farmers' kids do know how to party. He shares with two other students. They'll be able to tell you a bit more about him." She stopped at the end

Block and ran her finger down the buzzers. "C twelve, I think. That's right on the top floor."

She tapped in a code, the door swung open, and they went in.

At the bottom of the stairwell, Mullens stopped. "Is there a lift?"

"Really, it's only three floors."

"Saving my energy for the Hitler wincher," Mullens replied.

Kallie snorted with laughter. She took him back through the foyer to a set of two lifts.

At the top, she checked the door numbers. "C twelve, this one," she said and rang the bell.

It trilled loudly on the other side.

"They're all probably still in bed," she said.

"Or at lectures?"

"Are you serious?" She smiled and knocked again.

"Coming," a croaky voice sounded from the other side, and the door opened.

"Aye?" A young man in a washed-out t-shirt and pyjama bottoms peered at them through bleary eyes.

"Detective Sergeant Mullens from Kilwinnoch station. Can I have a word, sir?" Mullens flashed his lanyard at the startled student.

"What?" the befuddled young man said with panic rapidly rising on his face. "The keys were already in the tractor. We only drove it to the other side of the field. If it's anyone's fault it's the estates for leaving them in there in the first place." He spotted the girl giggling next to Mullens. "Oh, hi, Kallie." He attempted to fix the matted nest teetering on top of his head.

"I'm only pulling your chain." Mullens grinned, and the girl burst out laughing. "I'm looking for your flatmate, Fergus Dulhoon?"

"Oh right, aye, no bother." He glanced back into the flat. "Er, you'd better come in, er, I suppose. Ignore the mess. We haven't got round to cleaning up after the weekend yet," the flatmate said, cautiously entering their shared kitchen.

"I think we could press charges on the misuse of the term 'mess.' This is a work of art." Mullens surveyed the decomposing devastation in front of him.

"You need to open a window, Callum, the smell in here is terrible," Kallie said, raising her eyebrows.

"Aye, those herbs you're cooking with are mighty pungent. A few more minutes breathing that in and we'll all be high as kites." Mullens smiled.

The flustered student laughed nervously and opened all the windows.

"Is he in then?" Mullens asked.

"Who? Oh, Fergus, sorry, raging hangover. Do you mind if I get myself a drink?"

"Hair of the dog?" Mullens asked.

"Oh God, no." He gagged. "Irn Bru."

"Never again, eh?"

"Something like that." He opened one of the wall units, and a cereal box tumbled out, spilling cornflakes all over the floor.

"If that was me, I'd just pour the milk straight on and get tore in," Mullens commented.

"I see you'd fit right in here," Kallie said.

Callum found an unopened bottle in a near-bare cupboard, and with a loud fizz, downed half of the contents in one.

"Hey, that's mine, ya bastard." A second flatmate appeared, dressed and clutching a laptop. "Oh, hi, Kallie," he added with the same gormless expression. He then spotted Mullens in the corner, sitting on the last remaining chair that was free of debris.

"Dave, this is Detective...?"

"Detective Sergeant Mullens, and before you start, it's not about your adventures with farm machinery last night."

"Right, so?" The second student looked at his flatmate.

"The detective is after Fergus."

"He's not in. I knocked on his door this morning. I thought he'd finally come back last night, but it must have been one of you lot," the second flatmate said.

"Is it okay if I leave you now?" Kallie asked. "I have a lecture in ten minutes."

"No problem," Mullens said.

"Nice to meet you, and see you guys later," she said and left.

Mullens turned back to the two rabbits caught in the headlights in front of him. "So you're Callum?"

"Hargreaves," Worried Flatmate One replied.

"And you are?"

"Scott Meharg," the second worried flatmate stuttered.

Mullens removed his iPad from his bag, stared at the front for a second, then searched for the 'on' button.

"It's on the top, there." Callum pointed.

"Ta. It's brand-new, and I'm still finding my way around." Mullens fumbled with the buttons.

"You touch the screen, just tap it," Callum added.

Mullens thumped it with his fist, and nothing happened.

"No, lightly."

He tried again, but it still refused to comply.

"Fuck it." He dropped it back in his bag and swapped it for his old, reliable notepad.

"Old school." He smiled and flicked open to a new page, scribbling down their names. "Okay," he said with a sigh. "Let's start again, shall we? You mentioned he's been away. Has he been absent for a while, then?"

"A couple of weeks," Callum said, glancing over at his flatmate.

"I think it might be more than that, maybe," Scott replied.

"Do you know why he's gone AWOL?"

"He, er—" Callum began.

"What?" Mullens pushed.

"He was having a few issues paying his term's accommodation bill."

"Did he tell you that?"

"Aye, he was worried they were going to kick him out."

"Do you know why he wasn't paying it and if he has now?"

"I don't know. He never seemed to have any money. He was always cadging off us," Scott jumped in.

"Have you told the college he's missing?"

"He's not missing. I mean, we didn't think he was missing, but now you're here, maybe we should have. We just thought he'd maybe gone home to get his parents to pay up or something."

"Can I see his room?"

"I'm sure it'll be locked," Callum said.

"I've got a spare," Scott interrupted again. "He's always locking himself out, so he had an extra one cut illegally." He stopped and shot a look at Mullens.

"For a small fee, I won't tell the dragon in reception." Mullens grinned.

"Ah, right, you're joking," Scott replied with a relieved sigh. "I don't know why I agreed to take it as he's woken me up God knows how many times to let him in."

"Can you let *me* in?"

"Oh, aye, sure. This way."

Mullens prised himself out of the chair and followed the two flatmates to the end of the short corridor. Scott ducked into his room and re-emerged clutching the key.

"This is his room here, opposite," Scott said.

He fiddled with the lock for a moment or two, pushed it open and Mullens stepped inside.

The room was unexpectedly tidy. The single bed pushed up against the window was made, and an electric guitar rested across the top. The adjacent walls were covered with posters of various metal bands.

"Love Motorhead," Mullens said. "Is he a musician?"

"I think that might be pushing it. He can play two songs," Scott said.

"Over and over, loudly," Callum added, peering around the door.

Mullens glanced around the rest of the room. "Is he always this neat?"

"The housekeepers come every week. We have to clean our rooms before they get here, otherwise, we have to pay fines."

"I take it your kitchen falls outside of their cleaning rota, then?"

"I think they've given up even going in there," Scott replied.

"So, would they have been in since he did his disappearing act?"

"I would think so, yes."

Mullens went over to the study desk tucked under the window. Books and papers were stacked neatly on the top. He opened an A4 notepad and flicked through pages of scribbles, calculations, and crudely drawn mind maps.

"What's he like, then? Do you both get on with him?"

"Yeah, he's okay. Works hard but likes to go out as well."

"Okay?"

"I mean, good mates, yeah, but not around that much, to be honest," Callum elaborated.

"Big boozer?"

"We're agricultural students," Scott said.

"Aye, daft question. And this money worry thing. When did that start?"

"Can't remember. He was fine at the start of the first term, but things seemed to be getting worse."

"Did he talk about why he was skint?"

"Not really, no. I think he was a bit embarrassed about it," Callum said.

Mullens checked through a rack of clothes hanging in an open wardrobe. "Is that all his clothes?"

"Dunno," Callum said. He turned around. "His coat's gone." He nodded at the empty coat hook on the door.

"And boots as well. We're supposed to keep our muddy boots in these boxes," Scott said, holding up a recycling-sized plastic container.

Mullens spotted a bin by the bed and, kneeling, checked through its contents. Beneath two empty cans of Coke and a few chocolate bar wrappers, he retrieved some pink-coloured papers, twisted together in a tight bundle. He laid the knot out on the bed and unpicked it, disentangling one, then another until he counted eight in total.

"These are betting slips," Mullens said. "Was he into gambling?"

"News to me," Callum said.

Scott shrugged. "He was always on those online games, though, Cal."

"What online games?"

"The puggies, the slots," Scott said.

Mullens frowned. "Well, that's gambling, isn't it?"

"Just didn't think of it like that. Quite a few students are into it. Helps us chill out."

"While the companies fleece you for every penny."

"Ach, it's usually only buttons that people play with."

"Starts as buttons, but ends with the shirt off your back," Mullens replied. "It's a slippery fucking slope, lads, and you shouldn't go near. So, do you think he might have got into a bit of bother with his wee bit of fun, then?"

"It definitely would explain things."

"Do you know if he was borrowing from anyone?"

"Other students, you mean?"

"Anywhere: students, banks, loan companies, loan sharks?"

"Loan sharks?" Callum replied in surprise.

"If he has a problem with gambling, it's like a disease, as bad as heroin addiction. And when it gets bad, addicts will do anything to feed their habit, including visits to loan sharks."

"God, I don't know," Callum said.

"Any Hulk Hogan lookalikes at your door in the middle of the night, threatening to confiscate your bollocks?"

"He's not in trouble, is he? I mean, you don't think he's been nobbled or something like that?" Scott asked.

"We'd like to speak to him in connection with an ongoing investigation."

Callum shook his head. "I really don't think Fergus was a gambling addict. He would have said something."

"I dunno," Scott cut in. "He might have been totally ashamed to admit it."

"Often the way with addicts," Mullens said.

"He was definitely more preoccupied and moanier just before he left," Scott added.

"How moany?"

"He was just fed up. But we all were at the end of the first term. It's really long, with a shitload of assignments, you know?" Callum said.

Mullens flattened out one of the slips.

"This is a horse racing stub," he said. He pushed the fold at the top. "Do you know where Bonanza Bookmakers is?" He chuckled. "Fucking Bonanza, what a joke."

"Stirling High Street, I think," Callum said.

Mullens got up. "Right, thanks, lads. Here's my card. If Kenny Rogers makes a comeback, give me a buzz."

"Who?" Callum asked.

"Kenny Rogers, 'The Gambler'?" Mullens shook his head. "Never mind. Just let me know if he turns up, okay? And if you think of anything else that might help us find him, that would be grand."

They showed him to the door.

"Thanks a lot for your help."

"No problem, and if we hear anything, we'll ring you straight away," Callum said, holding up Mullens' card, and he shut the door.

Mullens made his way back to the reception car park. At the pool car, he called Baxter, but her phone rang out. He climbed in, but before he could turn the key, she rang him back.

"Don't tell me, you were out buying more shares in Golden Virginia?" Mullens joked when she answered.

"No!" Baxter retorted. "How dare you. I'll have you know I was powdering my nose, and before that, yes, I was out having my second of the day."

"And the rest."

"The whole truth and nothing but. Anyway, enough about me and my lungs, how are you doing, or should I say, how is the world doing with you back in it? Managed to cause any mayhem yet?"

"No, I leave that up to our boss. Listen, could you do me a favour?"

"For you, never," Baxter replied.

"Thanks. Could you look up active loan sharks operating in the Stirling area?"

"If you're short of a bit of cash for a deep-fried bridie, I'm sure I could stretch to buy you one."

"Why did you mention those? You know I'm banned from even thinking about them."

"Sorry, that was below the belt."

"Aye, and a rapidly shrinking belt it is, too," Mullens said.

"I'll get on that shortly. How did you get on at the college?"

"Dulhoon isn't here, but the trip may not have been in vain. Ring me back when you've got it, okay?"

"Where are you going now?" Baxter asked.

"To look for somewhere that sells silage and rabbit shit pretending to be a Sandino's fish supper. I've got the munchies something terrible."

"I'm not even going to ask," Baxter replied, and hung up before Mullens could elaborate.

"Right, Mark," he eyeballed himself in the rear-view mirror. "Just say no. Just say no," he muttered over and over and set off out of the car park.

TWENTY

When Bone and Walker arrived at the hospital, the injured bride had been moved out of the Intensive Care Unit into a high-dependency ward. Bone told the pair of family liaison officers to hang back in the corridor outside reception, and then they went in.

"At the moment, Mrs McDermid is stable, and the consultant surgeon is pleased with her progress, but she is still very poorly," the nurse on the desk said.

"Hold on, you know her name? Did one of my colleagues ring you?" Bone glanced at Walker.

"No, her parents came in about twenty minutes ago."

"What?"

"Clare asked for her mum, and we got their landline from the address she gave us. We were about to call you."

The nurse led the detectives through the reception and onto the small ward with four partitioned units. At the far end, she stopped at a door with the blind pulled on the window.

"Excuse me a sec." She went in and shut the door behind her. Moments later, the door opened, and she emerged with a second nurse, who was clutching a bowl half filled with yellowish-red liquid and saturated dressings.

"Only a few minutes, okay? She is still very weak and traumatised." She ushered them in.

Clare was propped up in bed with tubes and wires attached to her arms and face. Her parents were by her bedside. The distressed mother was leaning over her daughter, stroking her face gently. The father, a tall middle-aged man in a smart suit, was hovering nearer the bottom.

"I'm Detective Chief Inspector Bone from the RCU, Kilwinnoch," Bone said quietly.

The father spun around. "About bloody time. Have you caught the animal who did this?"

"I'm so sorry." Bone approached the bed. "How are you doing?" he asked the ashen-faced patient.

She closed her eyes and turned away.

"How do you think she's bloody doing?" the exasperated father exclaimed.

The mother turned on him. "James, calm down. This is the policeman who saved Clare, is that right?"

"No, I just found her. It was the courageous work of inshore rescue paramedics who saved her."

"Thank you," the mother whimpered, her face crumpled as she fought back more tears, and she resumed stroking her daughter's cheek. "My poor wee girl. What monster did this to you?"

The father took a deep breath and was about to speak, but stopped short.

Bone intervened. "Can I ask your names, please?"

"James Willerby, and my wife is Lynda."

Bone turned back to the girl. "Clare, we need to ask you a few questions."

"What, right now?" Mr Willerby snapped.

"It's often better to do this as soon as possible."

"But she's still very sick. Can't you at least wait a few more hours?"

"I'm afraid not."

"We hadn't been able to get a hold of her for days, I mean, before the blizzard, and we were worried she was back with him."

"Who?"

"That lowlife creep she was going out with," Mr Willerby replied.

Clare mumbled something.

Mrs Willerby leaned in. "What was that?"

"I want Laurence," she repeated, this time loud enough for the others to hear.

"Let's step outside for a moment, sir," Bone said to Mr Willerby.

He gestured to Walker, and she went over to the bed.

Bone took Willerby into the corridor on the other side of the ward.

"How much has the hospital told you about what's happened?"

"Very little. Something about her being found on some remote Scottish island. What the hell was she doing? Was she kidnapped, taken there? This lack of information is completely unacceptable. Our daughter is lying in there with critical injuries, and we're the last to know."

"I was the first to find your daughter and her husband on Balhuish Island," Bone interrupted Willerby's rant.

"Husband? What do you mean, husband?"

"When I found them, they were both dressed in full wedding ceremonial outfits: dress and morning suit."

"Oh my God, did she actually marry the bastard? This gets worse by the second. What the hell was she thinking?"

"You didn't know they were getting married?"

"No, as far as we knew, they'd split up, and I can tell you right now, the day she told me that, was one of the best of my life."

"I take it you don't like him then?"

"He's lowlife scum."

"What's his name?"

"So where is he, then? I hope you have him in custody, because if I get my hands on him, I'll wring his bloody neck. Laurence McDermid. I can't believe he's conned her into marrying him. What the hell were they doing all the way up there?"

"They'd booked into a five-star hotel, first to the 8th of April."

"Five star? Where the hell did they get the money for that, because it certainly didn't come from us?"

"They'd booked one of their honeymoon lodges. We're trying to piece together their movements leading up to the attack on Balhuish Island."

"If I were you, I'd start your investigations by interviewing that piece of filth, McDermid. He's obviously coerced Clare into something she didn't want to do, and I wouldn't be at all surprised if he's behind the attack."

"Did they have a rocky relationship then?"

"We tried time and time again to persuade her that he was rotten to the core and she could do so much better than him, but he had some kind of hold over her. I even threatened to have a court injunction placed on him, but she wouldn't listen. She wouldn't hear a bad word said against him."

"If you don't mind me asking, what do you do, Mr Willerby?"

"I'm director of a chain of solicitors in Bridge of Allan and Stirling, Willerby and Wilson. You see, in my profession, you come to spot the Laurence McDermids of the world. Scheming, selfish con artists who will stop at nothing to get what they want. If you check your records, you'll find a string of offences as long as your arm. The man is hard-wired to criminality."

"What sort of offences?"

"Theft, deception, you name it. He is a crooked, lying, manipulative, narcissistic monster, and I wouldn't be one bit surprised if all of this is his doing, another of his nasty schemes to get his hands on Clare's money, or ours, for that matter."

"Mr Willerby, we have every reason to believe that Laurence McDermid is dead. He didn't survive the attack on Balhuish Island."

"Dead?"

"I'm afraid so, yes."

"Oh, right." Willerby took a deep breath. "Well, that's tragic, but I won't be shedding any tears."

"Do you know of anyone who may wish to harm either your daughter or Mr McDermid?"

"My daughter is an angel, Inspector. She is loved by everyone who knows her. That scum, on the other hand, I'm sure he has plenty of enemies, all cut from the same filthy rag as him. I would even go so far as to hypothesise that he might still have been behind this, but somewhere along the line, things didn't go according to his wicked plan."

"Clearly."

He rubbed his forehead. "I still can't believe she'd get married behind our back like that."

"We don't know if they were actually married at this point in the investigation. But from what you've said, it sounds as though you wouldn't have given them your blessing."

"I would have done everything in my power to stop him from ruining her life."

"Really?"

"Legal powers, Inspector." Willerby frowned. "My worry is that he might have involved one of his pondlife criminal friends in all of this and they might come for our daughter again."

"That's why it's imperative that your daughter speaks to us as soon as possible."

"You saw how she is. It's as though the life has been battered out of her, and when she finds out McDermid is dead…" He looked up. "Does she have to know right now?"

"No, we can hold off on that for a short while. Did Mr McDermid have any family?"

"He told us his mother and father were both dead, but that's probably a lie." Willerby thought for a moment. "He mentioned an older brother once that he hadn't seen for years. No doubt he'd shafted him as well."

"You wouldn't have an address of contact for him, would you?"

"We had as little to do with Laurence and his toxic life as we could, but I do recall the brother was called Kenneth or Ken." He sighed again. "She would never have willingly excluded us from her own wedding like that. She knows how upsetting that would be for us."

"At least she's going to be okay."

"Physically maybe, but mental scars after something like that never heal, do they?"

"We learn to live with them," Bone replied, and Willerby glanced over. "Could you give me your address and contact number, and did your daughter have her own place?"

"Yes, she has a flat in Stirling."

"We'll need that address as well and a set of keys if you have them, along with your daughter's mobile number, landline if she has one, and that of her boyfriend."

"Hold your horses here. The last thing she needs right now is a bunch of police officers ransacking her flat and going through her private possessions."

"I'm sure you want us to apprehend the person who did this to your daughter as soon as possible, Mr Willerby. The officers will be very careful and treat your daughter's belongings and property with respect." Bone handed Willerby his card. "Send details here, please."

The solicitor stared at it for a few moments, as though he'd lost his bearings, then tucked it into his suit pocket.

"Shall we go back?"

"For my wife's sake, could you please not mention the possibility that our daughter may have married the bastard, not yet anyway? She's already so close to losing it completely. She needs to be here for Clare, and our daughter needs her close by."

"We will have to interview her again very soon, though, but in the meantime, if you could give us as much information as you can on Laurence McDermid, his life, and your daughter's relationship with him. Also, if you can think of anything your daughter may have been involved in that might have led to this assault?"

"This is down to him, not her!" Willerby exclaimed.

"Okay." Bone turned to go back.

Willerby grabbed his arm. "I don't mean to speak ill of the dead. I know that it's a tragedy for his family. I wouldn't wish that upon anyone. I'm not a bad person. But I'm afraid I cannot waste any of my strength on him. I need to help my daughter get over this and support my wife through this crisis."

They were interrupted by a loud, guttural wail. Mr Willerby dashed back in.

"Laurence is dead, James," the mother said, her face contorted with pain.

Clare cried out again, this time a searing near-silent scream, and she tried to get out of bed. Mr Willerby rushed over and stopped his daughter from climbing out and tearing the life support from her arms. A nurse came in and helped restrain and calm her down.

Walker dashed out and moments later returned with the family liaison officers who hung back at the door.

"My colleagues are here to help you," Bone said. "We are so sorry for your loss, Clare."

"Leave us alone, please," Mr Willerby snapped and continued to wrestle with his daughter's flailing arms.

"We've got this, sir," one of the liaison officers said.

The detectives left.

"That went well, then," Bone said on the way back to the car.

"She kept asking for him, pleading with me to go and get him. I felt she had a right to know."

"Absolutely. Did she say anything before?"

"She's severely traumatised and says she can't remember much of what happened, just flashes of a struggle, and then she fell."

"A struggle?"

"When I pressed her, she got very agitated, along with the mother."

"Could she remember any details at all about her attacker?"

"Vague recollection of a man in a ski mask. She thought he was the photographer."

"Jon Hoskins Photography? So, it was a photo shoot, or supposed to be? Let's get back and see what Buchan's found out." His phone pinged as Willerby sent through the details he'd requested. He was about to forward them to Baxter and Harper with an update on events when his phone rang.

"Were your ears burning, Will?"

"Sorry to interrupt. A few developments. CFO Cash just called through. Forensics ran a quick DNA sample check on the deceased male victim, and he popped up on police records."

"Laurence McDermid, I know."

"That's right. How did you manage to Top Trump me?"

"I can do better than that. I've just met Clare McDermid's parents."

"Who?"

"The female victim's mum and dad have turned up at the hospital."

"Did they know anything about what's happened?"

"Absolutely in the dark, and no idea that she might have married. The father had some interesting things to say about the groom, though. I'll fill you in later. Anything else?"

"When Cash phoned in the ID, we found a match on the weddings list. They were married three weeks ago, the 17th of March in the Monteith Registry Office. I called and spoke to the registrar there. She said she couldn't remember, but then phoned back to confirm that they were married alone with no other guests."

"Okay, so definitely married then. I can tell by the excited tone in your voice that you have something else to share."

"I've also been going through Trough's phone, and there were three calls and texts from the same number the day before the attack."

"What do the texts say?" Bone asked.

"They are kind of cryptic. Three in total. The first says: *Still on for tomorrow at two*? The second is Trough's response: *Legit?* And the third from the caller a few minutes later, a laughing face emoji."

"Can you trace the number?"

"Yes, I already have, and this is where it gets interesting. The caller's number is registered to a Mr L Kilpatrick of two Harbour Lane, Loch Gillan."

"Now that *is* interesting," Bone replied. "Okay, hold tight. We're on our way." He was about to hang up. "Oh, Will, are you still there?"

"Yes,"

"The victim, Laurence McDermid, has a brother who lives in Stirling, Kenneth McDermid. Can you ask Sheila to see if she can find out who and where he is? He's going to need family liaison as well."

"Sir." There was a pause. "Anything else?"

"No doubt, yes, but I can't think of it right now." Bone hung up.

"News?" Walker asked.

Bone smiled. "Potential front page. Come on, I'll explain on the way."

TWENTY-ONE

Mullens opened the plastic container of mixed bean salad and sniffed.

"Fuck's sake." He winced. "My farts smell more appetising than this." Cautiously, he spooned some of the thick brown sludge into his mouth, and his face contorted. "Good God." He spat the lump back into the box and quickly closed the lid. He looked back across the supermarket car park and was contemplating a return visit for something a little more edible when his phone rang.

"Saved by the bell," he said. "Good afternoon, Sheila."

"I've just pinged over the list of the loan sharks on our books or radar, as requested."

"Hold up." He opened the attachment and scanned down the list of names, and stopped.

"Craig Sneddon, he's still at it, I see. I thought him and his brothers were still banged up?"

"Early release last year after serving six years out of eight for good behaviour."

"Him, good behaviour? And now he's back at it?"

"It would appear so."

"And the brothers as well?"

"They're both still inside, but SCD believes they are still involved in his activities, one way or another."

"So SCD are investigating Sneddon?"

"Yes, for all the usual stuff, loan sharking, money laundering, extortion, blah, blah, but Craig is a slippery fish, and they haven't been able to pin anything on him as yet."

"Covert operations?"

"I think so, yes."

Mullens checked through the list. "I'm surprised there are more operating so near his neighbourhood."

"The list changes almost weekly."

"Aye, as he scares off the competition."

"Or worse."

"Let's hope so," Mullens replied. "Okay, I'll go and have a wee word with Mr Sneddon."

"Are you sure that's a good idea? You two have form, don't you?"

"Ach, it'll be entertaining."

"Do you want me to check with SCD and the Super that they are okay with you paying him a visit?"

"They'll only say no. Let's leave it until after I've been to see him."

"Not entirely happy about this, but okay. I have his address here, hold on."

"Don't worry, I know where he lives."

"Be careful," Baxter said.

"That appears to be my middle fucking name now," Mullens moaned.

"I thought it was bawheid." Baxter chuckled.

"Very good, Sheila. And one day I'll teach you to say that without that bag of public-school plums in your mouth."

***

Sneddon's heavily fortressed, ex-council house was located in the dark heart of the Raphorse Estate, or as the locals affectionately called it, The Ratarse.

Mullens weaved the pool car across an expanse of waste ground, avoiding burnt-out cars, rotting and rusting piles of fly-tipped rubbish. He turned into a cul-de-sac, and the presence of three bulked-up, shaven-headed bears at the junction indicated he was entering Sneddon's turf. He slowed and wound down the window.

"Afternoon, lads, can you direct me to Stirling Castle? I seem to have taken a wrong turn."

The men approached, one nudging the other, but when they got to the car, they both stopped.

"Thought you were on a wee bonus there, didn't you?"

One of the neds sniffed the air. "Smell that?"

"Aye," said the other. "Definitely pork maggot."

"Could you tell your boss I'd like a wee word, Mr Maggot?"

"That's no' ma name," the first thug retorted.

"Oh, really? So what *is* your name then?" Mullens reached into the top pocket of his jacket, feigning a search for a pen.

"He's no' in," the second ned said.

"Oh, I think he is, otherwise you two clowns wouldn't be hanging about here like two turds blocking a U-bend. Go tell him."

One of the guards set off up the middle of the street, his tree-trunk thighs colliding together as he slowly wobbled towards Sneddon's lair. Mullens followed in the car and slowly crept up until his bumper nudged against the guard's bloated calf. He spun around and thumped the bonnet. Mullens winked, and the ned crossed the road onto the pavement. Mullens pulled up alongside and got out.

The ned approached a black-painted door in the centre of a high, solid steel fence that encircled the property. A camera directly above their heads swivelled. Mullens waved at it and grinned, like a dad waving at a toddler. The intercom crackled.

"Polis," the ned said.

The speaker clicked and clacked.

"Does he have a warrant?" the voice on the other side hissed.

"Tell your boss it's DI Mullens and I have some good news."

The speaker whistled and screeched, and moments later, with three or four loud thumps, the door swung open, and a third identical heavy stepped out.

"Arms," the heavy ordered.

"Hugs? How lovely," Mullens replied. "I'm not wearing a wire or carrying, if that's what your boss is worried about, or were you hoping for a bit of *Die Hard* action?"

"Arms," the thug repeated.

Mullens reluctantly complied.

The heavy frisked Mullens, and he let him pass into a tarmacked front yard with a gleaming 4 x 4 BMW parked up alongside the house.

"Nice car. Those DSS payments must be really generous these days." He glanced over at the building ahead.

Sneddon had taken over two ex-council semis and knocked them into one. A pair of massive, ostentatious plastic white pillars straddled another reinforced steel door. Mullens laughed at the juxtaposition.

"Tasteful," he said, tapping the hollow plastic as he passed.

The heavy rang a second buzzer, and yet another Honey Monster greeted Mullens with a second frisk.

"Aww, foreplay over? I was enjoying that, ya big hunk of burning love," Mullens quipped when he was done.

Guard One led Mullens in, the second following close behind. Reaching a door at the end of the gloomy hallway, the henchman thumped it with his fist, and it swung open. The room opened out into an open-plan living space with three gigantic sofas grouped in an expansive semi-circle around a TV about the same size as the room. A video game was playing with the volume turned up to deafening levels. The screen was filled with blood-spattered carnage as giant cartoon gangsters shot, stabbed, and beheaded one another.

Sneddon was slumped down in one of the sofas with his back to the detective, facing the TV, his arms waving a game console from side to side. The bodyguard called over to him, but the screams and explosions coming from the PA-sized speakers were too loud. He went over and gently tapped his boss on the shoulder. Sneddon spun around as though anticipating an assault. Then when he saw Mullens, he resumed his game. Mullens approached. The bodyguard stepped in front of him to block his path. Sneddon stuck up his hand and gestured for his help to let him pass.

"Excuse moi," Mullens said and briskly stepped around him.

"Good afternoon, Craig. Long-time-no-see," Mullens hollered over the din.

Sneddon ignored him and continued to play. He was dressed in a pair of boxers and a holey grey t-shirt too short for his expansive gut that rolled out and over the top of his shorts. His face was wet with perspiration, and the sweat puddle extended down his t-shirt. He turned down the volume slightly but kept his eyes on the screen.

"The fuck do you want?" he barked.

"Charming. After all these years, is that the best you can do?" Mullens replied.

"Come to harass a hard-working pillar of the community again?"

"Aye, I saw your pillars outside. Where did you pick those up from, Pontins?"

"As you can see, I'm too fucking busy to talk to chipolatas like you." Sneddon sneered.

"That's hilarious. I see what you did there. Two insults in one. You're smarter than I remember."

Sneddon stabbed violently at the console, but the sound died, the game disappeared for a second, and then a 'game over' logo danced across the screen.

"Fucking hell!" Sneddon bellowed. "See what you made me do? I was top dog, and you made me fucking lose."

"Story of your life."

Sneddon tossed the console onto the adjacent sofa and ran the palm of his hand across the top of his bald, glistening scalp.

"I'll ask you again. What the fuck do you want?" he asked, his strong Govan accent making his growl even more grizzly.

"How's life in the hills these days?" Mullens asked.

"Small talk? Okay, let's do that. Fine, thanks. And how's that ugly horse's arseface of a sister you call your wife getting on?"

"Bloody hell, did you attend stand-up training while you were in prison?" Mullens joked through clenched teeth. "Your comedic timing has improved by leaps and bounds."

Sneddon jumped up suddenly. "Boo!" he shouted in Mullens's face.

Mullens jerked back in surprise.

"Ah, didnae work. Shame. Just thought I'd test that new heart of yours." Sneddon belched out a loud snort and adjusted the crotch on his boxers.

"It's amazing. I've the strength of a twenty-year-old now. I'm like Wolverine. I have to be very careful. I could easily break someone's neck with the slightest wee tap of my fist."

Sneddon's bodyguard shifted forward. Sneddon raised his arm, and the beast retreated again.

Sneddon stood up. "Right, enough of this bollocks, you're stinking out my airways."

Craig was shorter than Mullens remembered, but he wasn't worried. He was more than capable of punching his way out of most situations, even if he was outnumbered. As Sneddon turned to face him, Mullens noticed that Sneddon's left ear was completely missing.

"Wee accident there, Craig?" Mullens pulled at his own ear. "Does your colleague sign for the deaf as well?"

"I swapped it for the guy's entire face," Sneddon snarled. "Come on, Detective, spit it out, or are you more of a swallower?"

"Have you had any dealings with a man called Fergus Dulhoon?"

"Dealings?" Sneddon scratched at his boxers again.

"Oh, come on." Mullens sighed.

"I run a legitimate courier and taxi company. We deliver pizzas and ferry hens and stags to clubs."

"Did you lend Mr Dulhoon any money?"

"Those days are over, Detective Mullens. Keep up. I served my time, and thanks to the love and care I received from our wonderful prison service, I'm totally rehabilitated. I'm a reformed man."

"Oh aye, so are these all your boyfriends then, and the security fence is to keep your fans out?"

"You know better than many of your fellow chipolatas that I have accumulated enemies, many of whom would still like to skin, batter, and deep-fry me. As a result, I'm very cautious."

"Pizzas and taxis must be very lucrative to afford all this?"

"Surprisingly so. I thoroughly recommend it. I'm sure you could be making ten times or even more than that pathetic salary you're on."

"I'd rather have colonic irrigation through my eyeballs," Mullens replied. "How much did he borrow?"

"Oh, you're not listening, are you?" Sneddon turned to the bodyguard. "They never do, Clarence."

"Clarence?" Mullens said with a grin.

He turned to the fridge-freezer who was frowning so hard, the skin on his brow almost enveloped his eyes.

"That's a sweet name. I bet your mammy is so proud of you, Clarence."

The guard stepped forward again, but Sneddon shook his head.

"I've told you. I don't lend money anymore and I don't know this loser."

"Loser?"

"Well, anyone who gets themselves into debt is a loser in my book."

"Loan shark talk, that. You know there are people dead up at Loch Gillan?"

"Where?"

"Balhuish, too. Place is littered with bodies. If you get banged up again, especially if you're involved in any shenanigans up there, well, I'm sure you'll get ten times or maybe even more than those six years you've just served."

Sneddon stared at Mullens for a second and then dropped back down onto the sofa. "If you don't mind, I have things to do, places to be, people to meet and all that. So I'd be grateful if you could get the fuck out of my house and off my property."

"We're not done here, Sneddon," Mullens said.

Sneddon looked up. "I'd take good care of that heart of yours. You wouldn't want to leave your wife all alone with your miserable excuse of a pension. It's a big bad world out there."

Mullens erupted. "You fucking threaten my wife, and I'll punch a new arsehole in your skull and shit into your brains."

He made a lunge at Sneddon, but the guard rushed over and yanked him back.

Mullens threw his arms up in surrender. "Okay, cool it, cutie," he said, shrugging off the ned's huge excavator arms.

Sneddon readjusted his t-shirt and started up another video game. "Goodbye, Detective. Die a slow, painful death."

Mullens eyeballed the heavy for a second, and with a wry smile, he left the room. The guard who was still lingering in the hallway escorted him out and back onto the street and then slammed the steel gate shut with a loud clatter. Mullens jumped into his car, and with a deep frustrating growl, started it up, and accelerated out of the cul-de-sac, tooting at the two gormless stooges who had returned to their spot at the junction.

TWENTY-TWO

Jon Hoskins's studio was tucked away on a narrow street just off Drumgoil's main high street. Buchan stopped at the door and glanced at the selection of portraits arranged in a window display selling his wares. One of the shots was of a young couple arm in arm on a beach with a glowing amber sunset behind them. At first glance she thought it was the Caribbean or the Med, but then realised it was the tiny strip of sand on Balhuish Island, with the tiny jetty landmark behind them.

She went in, and a bell tinkled above the door. The front desk was empty, and there were various photos and card frames laid out across its surface. The walls around the shop were covered in similarly posed shots of happy couples in scenic Scottish locations, locked in romantic embraces.

"Can I help you?"

She turned at the thin voice. "Mr Hoskins?"

"Aye." The man nodded, removed his woolly hat, and flattened down an errant comb-over.

"Lesley, sorry, I didn't... I haven't got my glasses on. Have you recovered from all that Hogmanay karaoke yet?" he joked.

"Who the hell wasn't at that party? Anyhow, sorry, I'm here in a formal capacity, Jon."

"Oh, right. Let me—" He fumbled around his desk.

"Your glasses are attached to your hat," Buchan said.

The photographer sheepishly disentangled them.

"That's better," he said, adjusting the frames. "Sorry again, and for not answering right away. I was outside trying to get the boiler to fire up, but I think the vent's frozen up again. Has there been some kind of accident or something? I mean, the weather has been absolutely atrocious and—"

"No, we're investigating an incident over on Balhuish Island."

"That sounds ominous. What sort of incident?"

"You haven't heard, then?"

"No, the phones and power have just come back on, so we've been in splendid isolation over here."

"A newlywed couple was seriously assaulted on the island."

"Oh my God. That's awful."

"A Mr and Mrs McDermid."

"Laurence and Clare McDermid, the newlyweds?" Hoskins reeled.

"That's correct, yes. Do you know them?"

"I was, er, yes. I was supposed to do a photo shoot a few days ago."

"Supposed to?"

"Yes, they cancelled at the last minute. Are they okay?"

"Our investigations are ongoing," Buchan dodged.

"Did you meet with the McDermids, then?"

"Not face to face, no, and I only dealt with Mr McDermid via emails."

"Do you have a record of those and your booking?"

"Yes, of course." He sat at his desk, a pile of photos to one side, and removed an A4-sized book from a drawer underneath. "It was originally booked for the 3rd of April. Let me just check." He opened the ledger and flicked at the pages. "Here it is. I pencilled it in, but as you can see, I've scored it out." He turned the book around.

"When did he make the booking, and when did he cancel?"

"I'm not sure when he first contacted me, but the cancellation was just two days before the booking. I do remember that as I wasn't pleased, let me tell you. The cancellation policy on my website is very explicit, one week's notice. But to be honest, it was a lucky escape because I wouldn't have fancied getting caught in that mother of all storms."

"You said he emailed you? Can I see that?"

"Actually, I think he used the contact form on my website." He got up. "My computer is next door.

He took Buchan through to his house behind the shop and into a small office crammed full of photo equipment.

"Welcome to the nerve centre, or as my partner calls it, my nervous breakdown centre." He went over to a desktop computer, rammed up against the wall. He shifted a tangle of tripod stands out of the way and squeezed into a chair.

"Let me just fire this up a sec," he said and tapped at the keyboard a few times, sat back a second, then leaned over. "Ah, not plugged in, sorry. I'm all nerves now. Two secs." He fumbled with the socket and tried again.

"When people fill in the form, the message is sent to my business email." He stared at the screen for a few seconds. "April 2nd, there we are, sender: L McDermid."

Buchan negotiated the chaos around the desk to read the message, and leaned in.

> *Sincere apologies. Have to cancel tomorrow's*
> *appointment.*
> *L. McDermid*

Hoskins shrugged. "Just like that, no offer of compensation for the inconvenience or anything."

Buchan took out a notepad and scribbled down the entry and the sender's email address.

"Do you have the original booking?"

"Yes, I'm sure." He typed 'McDermid' in the search bar, but nothing came up. "Oh?" he said and scrolled back through the dates and then stopped. "There he is. And there, two on the same day. The first here, was a query about a photo shoot on Balhuish. He asked about charges and options. And I replied with my costs and available dates, here." He paused to let Buchan read the message. "Then he shot right back with a go-ahead, and I confirmed. All done and dusted in a matter of a few minutes."

"No deposit?"

"I do this on a trust basis, but I've had so many cancellations this year I'm thinking of introducing one."

"This email address is different," Buchan said, writing it down.

"Oh, I hadn't noticed that. That's why it didn't pop up in my initial search."

"Tell me a little bit about your services, Mr Hoskins?"

"I offer three-tier wedding packages, bronze, silver, and gold, where bronze is photos only at church, reception and so on. Silver might include special location shots, additional photographs for family and friends, and gold includes video, and with that, I subcontract to a business partner."

"So, Mr McDermid booked the silver option?"

"That's correct, yes."

"And do you shoot regularly on Balhuish Island?"

"I can shoot anywhere in the area. There's a list of favourite locations on the website, and clients can tick which one they prefer."

"And Mr McDermid selected Balhuish?"

"Aye, though my quote included a surcharge to include my own transportation to and from the island, as Mr McDermid explained that his wife and himself would make their own way from one of the cabins on the Balhuish Country Estate."

"Do you have many bookings from the Balhuish Hotel?"

"Oh aye, my bread and butter. The new cabins have proved an absolute goldmine for the hotel, especially with newlyweds and the romantic break market. But this is just a total nightmare. I mean, first and foremost for the unfortunate couple, but horrendous news like this will have a terrible impact on my business." He looked up. "Sorry, that sounds callous."

"Not at all. You have bills to pay like the rest of us, Jon. Is the island a popular choice?"

"Not the most popular, but certainly one of the top three. I think it's all that mysterious Celtic history, along with the stunning views from the top of the island that make it the dream spot for many couples. I'll show you."

He clicked through to the main page of his website and hit the gallery section. He scrolled slowly through a few spectacular shots of the island and clients in various poses. "I like this one in particular."

He paused on a couple arm-in-arm among the graves on top of the island. They were dressed in what appeared to be full Viking costumes, complete with shields, swords, and horned helmets.

"They actually arrived in a longboat that he'd built himself."

"Is that quite common, then?"

"Thankfully not, but it was very funny, and the couple were an absolute joy, totally off their rockers, but lovely all the same."

"So Mr and Mrs McDermid were going to meet you on the island?"

"Yes, as you can see in my reply here. I'd arranged to rendezvous with them. It's so awful. I can't understand why they would pull the plug, but still go over there, especially with that storm coming in."

"That's what we're trying to work out, Mr Hoskins. And you had no other contact with either Mr or Mrs McDermid after the cancellation?"

"No." He sat back. "There, but for the grace and all that."

"Okay, thanks for now. If anything else comes to you, please ring me." Buchan handed the shocked photographer her card.

"I'm not a suspect, am I, Lesley?" Hoskins asked.

"Try not to worry. We're just trying to piece things together."

Hoskins nodded and showed Buchan to the door.

"Thanks again, Jon. You have been very helpful."

"Oh, I do hope so, Lesley. And I would say it was lovely to see you again, but under the circumstances, that doesn't seem appropriate at all."

On her way back to the squad car, she turned, and Hoskins was still at the door, waving until finally, he went in.

Isle of the Dead

TWENTY-THREE

Back in Loch Gillan, Bone checked in on Harper. "Lesley not back yet then?"

Harper looked up from his laptop. "That was quick. I take it you were driving, Rhona?"

"The cheek of him." Bone shrugged.

"Oh, the SOC team has been over to the female victim's property."

"And?"

"Their inspection is continuing, but Laurence McDermid's belongings were there, so clearly he's been living with her for some time. They also sent over a scan of one of Laurence's bank statements they recovered from a bedside drawer." He clicked at his laptop and turned it around.

Bone scanned the image.

"I've highlighted the payment on the 14th of March for five hundred pounds from a K. McDermid."

"The brother, Kenneth?"

"Looks like it, yes. Oh and the Super's been on the phone, twice."

"Oh, God. I've forgotten to call him today. Am I in the doghouse?"

"He didn't say, but wants you over at the station for 4 pm."

Bone checked his watch. "Bloody hell. I'm just back from Stirling. Did he say why?"

"No, just said go to his office."

"Doghouse it is, then." Bone turned to Walker. "Could you do the honours and interview Kilpatrick, and I'll take Bertha out for a spin."

"Or a skid, stall, or stutter," Walker replied.

"I hold such high authority over my troops, don't I?" Bone glanced over at the empty percolator and sighed.

"Oh, sorry, sir. Lesley totalled that."

"Grass," Bone replied and left with Walker following behind. "When you're done with Kilpatrick, can you fill the team in on the fun and games at the hospital and let DCI Harris know what's going on? You can draw straws on that one."

"Russian Roulette." Walker winced.

Passing the bar, Bone glanced in. "Speak of the devil."

Kilpatrick was at the bar leaning over a pint of Guinness, with Junior hanging off the stool next to him.

Bone carried on to the reception. "If I'm not back later, I'm in Andalucía on full pension."

"Hasta luego." Walker waved, went in, and approached the inebriated pair.

"Can I speak to you, Mr Kilpatrick?"

"Aye." Kilpatrick smiled and took another large gulp of his beer.

"I mean in private."

Walker glanced over at Junior, who was now almost bent double. "What are you doing?"

"I'm showing the young lad here a few Tai Chi moves," Junior slurred, clearly the worse for wear.

"You practice Tai Chi?"

"He's a black belt or whatever the hell they call it," Urquhart said, emerging from the back.

He tried again to work his mouth. "Linway, lineudge holder," he slurred.

"Top level? Bloody hell, Junior. Is there anything you're not bloody good at?" Walker asked.

"Paying his bar bill," Urquhart replied. "And you're getting no more until it's settled, capiche?"

"Fuckinnobrot," Junior mumbled and, raising his empty glass, he toasted the company, then attempted to dismount his stool, but it slipped from under him.

Walker caught his arm before he fell.

"You need to go home and get something to eat, and soak up that booze, Junior," Walker ordered.

"Aye aye, Lieutenant Uhura." He giggled and accidentally sprayed Walker with beer. "Oops." He found his legs and forced them forward and out the door.

"Is he going to be okay?" she asked.

"The man will outlive Keith Richards," Urquhart replied.

Walker turned back to Kilpatrick, who was gulping at his pint. "I hope you haven't been keeping up with him."

"I have more volume capacity, Inspector." He rubbed his bloated stomach, bulging against his checked shirt.

"Could we use your office for five minutes or so, Gordon?" Walker asked.

"Oh aye, help yourselves. You have total run of the bloody place anyway," he scoffed.

"This way," Walker said.

Kilpatrick downed the rest of his pint and followed the detective around the bar and into the office. She shut the door behind them.

"Take a seat," she said, pointing at the only office chair in the room.

Kilpatrick slumped down on it and sighed a drunken sigh, filling the room with the stench of alcohol.

"How many have you had?" Walker asked.

"Lost count," Kilpatrick said through a hiccup.

"Any particular reason why you're getting bladdered?" Walker sat on the desk next to him, but was still lower than him.

"Oh, you mean aside from all the corpses piling up and getting flattened by the psycho who killed them? Nope. Can't think of anything at all." He pulled a face, and it seemed to stick. He rubbed his hand across his mouth to try and reset it.

"When DCI Bone called round to see how you were yesterday, he said it sounded like there was someone else in your house."

"That was the cat sleeping upstairs, I told him that. She's a big bloody useless lump."

"He also mentioned that you told him you'd just got up, but when he shook your hand, it was freezing cold, and your dressing gown was the same. Had you been outside somewhere just before he called round?"

"What? I could do with another drink. I'm bloody parched." He clicked his tongue.

"Had you been outside just before he arrived? There was blood on your doorstep."

"Aye, from this." He pointed at the bandage, half dangling from his matted hair.

"We recovered Vincent Trough's mobile from his property, and checking through his call records, we discovered a mobile number registered to you."

"What?" Kilpatrick looked up, confused.

"You rang and texted him three times the day before the attacks. Would you care to explain?"

"When was this?" Kilpatrick shook his head. "I'm a bit pissed. I don't remember—"

"The 2nd of April at 7:33 a.m., then at 1:22 p.m. One call and two messages. The first text said: *Still on for two p.m. tomorrow*? Trough replied with the word 'Legit' question mark, and then you replied with a smiley emoji."

"Oh aye, hold on, I know what that was. I was taking an outboard over to him to get fixed. I was just confirming it was still booked in."

"Did you take it over?"

"No, when I heard the storm was coming in, I didn't want to risk getting stuck there."

"Why did he use the term, *legit*?"

Kilpatrick thought for a moment. "Ach, we have this joke." He stopped. "*Had* this joke that I think he's a bit of a Del Boy and he thinks I am."

"And are you?" Walker asked.

"What?"

"A bit of Del Boy," she repeated.

"I'm always on the hunt for good deals, so I suppose I am, and Trough's like that, too. We could spend hours in the pub negotiating the price on a repair. In the end, we probably spent more on booze than whatever savings we managed to squeeze out of one another."

"And you still have this broken outboard?"

"Eh, well, I fixed it myself in the end." Kilpatrick yawned.

"And where were you on the day of the attacks?"

"Oh, bloody hell. I'm so thick. I see now. You think I'm involved, don't you?"

"Where were you?" Walker pressed.

"Jesus Christ. I took your boss over there and got fucking assaulted. Why would I do that?"

"Just answer my question." Walker leaned in further.

"I was riding it out at home in Loch Gillan like most sensible people. I knew from the forecasts it was going to be bad, and when the weather says it's bad, it's always worse up here."

"Did you speak to or see anyone that evening?"

"I was going to come here but changed my mind, so apart from my fat useless cat, nobody. The first person I saw was your boss the next day. Come on, Inspector, how the fuck would I be able to get over to the island and back again in that storm?"

"You were happy to take DCI Bone over there the next day, and the storm was still in full swing.

"It was daylight. I can tell you're not a sailor. If I'd gone over there that night, I wouldn't be sitting here gasping for another pint. Come on, Inspector. This is daft." He coughed and hiccupped at the same time, then chuckled.

"Okay, Lonnie, let's leave it there for now, but please don't leave Loch Gillan while the investigation is ongoing, okay?"

"House arrest, is it?"

"Just stay put."

"There goes my trip to the Bahamas then." He shrugged and clambered out of the office chair, almost toppling onto a filing cabinet behind.

"You need to go home, too, and sober up."

"Aye aye—" He stopped, raised his arms, and staggered back to the bar.

TWENTY-FOUR

Once Bone had cleared the three days of Ice Age permafrost piled up around his ancient Saab, to his surprise and delight, the engine started the first time. He was tempted to run back into the hotel to share the news, but decided it was probably best not to tempt fate and set off before his old faithful changed her mind. On the outskirts of the village a figure emerged from the trees and moved onto the road. Bone hit the brakes. The figure continued to the other side and disappeared. Bone got out, went over to the bank and peered down into a deep gully with a frozen stream at the bottom. There was no sign of anyone. He climbed back in and carried on. A voice in his ear whispered, *"Blood,"* and he shot a glance in the rear-view mirror. The creature's empty-eyed, charred skull loomed over him and what remained of its scorched lips curled into a narrow sneer, exposing a row of broken, blackened teeth. He stopped the car again and spun round, but his ghostly nemesis had gone. A van approached and the driver tooted her horn. He quickly manoeuvred the Saab into a passing place. "What's was the fucking point of that?" He rubbed at the scar on his forehead in frustration and set off again.

Back in Kilwinnoch, in the station's reception, Desk Sergeant Brody greeted him.

"Good God, it's the Abominable Snowman, escaped from captivity."

"Afternoon to you, Sergeant. How's tricks?"

"All back to normal now, give or take. That was a belter of a hoolie, wasn't it?"

"You should have seen it up there."

"Nut-freezing madness." Brody winced. "Talking of which, I hear there's been some trouble in your new neck of the woods."

"Understatement," Bone replied. "Is he in?"

"Waiting for you."

"What about Mark?"

"Already here. It was good to see him. I do miss that life-affirming tirade of personal abuse."

"Any clue what it's about?"

"I couldn't possibly comment." Brody buzzed him in.

Bone took the stairs two at a time up to Gallacher's office. At the door, he paused and then knocked.

"Come," the Super called from the other side.

Mullens was seated in front of Gallacher's desk with the boss sitting opposite.

"Afternoon, sir, Mark."

Mullens turned and gave Bone an unsubtle wink.

"You made it back okay then?" Gallacher gently tapped at a stray leaf of paper sticking out from the pile in front of him.

"Aye, once I got beyond Loch Lomond, you'd hardly think there'd ever been the storm of the century."

"Did you drive back in Frog Face?" Mullens asked.

"I did, and she behaved herself very well indeed."

Mullens sniggered. "That'll be a first."

There was another knock at the door.

"Come," Gallacher repeated.

A sharply dressed woman came in.

"Thanks for making it in, DI Kelly. I thought it might be best to deal with this face to face."

"Deal with what?" Bone glanced back at the DI who sat alongside him.

"Detective Inspector Kelly, this is Detective Chief Inspector Bone and Detective Sergeant Mullens."

The detective nodded.

"DI Kelly has come over from SCU."

"Ah right, I see," Mullens muttered.

"See what?" Bone cut in.

"Earlier today, DS Mullens visited the property of Mr Craig Sneddon."

"Craig Sneddon, the loan shark and all-round bad bastard, pardon my French?" Bone said, turning to Mullens.

"The very same," Gallacher confirmed.

"What were you doing going round to his? Don't you two have form?" Bone asked.

"I was just about to update you, sir, when the Super rang and told me to hold."

"This better be good," Bone squinted back at the stern-faced DI adjacent.

"Right, enough," Gallacher said. "Perhaps you could explain, DI Kelly?"

"For eighteen months, the SCU has been involved in surveillance operations, monitoring and recording Craig Sneddon's movements and activities since leaving HM Northlands Prison last year. We have substantive evidence that he is the ringleader of a vast criminal network that operates across the length and breadth of central Scotland. We have people on the ground who are operating undercover."

"So when bonzo here walked in, he threatened the operation? Bone asked. "Is that where this is going?"

Mullens interrupted. "How the hell was I supposed to know?"

"You should have cleared it with your boss, DS Mullens," Gallacher said.

"What he said," Bone cut in.

"I know, but I was on a roll and I've been going shit crazy— Sorry, *stir* crazy, at home. It felt good to be out hassling the bad guys again."

"So you've called us in to reprimand us?" Bone turned back to Gallacher. "Sir, I'd just like to remind you that for three days we've been attempting to run a major multiple murders investigation with our hands tied behind our backs. We've had no phones, power, or means of communicating with the station. Or each other, for that matter, and we are only now starting to catch up with ourselves."

"Stop," Gallacher interrupted.

"Sir, it has to be one of the most difficult—"

"I said, stop!" Gallacher bellowed.

Bone looked up, flush-faced from his rant.

"DI Kelly is not here to complain. She has come to offer her help and support and to share and exchange information."

"What?"

"That's correct," DI Kelly replied. "DS Mullens did us a favour and created a timely and necessary distraction that I won't go into."

"Well, that's a first," Bone said.

"On every level," Mullens added. "Glad to be of service."

"It would be useful to our investigation if you could share any information you have on Craig Sneddon," Kelly said.

"I found out today that a person of interest," Mullens started, then turned to Bone. "He is a person of interest, isn't he?"

Bone nodded.

"That one of our persons of interest in the current murder investigation we are conducting, a Mr Fergus Dulhoon, may have borrowed money from Craig Sneddon to cover a gambling addiction. All of this is speculation at this stage, but by Sneddon's reaction,

I'd say I'd lit a fire under his arse, excuse me." He glanced up at Gallacher.

"We believe Craig Sneddon may have upgraded his skill set while in prison," Kelly said, "and in addition to the list of criminal activities he was involved in, is also procuring financial gain from contract killings."

Mullens growled. "What a festering fucking scumwart."

"Language, DS Mullens," Gallacher said.

"But that's what the fuckturd is. There's no pleasant way to describe him."

"Sorry about him," Bone said to the DI.

"No, your colleague is right. Craig Sneddon poses a major threat to society, not to mention our police service. That's why we are so determined to get him off the streets and banged up as quickly as we possibly can, and preferably for a very long time."

"Along with his associates as well, I'd assume?" Bone said.

"Exactly, that's why our case needs to be watertight. Any leaks or cracks, and the whole thing comes tumbling down. He's not short a bob, so he will hire the very best and probably most corrupt lawyer he can find to defend him." She looked back at Bone. "This Fergus Dulhoon character. Why is he a person of interest?"

"We have very little to go on at this stage," Bone replied.

"But you will share anything you find that connects him to Sneddon?"

"Of course, and likewise? Does your surveillance include phone taps, covert filming, bank records, that sort of thing?"

"Any means necessary, DCI Bone." Kelly smiled.

"Then, we're interested in Sneddon's movements around late March, beginning of April. Anything that might link the two men together."

"I'm not sure I get it?" Gallacher interrupted.

"What don't you get?" Bone frowned.

"Okay, so this guy has gambling debts, and he's used a loan shark. That doesn't make him a killer."

"No, but it might make him desperate, and going on Sneddon's track record, if Dulhoon didn't pay up, then Sneddon wouldn't stop at threatening him, he'd be at his family and even friends as well," Kelly interjected.

"And if Sneddon's added hired killer to his portfolio, then maybe the bride and groom were a contract," Mullens said.

"So, you see, there's plenty to throw into this cake mix, sir," Bone replied.

"I can certainly check what we have on him around those dates," Kelly confirmed.

"Likewise." Bone sat back. "Well, this is very productive and not where I thought it was going."

"What would be ideal would be a confession that nails Sneddon once and for all, and if there's a possibility your investigation might produce that, then the potential reward outweighs any potential risk of blowing our cover," Kelly said.

"Do you have undercover officers inside Sneddon's operations, then?" Bone pried.

"I am not at liberty to share that information with you."

"Bloody hell, I might have almost lamped one of them," Mullens said.

Bone spun around. "You didn't, did you?"

"Almost, I said."

"Right, let's leave it there for now," Gallacher said. "Probably the best way to deal with this is for shared information to come via me. That way, we can keep tabs on it and I'm up to speed at the same time. Are you both happy with that?"

"Yes, sir," Kelly said.

"Absolutely," Bone agreed.

"Okay, thanks again for making the trip over from Glasgow."

"The SCU office moved last year, didn't it?" Bone said. "How are you finding your new home?"

"What's not to like? As a Glaswegian, it was an aberration to me to have to traipse over to Edinburgh every day."

"And deal with East Coasters," Mullens added.

"Weren't you born in Auchtermuchty, Mark?" Bone asked.

"I've never forgiven my parents for that."

"Okay, I'm sure we are all very busy people and we don't want to keep DI Kelly any longer," Gallacher said.

"Good to meet you, DCI Bone," Kelly said.

"It's Duncan."

Kelly nodded. "DS Mullens; sir," she said and left.

"You two are very lucky indeed. That could have gone shit-on-the-fan wrong," Gallacher said.

"Can't believe I actually helped her out," Mullens said.

"Not through trying," Bone replied. "In future, just keep me in the loop, okay?"

"And that goes for me, too, DCI Bone." Gallacher cut in.

"Sir," the two detectives replied together. They got up.

"Could you give us a second, Mark?" Gallacher said.

Mullens followed Kelly out. A moment later, she laughed on the other side of the door.

"How are you doing, Duncan?" Gallacher asked, returning to his desk.

"Aside from the multiple murders and impossible conditions to investigate the crimes, fine and dandy, sir."

"Just thought I'd check in on you, as it has been particularly trying for all of us."

"And you thought I might be going doolally again?"

"I didn't say that, but you know it must be very bad indeed when the old firm game was postponed, and you were stuck up there with no support while all that shite was going on."

"I handled it and I'm still handling it pretty bloody well, even if I do say so myself."

"And the swimming and all that shenanigans?"

"Counselling, you mean?"

Gallacher nodded.

"I still speak to Josh every week, sometimes fortnightly, if I've nothing to moan about."

"We always have things to moan about, Duncan."

"And what about you? Has everything been okay back here while I've been on my unwanted skiing holiday from hell?"

"It's been challenging with staffing, and we had to deal with stuck cars and stranded pensioners freezing their arses off, but aside from that, the weather curtailed a lot of criminal activity in the area, so although we were seriously stretched, we kept it under the radar."

He leaned over his desk and clipped his stapler, knocking it sideways. Carefully, he repositioned it back where it was and flattened down his over-lacquered pate.

"Good to hear about your progress, Duncan. Sounds like you've finally won the war with your PTSD."

"As soon as you start counting chickens, that's when the fox comes, you know?"

"Aye, but good stuff anyway. And thank your lucky stars, DI Kelly wasn't on the warpath. Our esteemed colleague could have been in serious trouble, heart bypass or no heart bypass."

"That would be my trouble, sir. Mark was only doing what he does best."

"Bull in a bloody china shop."

"Indeed, but you know, it sort of works."

"I do." Gallacher nodded. "Okay, Duncan. Thanks for the update, and as I said before, just keep me informed on your progress."

Bone stood again.

"So, back to Loch Gillan?" Gallacher asked.

"I think so, but I might call in to see Alice on my way. Is that okay?"

"I didn't hear that. What did you say?" Gallacher smiled.

At the door, Bone stopped. "Thanks, sir."

"Say hello to her for me, and to that wee lad of yours."

"He wants to be a policeman, you know. He keeps talking about it."

"God help him. I thought you would have put him off that idea years ago." Gallacher stopped. "Sorry, that was below the belt."

"No, no, accurate and worth it just to see your face regret saying it." Bone laughed.

"Get out." The Super gave him a dismissive wave.

Bone shut the door behind him. In the corridor, he took a deep breath and heaved a long sigh of relief.

Mullens was waiting in reception for him. "Your mates have arrived."

"Who's that?" Bone squinted out of the entrance door. A small group of reporters were gathered at the gate. "Oh no, how did they get wind?"

"Maybe something to do with this?" Brody leaned across the counter and handed Bone his phone.

"What's this?"

"STV news report from Lomond station. The DCI there has just given a press conference."

Bone pressed play, and Harris's bulbous, flushed face appeared on the screen, his foghorn voice filling the room.

"Who the hell's he?" Mullens asked, looming over Bone's shoulder.

"DCI Robert Harris, a man whose personality is used by MI5 as a method of psychological torture."

"You get a mention as well," Brody said. "Joint response and all that."

"Oh, dear God. That explains the ringworm brigade outside. I suppose it was only a matter of time, now that everything's up and running again. But he could have warned us." Bone's phone pinged.

"And there we are, bang on cue."

"Mackinnon?" Mullens asked.

"He's probably outside now."

Mullens looked out again. "Yup, right at the front." He stepped back. "Hold up, member of the public approaching."

The doors slid open, and a woman in a hooded raincoat battled to control her umbrella.

"Let me help you with that, madam," Mullens said.

The woman turned. "Thank you."

"Mrs Willerby," Bone said in surprise.

"I wasn't expecting all that out there," she said nervously, manically brushing the rain from her coat.

"Yes, sorry about that," Bone said.

She looked around at the three officers staring at her.

"I, er, rang your colleague, Detective Walker, and she told me you were here."

"Let's get you out of the entrance, Mrs Willerby. Come this way. Would you like a drink, a cup of tea or water?"

"No, I'm okay."

Bone buzzed her through, and he took her to one of the counselling suites. "Please, let me take your coat."

She removed and shook it again, then handed it to Bone along with her umbrella.

Bone hung her coat on the door. "Sorry again about the journalists outside. I'm afraid the news of your daughter's attack is now in the public domain. I would advise not speaking to any of them. I don't wish to alarm you, but as the investigation proceeds, they may try and contact you. If that happens and you feel harassed by them in any way, please let us know, and we will provide you with all the support you need. Please, take a seat."

Mrs Willerby stared at the sofa and matching armchairs. Bone sat on one of the chairs, and Mrs Willerby sat opposite.

"Have you some news you wish to share?" he asked.

She folded and unfolded her hands and looked on the verge of tears. "It's all been so shocking."

"It has, indeed." Bone shifted a box of tissues resting on the coffee table closer to her. "Take all the time you need."

She plucked one out, gently patted her eyes, and blew her nose. "I'm sorry I didn't tell you before, but when I heard that Laurence had died..." She sniffed.

"Tell me what?"

"It's just that James doesn't know, and I went behind his back."

"About what, Mrs Willerby?"

"It was me."

"Go on," Bone urged.

"I paid for the honeymoon."

"Okay."

"My daughter rang me up the night before they were due to be married and said that they were doing it in secret because she didn't want us to try and stop her." She blew her nose again. "I was so upset that she'd do that behind our back, but more upset that she felt we'd forced her into a corner like that. I never wanted that to happen. She's our daughter, you know? You can't just let things like that be, can you?"

"It must have been very upsetting for you."

"I just wanted my daughter to be happy, and if marrying Laurence was what she wanted, then I had no right, *we* had no right, to block it. I just knew that if I didn't do something to try and make amends, then I was going to lose her forever."

"So you paid for their honeymoon to make up for your disapproval of her partner?"

"We didn't trust him, but that didn't give us the right to treat him the way we did. Clare had told us over and over that he had changed, but we refused to believe her. There was so much about him to forgive and forget, you know? But there was no excuse on our part. We behaved abominably."

"So, what did you do?"

"The next day, I rang her back and offered to pay for a honeymoon as they couldn't afford one. But she threw it back in my face. So the following week I tried again, but this time I contacted Laurence in secret and told him I'd give him the money and he could pay for it, then she wouldn't know it was from us."

"How did he take that?"

"At first he said no, but then I sent him an advert for the lodges and the honeymoon offer they were running, and he called me back and accepted, so I met up with him and gave him the money to pay for it."

"You handed him the lodge fee, eighteen hundred pounds, in cash? That's a lot of notes. Why would you do that?

"He said it was best that way in case Clare spotted the transaction in his bank statement, the whole plan would be ruined. But there was something else." She paused and took a deep breath.

"Take your time."

"I thought that this could be a test."

"What sort of test?"

"To see what he did with the money. If he actually went through with it or just kept it for himself."

"Let me get this straight, you felt guilty about the way you'd treated him, offered to make up for it with your offer to pay for the honeymoon, but then used that money to tempt him to steal it?"

"It wasn't like that. Despite what Clare said, I needed to know that we could trust him, too. It's very difficult to accept your daughter has fallen in love with a convicted criminal."

"And you didn't think that if your daughter found out, she'd be even more upset about this arrangement?"

"It was a risk, I know, but I felt I had to do something to show that I cared about them both, even though I hadn't shown it before."

"What about the photo shoot on Balhuish Island?"

"I didn't know anything about that. He must have arranged that later on himself."

"So you didn't pay for that as well?"

"No."

"It's just that we found a newspaper cutting and a flyer for the wedding photographer's studio in among Clare and Laurence's things at the lodge."

"It was a complete shock when we heard they'd been found on that tiny island. That's why I thought she'd been kidnapped."

"So you have no knowledge of why he booked it and then cancelled it?"

"No, but I have my suspicions."

"Go on,"

"That he used my gift as an—" She stopped again, then sobbed.

"It's all right, Mrs Willerby. I understand this is very difficult for you."

She slowly composed herself again. "That my test went horribly wrong, and he used the money to set the whole thing up."

"What do you mean, set up?"

"Come on, Inspector. He arranged for her to be—" She took another deep breath. "Killed on the island."

"But why?"

"He'd got what he wanted, a marriage certificate, so then he could claim her estate. She had a flat, a healthy bank balance, and a savings account that we'd provided for her. So he saw an opportunity and took it."

"But he's dead, Mrs Willerby."

"Yes, I know that." She shifted in her chair. "But maybe something went wrong. Clare mentioned a masked man. Maybe he panicked and tried to kill them both, I don't know. But, put it this way, if Laurence had been a respectable, law-abiding, and morally centred person, would any of this have happened?"

"You'd be surprised. And does your husband know about this now?"

"No, I still haven't told him. He's so furious and emotionally charged about the whole thing. I've been too afraid."

"I think he has to know, Mrs Willerby."

"I'll tell him today, I promise."

"I'm going to have to ask you to make a formal statement about this."

"I am so sorry for not speaking up sooner. It's an awful lot to deal with."

Bone nodded.

"I feel sick to my stomach that my stupid meddling may have led to all of this and I'm prepared to face whatever the consequences. It's all my fault." She resumed her sobbing.

"Okay, go home for now, Mrs Willerby, and I'll arrange for officers to call round and take a formal statement. Are you okay with that?"

"Yes, of course."

He got up and retrieved her coat and umbrella. "Did you drive over?"

"My car is in the visitor's car park at the front."

"It might be a good idea to avoid the press. If you have your keys, I could move your car round the back and you can leave by the rear entrance."

"Oh yes, I'm in no fit state to deal with any of that." She rummaged in her handbag. "It's the Mini Coupe." She handed him the keys.

"Wait here. I'll be back in a moment."

Back at the entrance, Bone stepped out. When they spotted him, the mob of journalists surged forward to the bottom of the steps. Colin Mackinnon, the chief social affairs reporter at The Kilwinnoch Chronicle, was at the front, as usual.

"Any comment about the recent attacks up in Balhuish, DCI Bone?" he called out, his nasal whine sawing right through Bone's ears.

Bone marched down the steps straight at him.

Mackinnon reversed back into the mic-clutching arms and shouting faces behind him.

"Decided to export your incompetence to the mountains and glens, I see. I hope Lomond station knows what they're letting themselves in for." Mackinnon sneered.

Bone rammed past him and elbowed through the group towards the car.

"Is that why you've been demoted to second fiddle, then?" Mackinnon tried to rile him again.

Bone ignored the bait and unlocked the Mini, and the car let out a loud bleep.

"Nice wheels. I know you're living in Balamory now, but that's taking it a bit far, isn't it?"

There was a collective roar of laughter.

"I mean, does Josie Jump know you've nicked her car?"

The laughter continued. Bone turned back, and Mackinnon smiled.

"Go on, Inspector Bone, you know you want to."

Bone clenched his fist, climbed into the car, and reversed aggressively, stopping within a couple of feet of Mackinnon. He turned, tooted a very high-pitched horn, which drew more hoots and guffaws, and edged towards the crowd, making them part and let him past. At the gate, Mackinnon stood in his way. Bone rolled down the window.

"Out of my way, Mackinnon," Bone shouted.

"Come on, Inspector. I was only kidding. All we want is an update. The victims' names and which hospital they've been taken to, possible suspects. You know we'll find out sooner than later, anyway."

Bone juddered forward, and Mackinnon finally stepped out of the way.

Bone drove at speed out of the entrance, around the corner, and into the staff car park at the back of the station, making sure the automatic gate shut behind him.

He sat for a moment to allow his blood pressure to fall and his anger to subside.

He clambered out of the shrunken banana, slammed the door shut, and went to collect Mrs Willerby before he did something he'd regret, again.

TWENTY-FIVE

When Bone finally arrived at Alice's, a lorry was parked up in front of the farmhouse offloading building materials. Bone pulled up alongside the gate and climbed out. Alice appeared from behind the crane, lowering a crate of breeze blocks onto the gravel.

"Did you walk all the way from Loch Gillan?" Alice said, approaching.

"Feet are killing me." Bone smiled.

Alice gave him a very welcome hug. "I bloody missed you."

"And I missed you, too. Glad to have my freedom of movement back. It's been horrific up there."

"In more ways than one, I hear," Alice said.

Bone stepped back. "Who told you?"

"Mark. He rang to check how I was. I swear since that heart operation, he's like a totally different person."

"He certainly doesn't fart as much," Bone joked. "But still has a big gob on him."

"What's been going on, truthfully?" she asked.

"Can we get out of this racket first?"

Alice nodded, and he followed her around the back of the farmhouse.

"How's it all coming on?" Bone asked.

"The extension is in full swing now. The weather stopped it in its tracks, but glad to see the builders back on it. But I wanted to show you something else first."

They carried on around the side of the house to a set of outbuildings.

"Check out the ladies' new abode," she said, nodding at a brand-new wooden henhouse and run, surrounded by an enclosed fence. Five happy hens were running around scratching and pecking at the soil and feeding from gleaming steel trays.

"When did you do that?"

"The builders sorted it this morning. I'd been meaning to do it for weeks, but they put it all up in an hour. I've just this minute let the girls back in and look at them. They are loving it."

Bone knelt by the fence, and the hens clucked and circled him.

"At least they remember who you are," Alice said.

Bone glanced back at her. "I'm so sorry I got stuck and you two couldn't come up."

"Never mind, you're here now."

"Speaking of which, is bonzo back from school yet?"

"He's in the house. He had yet another day off. The school boiler is broken."

"Oh, Jeez. What did you do about your work?"

"I moved a couple of meetings online, so no sweat. He's been good as gold, obsessing over his new hobby."

"Another one? In under a week? What is it now?"

"You'll see, come on."

They went into the farmhouse, and Alice fired up the ancient Aga. "I assume you want coffee."

"You are correct in that assumption." He looked around the kitchen. "I hope you're not going to change much of your mum's old kitchen. It's kind of special, isn't it?"

"Give or take some white goods and a few more shelves and storage units, no. There are too many memories in these walls."

"Along with the grease and years your mum sweated over that Aga cooking for you and your dad."

"And sweated over her mounting bills as well."

"Is he in his room?" Bone asked.

"Aye, good luck." Alice smiled.

Bone carried on down a hallway and up a narrow staircase to his son's room in the attic. At the door, he read out the handwritten sign Blu Tacked to the front. *DO NOT DESTIRB.*

He smiled and knocked gently, but there was no response. He knocked again.

"Go away, I'm busy," his son called out.

Bone pushed the door open.

"Mum, please. I'm trying to do this." He turned around. "Dad!" he said and ran over to greet him.

"Hey, Michael," Bone said and gave his son a tight hug. He broke off. "If you want me to go away, that's okay."

"Not you, just Mum," Michael replied.

"That's not very nice," Bone said.

"Ach, she's always at me to do my homework and stuff, and I've done it all."

"I hear you had another day off school."

"Yeah!" Michael fist-pumped the air.

"Your mum said you're working on something?"

"I'm building this F14 Tomcat." He took Bone over to a bench laid out with plastic parts for a model plane surrounded by instructions, tubes of glue, and paints. The half-constructed fuselage was resting on its side. Michael picked it up, and his fingers stuck to the side. He disengaged and picked at the blobs of glue accumulated on his fingertips.

"Wow, that's amazing. What made you choose an F14?"

"It was all they had in the shop. It was that or Barbie's beach buggy."

"Fantastic," Bone said.

"You can help me, if you like. I'm not sure about a few bits on the map."

Bone gently lifted the side of the plane and examined it more closely. "Wow, the detail is amazing."

"There's even a pilot." Michael lifted a rack of parts.

"You know, your grandfather was into model building. We used to build galleons and rockets together when I was a kid."

Michael nodded enthusiastically. "A galleon would be good."

"What made you want to try this?"

"My friend, Adam, at school has a magazine with some models in it."

"Right, let's see what's what."

Bone squeezed in alongside his son on the stool, and they worked together on the fuselage, flitting back and forth between the work in progress, the instructions and the array of parts still packed into the box.

A few minutes later, their silent concentration was interrupted by Alice.

"Ahem, your coffee's getting cold, along with your scrambled eggs on toast."

They both looked over, their eyes a little glazed from the smell of the glue.

"And I've made you some, too, Michael, so can you both put that thing down and return to the kitchen?" She about-turned.

Bone pulled a face, and his son copied it.

"We'd better go, otherwise we're dead meat," Bone helped his son from the stool and they followed Alice back downstairs.

"Now these are our ladies' eggs, so you'd better say nice things about them." Alice spooned a mound of food onto Bone's plate. "I guessed you won't have eaten for at least a week, so tuck in."

"Bloody hell, how many eggs did you use?" Bone asked, staring at the small mountain of yellow protein before him.

"Eight or nine. They lay a lot of eggs, and they have to go somewhere."

Michael sat next to his dad and slopped a huge dollop of ketchup onto his plate.

"God's sake, Michael. All you'll taste is sugar."

"I like it on my eggs." He pounded the bottom of the bottle until another blob spurted out.

"This is too kind, Alice. I don't deserve such attention."

"No, you don't," Alice replied and sat opposite with her own plate.

Bone took a sip of his coffee. "Ah, now that's what you call a decent cup. The stuff at the hotel was beginning to taste worse than the tarmac we drink at the station." He slurped again, then shovelled in a huge mouthful of egg and toast.

"Steady on. We don't want to lose any cutlery down there," Alice joked.

Michael copied his dad but then choked on his.

"See?" Alice shook her head.

Bone rubbed his son's back until he stopped.

"I think I swallowed one of the ladies," Michael croaked with another giggle.

"Just be careful," Alice said.

They ate in silence for a minute or so, then Alice put her knife and fork down.

"So, are you staying the night, or longer?" she asked.

"Would it be okay to stay? It's getting a bit late to go back, and to be honest, I could do with a breather."

"Happy to oblige," Alice said with a frown.

Michael cheered. "You can help me finish the F14."

"But I'll have to get back up there in the morning. We're in the middle of—"

"An investigation, I know," Alice interrupted.

"I'll definitely be back at the weekend, or if we sort things out up there, then you two could come up as we originally planned. How would that suit?"

"Yeah!" Michael fist-bumped the air again. "Could we go out on the canoe?"

"It's too cold and dangerous, Michael," Alice said.

"Your mum's right. But if you bring your model, we can work on that. And maybe start another one if you fancy?" Bone smiled at his son.

"You've got egg on your chin," Michael said.

"What?" Bone looked down at his trouser fly.

"No, actual egg," Alice added, trying to suppress a laugh.

"God, some crime fighter I am, eh?" Bone nudged Michael.

"Super Egg Man," Michael said in his Hollywood voiceover voice.

"Alice, what do you think?"

"It is what it is," she said and pushed her plate to one side. "At least we have you for tonight."

"All being well, you want to come up?"

"I'll need to see how it goes with the builders. To be honest, it's kind of hectic with them here, so I just don't know right now."

"Aww, Mum, come on." Michael huffed.

"Can we decide closer to the weekend and see how things are here?"

"Whatever you want, always," Bone replied.

"Really?" Alice picked up her plate and carried it over to the sink. Bone followed.

"Really. I'll fit in with you, but right now I have to be at Loch Gillan." He leaned in closer to her. "We have to catch this maniac before it gets totally out of hand," he whispered, so that Michael couldn't hear.

"I heard that," Michael said and shovelled more ketchup-coated egg into his mouth.

Bone gestured to his wife, and they went out into the hallway.

"There are multiple deaths, and the suspect is still on the loose. I can't just walk out and leave my team up there."

"There's always some maniac on the loose, Duncan. It just gets very tiring. You promised a more normal life after we got back together, but this is fucked up. It's still fucked up." She sighed.

"I know and I'm sorry. I don't know what else to say."

"You could say, I'm going to quit or take early retirement, or stay behind your desk and do the job a DCI is meant to do," Alice started.

"If you want me to do that, I will."

"I want *you* to *want* to do that, not me. You'd never forgive me if I made you leave your true love."

"It's not my true love. Oh Jesus, why do we start on this every time?"

"Because it's never been fixed. It's never gone away. I'm the mistress in this relationship, and you'll never leave your job for me or yourself, admit it."

"I can't do this right now." Bone rubbed at the scar on his temple.

"The elephant in the room, you mean?" Alice replied. "Well, excuse me while I break my neck trying to get past it and back into the kitchen. I need to sort out my son's school bag for tomorrow." She stormed off.

Bone let out a long, deep sigh.

"Life," he muttered, and followed her back in.

"Are you two splitting up again?" Michael asked, still avoiding eye contact with both of them.

"We're just working through a few things, Michael, don't worry," Bone said.

Alice tutted, turned on the tap, and dropped her plate and cutlery into the sink with a clatter, filled the sink with warm water, and plunged her hands in up to the wrists.

"Sorry," Bone said, approaching cautiously, and putting his arm around her waist.

She slowly turned. "I'm sorry, too."

They embraced.

"It's just everything that's going on, the builders, my work, Michael still off, and just being among my mum's stuff I'm feeling a bit frayed."

"And I'm no bloody help."

"No, you're not." She shoved him away playfully. "Sorry, I've soaked your shirt."

She flicked water in his face, and he grabbed her, pulled her to him, and they kissed.

"Yuck!" Michael cried out from the table. "I'm going to boke."

Bone ran over and pretended to retch over Michael. Michael jumped up, and Bone chased his son through to the living room, shoved him onto the couch, and tickled him.

"Stop, you two, or someone really will throw up," Alice called after them and resumed clearing up the mess they'd left behind.

TWENTY-SIX

Early the next morning, Bone's phone woke him from one of the best sleeps he'd had in weeks. He snatched it off the bedside table, fumbled with the call button, and pressed hold.

"What time is it?" Alice mumbled from under the duvet.

"Too early, go back to sleep."

She moaned, turned over onto her front, and carried on snoring. Bone got out of bed and, closing the bedroom door gently behind him, answered the call.

"Morning, Rhona."

"Sir, did you decide to go to Puerto Banús, after all?"

"I wish. No, next best thing. Kilwinnoch. I decided to kip here last night." He checked his watch. "Jesus, it's only 6 a.m." He rubbed his eyes.

"Sorry, but Laurence McDermid's brother, Mr Kenneth McDermid, has been found, and we have an address for him in Stirling. Sheila also found in police records that he was cautioned in 2003 and then again in 2007 for instigating an affray at his brother's flat in Stirling."

"So, no love lost between them, then?"

"A little more serious than sibling squabbles, perhaps."

"You got the message I sent you last night?" Bone asked.

"Yes, and I assumed from the text that you didn't want me to call you back."

"Correct, I had a run-in with Mackinnon at the station last night and wasn't in the mood for conversation."

"Yes, I saw the laughing policeman's press briefing, and you'll be pleased to hear they're here, too."

"Christ almighty. Like rats at a landfill," Bone grumbled.

"Okay, so regarding the mother's revelation, we haven't found anything that would raise so much as an eyebrow. Upstanding pillars of the community and all that guff."

"Always raises my suspicions when people acquire those sorts of labels."

"Cynic."

"Occupational hazard. How are the search teams getting on?"

"Absolute blank. They've shifted their focus to the surrounding hills. Matheson and mountain rescue are helping."

"Is Cash and co still there? Sorry for all the questions."

Walker laughed. "You've only been gone twelve hours, for God's sake. No, they've gone. The Lomond forensic teams are still out on the island and in Balhuish."

"And nothing else from them?"

"Nada, though Will has confirmed that one of the emails sent to the photographer was definitely sent by Laurence McDermid. He's working on the second."

"So all eyes on Laurence McDermid at the moment, then?"

"And his accomplice, the mystery balaclava-clad killer."

"That's jumping ahead a little, isn't it?"

"Just putting the idea out there to let it percolate."

The bedroom door opened. "What's all that chatter?" Alice muttered, pushing her messy fringe from her face.

"Got to go. Text me the address, and I'll call in on the way back up." He hung up. "So sorry, love. I didn't mean to wake you."

"Well, I'm awake now."

"I have to get going."

Alice sighed, went to the kitchen, and filled the kettle. "Are you back tonight?"

"I don't know, sorry. I'll call you."

He went over to hug her.

"Don't. My head is pounding." She shrugged him off.

"Would you like me to stay a bit longer and help you get Michael ready for school or sort out the builders?"

She squinted over at him. "Go on, bugger off." She smiled and waved him away. "I'll be fine after some coffee." She turned back to the kettle.

Bone watched her for a second, fumbling with the switch, her hair everywhere, and the belt on her dressing gown trailing behind her, making her look like a sleepy lion. He smiled and went for a shower.

***

Kenneth McDermid's house was located on a tree-lined street, within spitting distance of Stirling Castle. A squad car was parked outside with two officers inside. Bone tapped on the driver's window.

He flashed his lanyard. "DCI Bone. Liaison officers?"

"Yes, sir. We've just tried to offer our support, but his wife wouldn't let us in."

"Okay. Let me try."

Bone rang the bell, and a woman answered. She was flush-faced as though she'd been crying.

"I'm DCI Duncan Bone for Kilwinnoch station—"

"I told you, my husband doesn't want any support at this time. If that changes, I'll let you know."

"No, I'm Detective Chief Inspector Bone from Kilwinnoch Police Station. I'm leading the investigation into Laurence McDermid's death and the serious assault of his wife, Clare."

"Oh, right. Sorry. I'm Mrs McDermid, Susan. You'd better come in then, but I warn you, Ken is in no fit state to do much talking. We are all devastated."

"I'm so sorry for your loss," Bone said, and followed her into an elegantly decorated living room.

Kenneth McDermid was propped up at a table by a window with commanding views of the castle outside. He was clutching a glass, and a bottle of Bells was resting by his elbow.

"Ken, this is Detective Bone," Susan said.

"My sincere condolences, Mr McDermid." Bone approached.

McDermid glanced up and took a sip of whisky. "I'm raising a glass to my brother."

"Ken, please don't drink too much. It isn't going to help." Susan went over to the table and attempted to pick up the bottle.

He snatched it away.

"No, this is for Laurence." He took a large swig.

"Sorry, Inspector, he's just got back from the mortuary."

"That's right, it's not every day you get to identify your brother's dead body. Cheers!" He raised his glass again.

"Ken, please," his wife pleaded.

"I'm so sorry, Mr McDermid. I didn't realise."

"Realise he's lying like a slab of meat on a butcher's block in Stirling Royal?"

Bone sat next to him.

Mr McDermid smiled at Bone. "Susan, get the inspector a glass; we can toast together."

"No, you're okay."

"The inspector is here to help, Ken," Susan said, trying again to edge the bottle away, but his grip was too tight.

"Help? How? Are you Jesus Christ? Can you bring him back to life?"

"Ken!" Susan interrupted.

Bone raised his hand and nodded to her. "Mr McDermid, we're trying to gather as much information as we can about your brother and his wife leading up to the attack."

"Have you caught them yet?"

"Not yet, no, but we are working round the clock."

Mr McDermid laughed. "It's ironic."

"What is?"

"He was always the black sheep, the prodigal son, fucking up his life at every fucking turn. In and out of trouble with the police." He looked up. "He stole cars. I'm sure you know that by now, though."

"Yes, he had a criminal record."

"More records than HMV, that's what our old man used to say. I was always Mr Goody Two-Shoes—university, good job, career, stable family—but he was nothing but trouble for Mum and Dad." He took a large gulp of whisky and topped up his glass.

Susan muttered again and wrung her hands.

"But he was still their favourite."

"That's not true," Susan interrupted.

"Oh aye, it is. Despite all the pain and endless heartache, he could do no wrong in their eyes."

"They worried sick about him, you know that," Susan said.

"Here's to the prodigal son." He downed another mouthful and grimaced.

"Do your parents live in Stirling?" Bone asked.

"Both dead, cancer and heart attack. Cheers, prodigal son." He winked at the ceiling.

"You said it's ironic. What did you mean?" Bone asked again.

"He'd turned his life around, Inspector," Susan said.

"That's right, darling. He had." He attempted to sing the song, "Isn't it ironic?"

"In what way?"

"It was when he met Clare. He changed. He stopped stealing cars and got help for his addiction. For the first time in his life he was actually working," Susan answered.

"Doing what?" Bone asked.

"Just some basic labouring jobs and supermarket packing. It was hard for him having a criminal record, but he was determined to change."

"That's right, you see, Inspector? Isn't it ironic," Kenneth said. "That's how God rewards us for our repentance. Do good and ye shall be murdered."

"For God's sake." Susan snatched at the bottle.

They grappled for a second or two, and then Mr McDermid gave in and let it go.

"And this all started when he met Clare Willerby?" Bone double-checked.

"She was good for him," Susan said. "She seemed to calm all that restlessness he had before."

"All the good it did him." McDermid stared into the remainder of the whisky lining the bottom of his glass.

"You didn't get on with your brother, then?" Bone asked.

"Not really, no. Not until this last year when he met Clare, then things improved between the two of them," Susan answered for him.

McDermid smiled and then winced. "Aye, we were bosom buddies."

"I'm sorry to have to mention this, but you were twice cautioned by police for fighting with your brother, is that right?"

McDermid chuckled. "We fought with each other our whole lives. He had a way of winding me up. I'm not proud of it, but you know, sometimes he deserved a good slap. I was just trying to get him to wake up and come to his senses instead of throwing his life away."

"And since 2007, have there been any other incidents?"

"Please don't tell me you're asking if Ken could have done this to his own brother?" Susan interrupted.

"I'm sorry. It's my job to check through all the details in an investigation."

"It's all right, Susan. The inspector has a point, and a few years ago, I would have gladly taken a hammer to my brother's thick skull."

"That's a terrible thing to say!" Susan exclaimed in horror.

"No, it's true. He was making all our lives a living hell, especially my mum. She worried herself to an early grave, for Christ's sake." He glanced back at Bone. "So to answer your question, Inspector, no, we decided it was probably best to keep out of each other's way for a while. What you'd call an uneasy ceasefire, and to be honest, I hadn't heard from him for a couple of years until he contacted me out of the blue."

"It was Clare who persuaded him," Susan said.

"Aye, and things were a lot different, better."

"Did you know about their wedding?"

"He rang me up and told me they'd just got married. I told him that not involving her parents would end in bloody tears, but was happy for them both. Unlike her side of the family."

"Her parents?"

"Aye, especially her father, what's his name?"

"James Willerby," Bone confirmed.

"Aye, him. Never liked him. He's what you call a right fucking snob."

"Ken!"

"He is, though. Lording it up over in Bridge of Allen with his law firm branches all over the west of fucking Scotland."

"So you've both met them?"

"Once, and that was too many." McDermid winced.

"I quite liked Lynda," Susan said. "I thought she just wanted the very best for her daughter and could see Laurence was making a huge effort to change."

"If you don't mind me asking, what is it you both do?" Bone asked them.

"I'm a finance officer at a local engineering firm," Susan said.

McDermid laughed again. "And I run a car dealership in Bridge of Allen. Now, isn't *that* fucking ironic?"

"We recovered a bank statement from your brother's house, and you transferred five hundred pounds into his account on the 14th of March, three days before their wedding."

McDermid's eyes welled up.

"Just a small gesture to show Laurence and Clare they had our full support. He said he had something special planned for his wife and he'd use the money to help pay for it." He finished the remains of his whisky.

"Do you know of anyone who could have done this to them?"

McDermid shrugged. "He lived for years in the arsepit of the world, Inspector. He made plenty of enemies. Maybe they didn't like it that he'd told them all to fuck off."

"Do you know who any of these associates might be?"

"Associates. That's a very polite word for them. No bloody clue. He was stealing cars to order at fifteen, so that's a very deep slurry tank of shit." He put the glass to his lips, then changed his mind and slammed it down on the table. "He was always a bloody idiot, but he was my wee brother." He pushed his fist against his mouth.

His wife rushed over and put her arms around him.

"I'm sorry to intrude at this impossible time for you both. I'll just leave my card here and let myself out. If you think of anything at all that might help with our investigation, even if you think it's just a small or trivial thing, give me a call. And family liaison officers are just outside."

Susan nodded and continued to console her distraught husband.

"I'll let myself out," Bone said and retreated out into the street.

In the car, he called Baxter and asked her to check through Laurence McDermid's criminal record again to see if it drew in any familiar names in amongst the charges.

TWENTY-SEVEN

Walker sat back from her laptop. "Right, I'm off out for some fresh air. I've been at this since five-thirty this morning, and my brains are fried."

Harper sat back from his desk. "I noticed you beat me in this morning. Why so early?"

"I couldn't sleep, and my bed has more lumps in it than the hotel porridge. What's yours like?"

"Bliss." He yawned and stretched.

"Wanker," Walker mumbled and grabbed her coat.

"Before you go," Harper interrupted. "Could you have a quick nosey at this?"

Walker yawned. "Sorry, it's not you. Well, it is but—" She smirked.

"The Super sent through some surveillance footage from the STU team. It's of a pub in the Raphorse estate, The Curlew Bar, known to police as Craig

Sneddon's local, where he conducts some of his, ahem, taxi and logistics business."

"How glamorous." Walker rubbed her eyes and peered at the grainy black-and-white image filling the laptop screen.

"It's time-lapse stuff, but I've isolated and worked through the footage of the time period around the attacks." He hit the pause button. "So this is March 30th, a few days before the victims arrived at their holiday lodge."

"What am I supposed to be looking at?" Walker continued to squint.

"See that car parked up at the far end of the street?"

"Barely?"

"I asked digital if they could run the frame through their clean-up software and—" He leaned over his desk and produced a printout of the frozen shot. "This is a copy obviously, but of the image-enhanced version, with the reg plate now visible."

"Is that a Mercedes?"

"It is."

"I can tell by the rising pitch in your voice that you've traced the plate, so go on, before you give yourself a hernia. Who owns the car?"

"It is registered to Willerby and Wilson Solicitors."

"James Willerby's car?"

"His company's car."

"Well, you know how to put a cat amongst the pigeons, I'll give you that, Will."

"Thought that might wake you up."

"Okay, hold that lead. I'll be twenty minutes."

She left the hotel by the back entrance to avoid the media vans camped outside, and cut through the rear garden onto a path through the trees, then out onto the main road out of the village. At the first stile, she climbed over and started her ascent up the mountain track, now almost clear of snow. A truck raced past on the road below, and she caught a glimpse of Lonnie Kilpatrick's hulking frame in the driver's seat. The Toyota continued up the main road and disappeared over the brow of the hill.

"Where's he going in such a hurry?" she wondered and with a quick, frustrating glance up towards the sunny summit, she clambered back over the stile and returned to the hotel.

"Les, grab your coat," she said, bursting into the makeshift incident room.

Buchan had just arrived and was helping herself to a coffee. "What, now?"

"Right now."

Buchan looked at her empty cup and, with a sigh, put it back on the trolley.

"Where are we going?" she asked, following Walker out.

"Want me to come as well?" Harper asked.

"No, you stay here and hold the fort."

The detectives found Urquhart in his office.

"Do you have a car we could borrow?" Walker asked.

"Is the entire hotel and most of the village not enough for you lot, then?" Urquhart said.

"Like right now?" Walker said.

"What's wrong with the dozen or so vehicles, boats, helicopters, and drones you have outside then?"

"Too conspicuous. Do you?" she urged.

"Okay, take the utility. It's insured for any driver. But if you wreck it, I'll be wanting Police Scotland to compensate me in full with an equivalent replacement."

"We're not going to trash it, but of course," Walker replied.

"A Lamborghini should suffice, but I'd settle for a Ferrari if your budget doesn't stretch." He fished the keys out of his pocket and chucked them over.

Walker snatched them up and dashed for the door.

"You'll be wanting to know where it's parked," Urquhart said with a smile. "Round the back of the public bar, so Hollywood out there won't see you."

They ran out and jumped into the white utility van with the hotel logo on the side.

"Where are we going??" Buchan asked again.

"I just saw Lonnie Kilpatrick heading out of the village towards the main road. If we're quick, we might catch up with him."

"In this thing?" Buchan grimaced.

"Let's see," Walker started the engine and van screeched out of the car park, past the group of journalists too busy gorging on Urquhart's morning rolls to notice them.

"Good job the snow's melted," Buchan said through gritted teeth as Walker took another sharp corner at breakneck speed. "I remember your driving from police training."

"Keep an eye out for his blue Toyota estate and any oncoming vehicles, like this one." Walker hit the brakes, and the van screamed to a halt a few inches from the bumper of a delivery van. She rammed into reverse and swung into a lay-by. On their way past, the delivery driver shook his fist at her, and with a returned gesture, she tore off again.

"We're about half a mile from the main road," Buchan said, checking her phone.

"Do you see him?"

"No."

"Shit." Walker hit the pedal. The van lurched around another tight bend and roared on.

"Main road in two hundred metres," Buchan said a few minutes later.

"Still nothing?"

"Still can't see him."

They approached the junction and screeched to a halt. A juggernaut tore past, almost taking the front off the utility.

"Jesus!" Buchan exclaimed.

"See him?" Walker checked left and right.

Buchan pointed. "There!"

"Where?"

"Go right, go right."

Walker pulled out in front of an oncoming car and just managed to screech past. The car horn blared angrily at her.

"I can't see it," Walker shouted.

"Keep going."

She accelerated on. The road ahead was clear.

"Are you absolutely sure about this?" Walker wiped at the build-up of condensation on the windscreen.

A crossroads loom with lights on red, three cars waiting.

Buchan leaned against the passenger window.

"Blue Toyota at the front of the queue," she said.

"Got him." Walker slowed to join the line of traffic and stopped.

The lights changed, and the Toyota turned right towards Balhuish along with the car next in the queue. Walker followed behind, using the car for cover. Approaching Balhuish, the road narrowed, then the Toyota turned off. Walker pulled up by the junction and waited a moment or two, then continued.

"Where does this go?" Walker asked.

Buchan flicked at the map on her phone. "It leads to some farms. It doesn't go anywhere else."

The road surface deteriorated until they were driving on a muddy track.

"Where the fuck is he now?" Walker checked ahead.

"He must have turned off again." Buchan checked the sign. "Dulhoon's farm."

"Interesting," Walker said and stopped the van by the farm's entrance gate.

"Let's get some support over here," Walker said.

Buchan called it in.

They climbed out and, approaching the farm entrance, Walker poked her head around the gate. The Toyota was parked up in the yard, the driver's door open.

"Shall we?" Buchan said.

***

Walker knocked on the front door, and a dog barked somewhere on the other side. She knocked again. There was still no reply. "Round the back."

They followed the path to the rear of the farmhouse. Passing one of the windows, Walker spotted Kilpatrick and another figure skulking in the hallway. She rattled the pane, and they disappeared.

"Stay here." Walker ran back around to the front of the house.

Kilpatrick was climbing into his truck.

She grabbed the door before he could slam it shut. "Going somewhere, Mr Kilpatrick?"

Kilpatrick jumped back. "God, you gave me a fright." He attempted a smile.

"What are you doing here?" Walker asked.

The farmhouse door opened.

"He's come to see us," Mr Dulhoon interrupted from the entrance. "Who are you?"

"Detective Inspector Walker. I work with DCI Bone, who I believe you've already met?" She turned back to Kilpatrick. "You seemed to be in an awful hurry there, Lonnie."

"I forgot I have a dental appointment in Balhuish. I swear this bloody knock on my head has given me dementia."

"Can we go back inside, please?" Walker insisted.

Kilpatrick checked his watch. "I'm going to miss it, and they'll probably bloody charge me."

"The idiot came over to help me fix my bailer," Mr Dulhoon said.

"After you, Lonnie," Walker insisted.

They went in.

"Is this about my stolen quad bike and the recent spate of robberies?" Mr Dulhoon asked, returning to the kitchen.

"There was a third person here with you a moment ago," Walker said.

"Is that your colleague hanging about out there?" Kilpatrick pointed at Buchan who had her face pressed up against the kitchen windowpane.

"Ah yes, could you let her in, please?"

Mr Dulhoon opened the back door, and she joined them.

"This is—"

"Yes, we know who she is. Hello, Lesley," Mr Dulhoon said.

"It's DI Buchan today, Jock," she replied.

"Where is the third person who was with you?" Walker asked again.

"My wife's—" Mr Dulhoon started.

"How do," Fergus Dulhoon said, entering from the hallway. He was a tall, well-built young man with the same shock of blond hair as his father.

"The elusive Mr Fergus Dulhoon?" Walker asked.

"Yes, that's correct, though not sure about the elusive bit." He glanced over at Buchan. "Good afternoon, Lesley. Sorry, DI Buchan."

"That's quite a shiner you have there," Buchan said.

"Aww, this?" He patted at the extensive bruising around his left eye and cheek. "A tractor door blew back in my face at college. Some numpty left it unlatched."

"Can you tell us why you all ran off when we knocked?" Walker pressed.

"I was just upstairs in the loo. I didn't run off," Fergus replied.

"Well, that's not how it looked from where we were," Walker added.

"And I told you I have a dental appointment, and it's now gone half two and I've missed it," Kilpatrick interrupted.

"I would say that in my twenty or so years as a police officer, I don't think I've come across a group of people acting as suspiciously as you lot."

"I was in the loo. You can go and smell it if you like," Fergus insisted.

"Can you all sit down for a second? I don't like you looming over us."

The three men sat at the kitchen table.

"Where's your wife, Mr Dulhoon?"

"She's gone over to her sister's. She's on chemo treatment, and my wife helps her out."

"What are you doing here, Fergus?"

"I wanted to check up on my parents after all the bother there's been, and with the weather on top of that as well, I was worried about them."

"I told him we were fine and we can look after ourselves, but he insisted on coming, and I couldn't persuade him otherwise," the farmer jumped in.

"How's college?" Buchan cut in.

"Fine, going well." He dropped eye contact.

"My son's at Agricultural College in Stirling, Detective Walker."

"Aren't you missing classes, though?" Buchan asked.

"Only a couple. I thought I'd nip up here before practicals start."

"So how long have you been here?" Walker continued.

"Came over last night," Fergus shot back.

Walker turned to Mr Dulhoon "And did you know your son was visiting?"

"Not a clue. But it's good to see his ugly face."

"You didn't travel up before the storm then?" Buchan asked.

"God no, and get stuck on the road? People die in weather like that."

"Don't they just," Walker replied. "Glad you got your quad bike back, Mr Dulhoon. I hope it wasn't a complete write-off."

"Just a bent handlebar, easily fixed. We were lucky this time." He glanced over at his son, who dropped his hands off the table.

"When are you planning to go back then, Fergus?" Buchan asked.

"Probably tomorrow. There's a field trip I can't miss."

The door rattled, and Mr Dulhoon almost jumped out of his chair. There was a second knock. "Shall I answer that?" he said, finally.

Walker nodded. Moments later, he was back.

"There are two police officers outside," he said. "What's going on?"

"DI Buchan, could you speak to Mr Kilpatrick in the living room? Mr Dulhoon, could you wait with the officers outside," Walker said.

"What about me?" Fergus asked.

"I'd like to speak to you."

"Why, what have I done?" He raised his arms in dispute.

"Only take a minute," Walker said.

Buchan followed the two men out, and shut the door behind them.

"My colleague visited your college accommodation," Walker said.

"Oh, aye?" Fergus shifted in his chair.

"Your flatmates haven't seen hide nor hair of you for over two weeks, maybe longer."

"I've been, er, out and about, you know, staying over places."

"Out and about in Balhuish as well?"

"No, in Stirling, just partying and sleeping at mates' flats, on floors, or if I'm lucky, not." He chuckled to himself.

Walker continued to stare at him. "My colleague also spoke to the college registrar. You haven't been paying your accommodation fees, and they've issued you with a final warning."

"That's just a stupid mix-up. They had the wrong bank details. I was going to sort it when I go back tomorrow." Fergus patted his face again which was now a little shinier with sweat.

"Feeling a bit warm in here?" Walker asked. "I'd open the back door, but I think you might want to run off again."

"I told you I didn't run off, I was taking a shit," Fergus grumbled, his anger rising.

"Do you have money problems?" Walker continued.

"I'm a student, of course I do."

"Big enough to visit a loan shark?"

"A what?"

"Have you borrowed money from an illegal money lender, who may be threatening you in some way?"

"Christ almighty. I have an overdraft that's in and out of the red. My bank shouts at me and I pay it off. You must think I'm totally thick to go to one of those crooks."

"And do your money problems stem from a gambling habit?"

"What? No," Fergus returned in surprise.

"Hence your inability to pay your accommodation fees?"

"This is nuts. I'm just a student having a bit of fun while working hard to pass my course so I can help my dad transform this place into a farm that's actually going to make us some money. Where's the bloody crime in that?"

"No crime, but in case you are unaware, there have been plenty round here of late."

Fergus folded his arms and sighed. "Are we finished? I'd like to carry on catching up with my mum and dad, and my old school friend."

"No, I'm afraid we're not done. I'm just not satisfied with your responses to my questions."

"I don't care if you're satisfied or not. It's the truth."

"That remains to be seen." She found her phone and turned it on.

"What are you doing?"

"I'm calling ahead to Lomond station to prepare the interview room for you. I'm taking you in."

"You're what? Am I under arrest or something? Oh, come on, what is this? Surely, you don't think I'm involved in those murders."

"Connecting," Walker said.

Fergus huffed and shuffled in his chair.

"Good morning, this is DI Walker."

"Okay, wait. Listen," Fergus interrupted.

"Can you put me through to DCI Harris, please?"

"Stop!" Fergus cried out.

"I'll call you back," Walker said and hung up.

"Okay, I have got myself into a bit of bother with debt, I've just told my dad about it and he's a bit upset. The last thing he needs is to be carted off in some pig wagon." He looked up. "Sorry, but he's not involved in my problems."

"Gambling?"

"Yes, it's got out of control of late. But I'm trying to get on top of it."

"How are you doing that?"

"That's why I'm here now. I came over to ask my dad for a loan to put an end to this once and for all. I've even signed up for Gamblers Anonymous. I can show you the emails. I am trying."

"And did you borrow from a loan shark?"

"No! The bank wouldn't lend me anymore and demanded their money back, so in desperation, I went to one of those payday loan companies. But now the interest on that is more than the original payments back to the bank. It's just a fucking nightmare." He bowed his head and took a deep breath.

"Are you able to show me your payday loan contract and bank records?"

"Of course, aye."

"And you insist that you arrived here last night?"

"Aye, I've been dreading it. My dad thinks I'm a bloody disappointment at the best of times."

"How did you get up here?"

"Bus, and then I walked over from Balhuish."

"Do you have a ticket?"

"No, I don't think I kept it."

"And how did you pay?"

"Cash."

"So there's no paper trail of you ever being on any bus?"

"I was on the bus. The nine-oh-three from Stirling to Gillan Pass."

"Was it busy, and did you know anyone? There must have been someone who got off with you at Balhuish."

"I didn't see anyone. I was so worried about what I was going to say to my dad, I just kept my head down."

"This is not good, Fergus. No receipt record and not a soul you know on a rural bus travelling back to your home village. You know we will ask the bus company to hand over their CCTV recordings of the journey. Most buses have that now."

Fergus looked up and stared at her for a second. "I came up on the bus. That's how it was." He shrugged.

"Can you wait here a moment, please?"

"Are you still going to arrest me?" he called out.

Walker ignored him and went to find Buchan. Mr Dulhoon met Walker in the hallway.

"Could I speak to you for a moment?" She took him back out to the yard.

"Look—" He rubbed at his temple. "This is very difficult. My son has got himself in a bit of bother."

"What sort of bother?"

"He's been gambling quite a bit, apparently, and fallen into a hole with it. This was all news to me until today, and I'm not right in the head with it. Bloody idiot!" He cursed. "But that's why we were behaving so... you know. We thought you were the bailiffs."

"What for?"

"Not paying his way. He said the payday loan company was about to report him."

"And he's up here to ask you to bail him out before the heavies get to him?" Walker asked.

"That's right, yes. I don't know about heavies, but certainly before he gets in any bother with the law or something daft like that. The last thing the boy needs is a police record."

"And are you going to help him out?"

"We just don't have that kind of money."

"How much exactly?"

"He hadn't told me yet, but by the look on his face, I suspect it's thousands, the stupid bloody idiot." He sighed. "I mean, we're on our bloody knees with this farm."

"You know that perverting the course of justice is a criminal offence, Mr Dulhoon? If you're lying to me and we find out, it could be very serious for you."

"That's the truth of it, Inspector. I wish it wasn't, but he's my son, and we just try to do our best by them, even when they don't bloody deserve it.

"Okay, thanks, and while we're being honest. When did your son arrive?"

"I told you, last night."

"And that's when he told you about his debts?"

"Yes."

Walker nodded. "Wait here with the officers, please." She nodded to a pair of PCs lingering by their car and went to find Buchan.

"It's like trying to herd cats," Walker said when Buchan stepped out of the living room and shut the door. "How did you get on with Kilpatrick?"

"Talking nonsense. Keeps ranting about some imaginary dental appointment. If I had a concussion, I think a dental appointment would be low on my list of priorities, but easy enough to go fib spotting. What about the son?"

"Stinks to high heaven. A few minutes ago he admitted to having debt problems and was about to ask his dad to bail him out, but then his father just told me that was the reason they were all acting weird because they thought we were the bailiffs."

"The cheek. I mean, do we look like bailiffs?"

"I'm afraid we probably do."

"The boys are falling over their lies, like rabbits with their feet caught in their own traps."

"Without any of the luck," Walker added. "Does your station have rooms where we could interview the pair formally?"

"Drumgoil? Are you serious? It's a two-room matchbook with a holding cell that doubles as a staff toilet. I think we'd have to take them back to Lomond."

"Oh, Jeez, and more fun and games with DCI Harris?"

"I'm afraid so."

Walker blew out her cheeks. "Okay, get them over there and see if we can unpick this mess."

"What about the dad?" Buchan asked.

"Jury's out on him, though he seemed genuinely shocked and upset about his son's financial predicament. I'd say let's focus on the likely lads for now and see where that goes."

"Agreed," Buchan replied.

"I'll deal with Fergus. Do you want to drop the good news on his co-conspirator?"

"Okay," Buchan said.

They went back in.

"Mr Dulhoon, I'd like you to accompany us back to Lomond station so that we can go through your story in more detail," Walker said, returning to the kitchen.

"What, no!" Fergus exclaimed. "I thought we'd cleared everything up! I'm telling you the truth."

"If that's the case, then you've nothing to worry about."

Walker helped him up, but he shrugged her off.

Out front, Walker took Fergus over to the squad car, and before he could complain any more, the PC waiting there lowered his head into the backseat. Buchan appeared in the doorway with Kilpatrick, Jock Dulhoon following behind.

"This is bloody ridiculous," Mr Dulhoon complained. "On what grounds are the boys being dragged all the way over to—" He scowled at Walker.

"Lomond station," she replied.

"I told you what was going on in good faith, Inspector."

"We'd just like to clear up a few more things. It's in your son's and Mr Kilpatrick's interest to cooperate fully with us."

"I told you, Inspector, my son arrived late last night. If you think for one second that him or Lonnie are involved in any way in recent robberies or break-ins or even the attacks on Balhuish, then you are very wrong."

Buchan deposited Kilpatrick in the second squad car.

"If you go with Kilpatrick," Walker said to Lesley, "I'll take the hotel van back and I'll meet you at Lomond station. The DCI is on his way."

"Fine." Buchan nodded.

"I need to chase up something first, so when Duncan gets there, please crack on with the interviews, and I'll get there as quick as I can."

"Where are you going?"

"Just something Will found. I'll fill you in when I get back."

"Okay, I'll see you over there, though are you sure that's not some lame excuse to avoid seeing Harris again?"

"No, but now that you've reminded me, it might take me a little longer to get back than I first anticipated."

"Too cruel." Buchan climbed in the front passenger seat of the squad car, and the PC started it up.

"Aww, please shut up," she shouted at Kilpatrick who was still complaining in the back.

The car set off, and the second followed close behind.

TWENTY-EIGHT

An overly harassed administrator took Walker through the law firm's reception area to James Willerby's office at the rear of the building. When she went in, the solicitor was on the phone. He nodded, turned his back to her, and carried on with his heated conversation. Walker stood for a moment, but her impatience got the better of her, and she coughed loudly. The solicitor swung around, shook his head, and then finally hung up.

"My sincere apologies, Detective. We are dealing with a rather demanding client at the moment, and he'd test the patience of a saint. Have you some news?"

"I wanted to clear up a couple of things, if that's okay?"

"Of course, anything to sort out this horrific nightmare. At least our daughter is recovering physically, but God knows what mental scars she'll have to live with after all this. Please take a seat. Did Fiona offer you a tea or coffee?"

"I'm fine, thanks." She sat down opposite the desk. "I must say I was surprised when your wife told me on the phone that you were at work today after everything that's happened."

"It was Lynda who suggested I come in. I'm so angry about the whole thing. I'm struggling, if truth be told, and work is a distraction."

"I won't keep you. I just wanted to double-check that you were unaware of your daughter's marriage to the deceased, Laurence McDermid."

"Absolutely, and I was completely shocked and somewhat dismayed when Lynda told me she'd paid Laurence for the honeymoon. But she did what she did, and we can't change it now."

"And you are adamant that he was a bad influence and an unsuitable husband?"

"Totally, and this awful attack proves my point. I'm sure he was behind it and had it all planned from the start. A nice little earner for him when all her assets, including her flat, were handed over to him." He paused. "Where is this going, Detective?"

"I'm asking you again because aside from you, all of the people we've interviewed claim Mr McDermid had turned his life around and he had rehabilitated himself with the help of your daughter."

"I've told you before and I'll tell you again, people like him are never rehabilitated. They are born social pariahs, and I should know, I've had to defend quite a few in my career."

"Can I show you something?" She opened her bag and produced an A4 photocopy of the screen-captured image of The Curlew Bar and the adjacent street. She placed it down on his desk and pushed it under his nose.

"What's this?" he asked, removing a pair of glasses from a case.

"This is The Curlew Bar on the Raphorse estate."

"One of McDermid's haunts, I presume?" He scanned the grainy photo.

"Have you ever visited this pub?"

"This bar is notorious. Do you think I have a death wish or something?"

"Can you see that car parked farther up the street, beyond the pub?"

"It's not very clear." He squinted.

She produced a second printout, this time of Harper's enhanced close-up of the vehicle. "The car is a white E-Class Mercedes."

"Drug dealer scum, no doubt."

"I saw a Mercedes in your car park, Mr Willerby. It looks like a drug dealer may have nicked your designated space."

"I think you'll find there's a vast difference between someone like me who has studied and grafted and worked day and night to build a career and business, a valuable asset to their local community and economy, and the sewer scum who probably stole this one here."

"Has your car been stolen recently then?"

"No, why?"

"We traced the plates, and the registered keeper is you," Walker replied.

The solicitor looked up. "What?"

"That's your car, Mr Willerby."

He scrutinised the printout. "You can't make out the registration plate from this."

"We have technology that deciphered it, and it is definitely your car."

"Oh." He stared at the image for a moment.

"Mr Willerby?" Walker prompted.

"When did you say this was taken?"

"March 30, four days before the attacks," Walker said.

"Let me just check my diary." He searched his suit pocket and produced a mini Filofax.

"Thirtieth, you say." He flicked at the pages. "Ah yes, I remember now." He closed the book. "I needed to speak to a client who was on bail and due to appear in court that week."

"Who was this client?"

"I was afraid he was going to go walkabout, so I had to make sure he didn't. The last thing I need is complete humiliation in front of the magistrates. One gets a sixth sense about runners, and he was definitely ringing alarm bells."

"What was his name?"

"Hmm… what was his name? We deal with so many that they all tend to blend into one single waste of space after a time." He stroked his chin. "Barraclough, I think that's it. I can check our records and get back to you with that. But as predicted, he wasn't there to meet me."

"How long did you spend in the pub?"

"Oh, less than a minute. I went to his property first, and his girlfriend, if it was his girlfriend, told me he might be in The Curlew. He lives a few streets away, as you would expect. I didn't want to hang around and find myself at the sharp end of a fist, knife, or firearm. So I got the hell out of there before I lost my car."

"Do you regularly go to dangerous estates after work, in the dark?"

"As I said, I was concerned he was going to jump his court appearance and it was a last resort, and looking at the expression on your face, one I now regret."

"I thought you would have assistants or juniors who would do that for you?"

"I didn't want to risk sending some naïve graduate in there. They'd be eaten alive."

"Do you know a man called Craig Sneddon?"

"Of course. He's one of Stirling's most notorious gang leaders."

"He also operates as a loan shark, amongst other things. He often uses The Curlew as a base for his criminal activities."

"Exactly, and the very reason I didn't want to hang around there."

"So you've never met him?"

"Never, thank God. I've met a few of his victims and so-called employees who we've had to defend, but never the king cockroach himself."

"Do you know that he's branched out into contract killing?"

"No, I didn't know that, but I'm not surprised." He stopped. "You don't think Sneddon was involved in the attack on my daughter?"

"Our investigations are ongoing. We're just trying to clear up a few anomalies. But thank you for helping us out with that one."

"Oh my God. I see now." Willerby nodded. "McDermid employed the services of Sneddon to murder my daughter."

"As I said, there are a number of leads we are following up on."

"I've dealt with many an evil bastard in my time, but this reaches the depths of depravity."

"Thanks for your help." Walker got up to leave.

"For all our sakes, please make this stop."

Walker nodded and left.

Out in the street, she called Baxter and asked her to check Willerby's story, then messaged Buchan to let her know she was on her way.

TWENTY-NINE

When the squad cars arrived at Lomond Police Station, Buchan checked in the two men, and they were taken down to two separate holding cells, and before Harris got wind she was there, she went for a walk along the banks of the loch to wait for Bone and Walker to arrive.

A short while later, she spotted a squad car pulling up in front of Lomond station's prefabricated extension stuck on the side of a converted bungalow, and Walker stepping out.

She went over to greet her. "So, are you going to tell me what you were up to?"

"Willerby's car's been spotted at Sneddon's favourite drinking den. I went to check out what he had to say about it."

"And?"

"He came up with some shaky alibi. I've asked Sheila to look into it and get back." Walker glanced across the loch. "These views never stop, do they?"

"Apart from that carbuncle." Buchan pointed at the station. "The pair are in holding cells."

DCI Harris appeared in the station entrance.

"Oh, Jeez," they muttered in unison.

"Welcome to our humble abode, DI Walker. Do come in," Harris said.

They reluctantly followed him inside.

"It's probably not a patch on your gaff, but at least we have better effing views, eh, Les?"

He cackled loudly, and the sergeant on the desk pulled the glass screen a little further shut.

"DI Walker, meet Desk Sergeant Fleming, a man for all seasons, but mainly winter, wet and windy ones." Harris laughed so hard the screen rattled in its hinges.

Sergeant Fleming nodded a hello.

"So you've brought two sissies in, I mean sussies," Harris continued.

"What?" Walker asked, already feeling a bit punch-drunk by Harris's overbearing presence.

"Sorry, persons of interest. Note to self, must use wokey lingo."

"Would you like to join us when we conduct the interviews?" Buchan asked.

"Me? Are you kidding? I thought you knew me better than that, Les. No, I'll be in my office, shuffling papers from one side to the other in an important manner as all DCIs are supposed to do." He looked up at her.

Here it comes, Buchan thought.

"Did I say paper? *GQ* effing magazine, more like." He literally belched out a guffaw.

Walker recoiled.

"Enjoy. Toodle-pip!" he said and set off up the stairs.

"Sir," Buchan called back. "I'll come up and brief you."

"Oh, how splendid. There was me thinking I'd effing dodged that bullet. Right, come on then. Let's make it snappy. *Escape to the Country* is on in ten minutes." He snorted. "Your face, DI Walker."

He about-turned and dashed up the stairs, Buchan reluctantly following slowly behind.

The desk screen slid back open.

"It's okay, it's safe to come back out," Walker said to the sergeant who peered around the gap in the window.

"Sorry about him," he said.

"How do you put up with him day after day?"

"Drugs, and then more drugs."

"I'm going to leave those two down there to sweat for a bit while we wait for my boss to get here."

"DCI Bone, isn't it?"

"That's right."

"I heard he was back on duty at RCU."

"A couple of years now."

"If you don't mind me asking, how is he to work for?"

"Pain in the arse. Aren't all bosses?" She smiled. "No, I've had a few in my time, and he's the very best by a mile, but for God's sake, don't tell him I said that."

"I might apply for a transfer." He chuckled.

"Go for it, but you'd be swapping the Bonnie Bonnie Banks for food banks."

"Oh, we have those here, too, don't kid yourself."

"I know, I grew up in Lewis." She looked around the tiny foyer. "Is there anywhere to grab a coffee?"

"There's a small canteen area on the first floor, but it's..." —he leaned over the counter and whispered— "next door to David Brent."

"Anywhere else?"

"The village café is at the end of the road, turn left. You can't miss it. It's between the chapel and the pub."

"Thanks, good talking to you."

"When the DCI arrives and DI Buchan comes back, shall I send them round to you?"

"That would be great, but no one else." Her eyes widened.

"I've no idea where she went, sir," Fleming said. The phone rang and, with a nod to Walker, he picked it up.

***

The postage-stamp-sized Bonnie Brae Café was deserted. A lone old codger was sitting hunched over a paper in the corner stirring heaped teaspoons of sugar into a frothy cappuccino. When he saw Walker come in, he saluted her and carried on.

"What can I get you?" a young woman in dreadlocks and a rainbow t-shirt asked from behind the counter.

As Walker scanned the board, she yawned and then, after recovering, yawned again. "Quiet, isn't it?"

"Aye." The girl sighed.

"Thought you'd have more tourists by now."

"The weather put paid to that for now. They'll all be back in their squeaky pac-a-macs in a couple of days, don't worry." She looked Walker up and down. "Are you on holiday yourself?" She attempted a fake smile, perhaps oiling the wheels for a potential generous tip.

"I'm over at the station."

"A copper?"

"'Fraid so." Walker smiled.

"Are you a detective, then?" she asked, staring at Walker's lanyard.

"Yes."

"You'll be wanting a black coffee then," she replied.

"Are we that predictable?"

"Yup." She stopped. "Is that for one, or…?"

"Yes, you'll be delighted to hear, I'm sure." She winked.

Walker sat in the window to take in the views across Loch Lomond.

A few moments later, the girl brought her drink over, with a slice of sponge cake.

"Sorry, I didn't order that."

"On the house. Well, actually, it's so quiet at the moment it'll probably end up in the bin at the end of the day, or I'll be tempted to eat it, so I've cut my losses."

"Well, thank you," Walker said.

The girl returned to the counter.

Bone appeared in the doorway. "Caught you, stuffing your face."

"That was quick," Walker said.

"Roads were quiet. I think people are still nervous about travelling around up here."

Bone sat opposite. "It's all been happening then?"

"You could say that. Lesley just dropped Lonnie Kilpatrick and Fergus Dulhoon at Lomond station. They are cooking away in a couple of cells over there."

"So, why the station interviews?"

"We followed Lonnie Kilpatrick over to Jock Dulhoon's farm, and when we made our presence known, he tried to do a runner, along with Jock Dulhoon's son. Or at least that's my conclusion, but they were both insisting they urgently needed to be somewhere else."

"I think we've heard that one a few times before, don't you?"

"Exactly. The pair of them were acting about as guilty as a kid with a mouthful of Pick n Mix in a Woolworths."

"Where?" Bone asked.

"Don't start."

"So why did Lonnie Kilpatrick go over there in the first place?"

"That's what we need to find out. And also, what Fergus was doing there."

"Did the son say when he arrived?"

"Oh, the night before; that was the mantra both him and his father were sticking to."

"And what about the dad? If you think he's covering, why didn't you bring him in as well?"

"Lesley and I both thought the dad seemed genuinely shocked by the sudden surge of bodies through his door." She stopped. "Sorry, wrong choice of words. He was still reeling from the news his son was up to his arse in gambling debt.

The barista approached the table.

"Black coffee?" she asked.

"Yes, how did you know?" Bone asked.

"Long story," the girl said. "Anything to eat?"

"No, you're fine," Bone replied.

"We can share this monster," Walker said, prodding the triangle of sponge with her spoon.

The girl walked away.

"Lesley is updating DCI Harris; she'll meet us here in a bit," Walker said.

"I've been meaning to ask about you two."

"Us two?"

"Were you an item when you were at training college?"

"Oh, don't hold back, sir."

"Sorry, that's nosey of me, don't answer that."

"I see what you're doing, you're playing the classic double bluff, so that I now say, *no, no, of course you're not being nosey, I'm happy to answer that*, otherwise you'll think that we did go out." She looked up. "But, with respect, sir, you are." She shook her head.

"Sorry, you are quite correct. That was inappropriate of me." He paused for a second. "I knew it," he muttered quietly.

"Okay, you're right. We went out very briefly in our first year, but it was over before it started."

"It was obvious the minute I saw you together."

Walker shook her head again. "Aye, right." She shrugged.

"Oh come on, you both blushed like a couple of teenagers, for God's sake."

"That's what you call embarrassment. We were just kids messing about back then. Have you never bumped into an old girlfriend?"

"Thankfully, I never had any to bump into."

Walker shook her head. "Now who's lying? Anyhow she's going to come over to ours to meet Maddie and Erin. She was so excited to hear that Maddie and I have a daughter. And before you ask, Maddie does know everything."

"Everything?"

"Yes, everything, and way more than I would ever dream of telling you, gossip face. I mean, sir."

The barista returned with Bone's coffee.

"Americano." She placed it down on the table. "Now, let me guess, two sugars but sometimes three when you're stressed?"

"What is this?" Bone sat back in surprise.

"Our cover is blown, sir," Walker replied. She turned to the girl. "You were born to be a detective."

"I'm still confused," Bone said.

"It's an age thing," Walker said to the girl.

Bone took a sip of his drink. "Oh, that's bloody good."

"Another reason to join. They're never going to turn down a barista-trained recruit," Walker said.

The girl smiled. "Good point," she said and left.

"Anyhow, never mind my love life, have you managed to see Alice and Michael yet?" Walker asked. "I'm sure they'll have been worrying about you."

"Don't mention it."

"What's happened now?"

"Nothing really, just the usual."

"Work-life balance issues?"

"Life-life balance. Big gob, Mark, had already filled her in about the killing up here, so she was stressed out about that." Bone sighed. "I don't know. This job and marriage are maybe just not—"

"Made in heaven?"

"Something like that, but you two seem to manage okay."

"We have our moments, too, don't kid yourself. The trick is to shut the door on it when you get home, and Erin definitely helps me do that."

"Something I've never been good at, but since my rehabilitation, I thought I was doing better, but Alice still hates what I do, and that's never going away."

"Just keep on keeping on, that's what I say. You two are soulmates. Sometimes you might need a bomb up your arses to realise it, but it's out there in plain sight. You've just got to keep looking for it."

"You think?"

"I know. Now drink your coffee, and let's get this investigation wrapped up so you can get the fuck home. Pardon my French, sir."

Bone raised his cup. "Say it like it is, DI Walker." He took a couple of long sips.

Buchan stumbled in through the door and approached the table.

"I need a coffee." She slumped down next to Bone. "Morning, sir. Briefing with DCI Harris complete. I need a gas oven to stick my head in." She glanced over. "Sorry, that wasn't very professional of me."

"Our thoughts are with you at this most difficult of times," Bone said.

"Right, five minutes to fill me in, then we go and see what Tweedledum and Tweedledee have to say for themselves."

Buchan called the waitress over and ordered a double espresso.

THIRTY

Lonnie Kilpatrick was waiting in a tiny interview room in the station's equally tiny basement. His huge frame was squeezed into a chair between a narrow interview table and the wall. When Bone entered, he sat back in anxious surprise,

"Sorry to keep you." Bone sat opposite, uncomfortably close. "Would you like a glass of water or anything? You're looking a little hot."

"I've been sitting in here for more than half an hour without a word of explanation." Kilpatrick huffed and wiped his sleeve across his moist, ruddy brow.

"Thanks for your patience. There's just a couple of things we need to clear up, then you'll be free to go." Bone turned to the recording device resting at the end of the table, an ancient front-loading cassette player.

"Cutting edge, eh? You don't mind if we record the interview?"

"Seeing as I haven't done anything wrong, why should I mind?" Kilpatrick replied.

Pushing back, Bone found a drawer in the table, and inside there were three or four unopened cassette tapes.

"I bet you haven't seen one of these before." Bone unwrapped the tape and dropped it into the machine. "Sometimes being an old fart has its advantages." He set the counter and pressed 'record' and ran through the preamble.

By the end of the spiel, Kilpatrick was fidgeting with his hands under the table.

"Okay, so let's go back to when you took me over to the island."

"When I was assaulted?"

"Exactly, yes. About that assault… I spoke to Doctor Cropper and asked him if it was possible your injuries may have been self-inflicted, and he certainly didn't rule it out."

"What? So you think I lamped myself? What for?"

"And then a little later, we found your number on Vincent Trough's mobile."

"I told you that I was booking in a broken outboard for repair." Kilpatrick sat back. "Hold on, I'm not done with this injury thing. One, the doc is a piss artist and should have been struck off years ago. I wouldn't trust any of his diagnoses as far as I could quack, and two, why would I volunteer to take you, a police detective, over to the island, the scene of the crime, when I was trying to cover up something?"

"You've hit the nail on the head there, if you pardon the expression, but though maybe not something, more like some*one*."

"Who? Oh, wait, you think Fergus is involved somehow?"

"You said it, not me. You've been best mates for how many years now?"

"We're not best mates, we're mates."

"You went to primary and secondary schools together, is that right?"

"So? I think you'll find nearly everybody in Loch Gillan and Balhuish went to school together, that doesn't naturally make them co-conspirators in a murder." He looked up. "Oh, except for you, of course. Everything was fine before you decided to trespass on our community and bring on this fucking carnage."

"Charming. It'll be pitchforks and flaming torches at dawn next. What are you going to do, run me out of town, Lonnie?" From his rucksack, Bone removed a notepad, flicked it open theatrically, and plucked a pen from his pocket. "Excuse me a second while I check back through all your suspicious activities I recorded here. My memory isn't what it used to be. I need one of these, eh?" He tapped the top of the cassette player and smiled.

Kilpatrick grimaced.

"Let's park that one for now and move on to events later that evening, once we'd returned to Loch Gillan from Balhuish Island. Do you remember when I called round to your cottage?"

Kilpatrick shrugged. "And?"

"You recall the blood on your doorstep?"

"My blood from my head from a deep wound inflicted by the person who attacked the people on the island."

"And the noises upstairs?"

"My cat, yes?"

"I'm sure I said it before, but it must be an awfully big beast, this elusive cat of yours. Is it a man-eating tiger you keep upstairs in that tiny cottage?"

"So my cat's made up now as well?"

"I shook your hand," Bone interrupted. "It was very cold. In fact, you were freezing, like you'd just been outside."

"The power was off, remember?"

"You have a log burner, and it was toasty in your house. I remember feeling quite envious. My cabin was like a mortuary." Bone leaned in. "You'd just been out helping your best friend, Fergus, make it back after injuring himself on the quad bike he stole from his father's farm. Have I missed anything?"

"That's total bollocks."

"If it's bollocks, you won't mind sharing your phone with us so we can check your call records."

"You can't do that! You'd need to arrest me and get a warrant or something!"

"Calm down, Lonnie. Talk about overreacting. Have I touched a nerve?" Bone smiled.

"If you are going to carry on with this fiction, then I want to speak to a solicitor."

"You have a right to speak to a solicitor and we can arrange that for you, but if I were in your shoes I'd rather just clear up this misunderstanding before it escalates further."

Kilpatrick sighed.

"Look, I'm simply trying to establish the facts here. If you have nothing to hide, then tell me what's actually going on."

"I'm telling you what's *actually going on*," Kilpatrick replied sarcastically.

"You got into a bit of a scrape with your best friend at the Hogmanay party in Balhuish a few months back, is that correct?"

"No," Kilpatrick sat back.

"I have plenty of witnesses who can corroborate, including two police officers who intervened. What was that about?"

Kilpatrick stared at the wall opposite for a second or two. "Oh, that? I remember now. It was nothing, just too much booze and a misunderstanding."

"About what?"

"I can't remember."

"About your friend's debts? Did he ask you to help him out?"

"Oh, for God's sake. We'd had too much drink and it was probably about a girl or something."

"Do you and your best friend argue a lot?"

"It was nothing, I'm telling you." Kilpatrick sighed.

"Is your best friend top dog? Does he cajole you into doing things, or bully you?"

"No, we're just—" He sighed and spread his hands out on the table.

Bone continued to stare at him. "You know, accessory to murder carries the same life sentence, Lonnie. As far as the criminal justice system goes, you are a murderer."

"I haven't done anything," Kilpatrick pleaded, his voice quivering.

"And then pile on top of that harbouring a known killer."

"I had no idea what had happened over there."

"Come to think of it, even as an accessory, I don't think a judge would hesitate to hand out a life sentence, especially in light of the hideous and brutal nature of the crimes. But if you co-operate with us and confess to your involvement then—"

"I've nothing to confess!" Kilpatrick cut in. "I'm not going to jail, that's just fucking stupid."

"It's stupid that you are protecting a so-called mate who has landed you right in it. That's not my definition of a friend, especially one you went to primary school with. If I were you, I'd be feeling angry and betrayed. I bet you a fiver that your so-called mate is next door right now turning himself inside out to land you up to your neck in it, while cutting a leniency deal with my colleague."

Kilpatrick wiped more sweat from his face and took a long, anxious breath.

"Let's go back to your relationship with Trough. You mentioned before that you did a lot of work together, shared jobs, that sort of thing."

"No, not share. He'd pass me jobs that were too technical for him. He's not good with modern boat engines, electronics, that sort of stuff." He looked up. "Was good, I mean."

"Yes, you mentioned the outboard, but did you sometimes fix whole boats?"

"Aye, if the boat had an inboard engine and it was too techy for him. He'd ask me to check it over."

"Like the boat, the house thief who broke into my home took off in the other night?"

"I've no idea what boat it was."

"A boat with an inboard, belonging to Trough, that mysteriously reappeared in Balhuish Harbour. I'm thinking maybe you were fixing this boat for Trough and this thief—let's call him Fergus—somehow magically acquired the keys and made off with some vital evidence that would implicate him in the murder and serious assaults that took place on the Isle of the Dead."

"That's utter shite. Vinnie was always back and forth from Balhuish on his boats. Sometimes he'd leave them over there for weeks.

"That doesn't explain how the thief got the keys."

"Ach, Vinnie would often leave them in the ignition, especially if he'd been on the sauce."

"And the thief would have known this?"

"Or got lucky?"

Bone sighed and sat back. "Nope. Not buying it. There's no way around this. He's dumped you right in it, Lonnie. What sort of person does that to their best friend?"

"Total fantasy." Kilpatrick folded his arms.

"Come on, Lonnie. Do the right thing. You're better than him, and you're better than this nightmare that he's happily dumped you in. He's busy cutting a deal that will send you away for a long time. You honestly think he's in the next room making sure you're cleared of all suspicion?"

Kilpatrick's face crumbled. "Ten years, you said."

"If you're lucky. And a young, handsome lad like you in Northlands Prison or somewhere even worse… Jesus." Bone grimaced.

Kilpatrick closed his eyes, and Bone held his tongue.

"I didn't ask for any of this," Kilpatrick said, finally. "It's all got out of hand." He sniffed and quickly rubbed at his eyes.

"It's okay, mate," Bone said.

"If I tell you what I know, will you help get me out of this mess?"

"I'll do everything I can. I know you've been suckered into something."

Kilpatrick took a deep breath. "About a week before the storm, he rang me."

"Who?" Bone pressed.

"Fergus. He told me he was in trouble, that he owed some loan shark a load of money, and the only way out was to do this thing for him."

"What was this thing?"

"He didn't tell me. I swear that's the truth. All he said was it was best I didn't know, but he promised me it wasn't serious and it was the only way to clear his debts with this gangster. The guy was threatening to harm Fergus' family if he didn't do as he said."

"And you believed him?"

"I've known Fergus nearly my whole life, and I've never heard him like that. He was genuinely shitting himself and worried sick this loan shark would kill his parents."

"And what did he want you to do for him?"

"He asked if I could lend him a boat."

"To go to Balhuish Island."

"That's right, aye."

"On the day of the assaults?"

"Aye, but I told him he didn't have the experience to sail any of mine, but Vincent Trough might let him rent one of his motorboats. He said okay, but asked if I'd ring Vinnie to sort it out."

"Did he say why he wanted you to do that?"

"He didn't want the word out that he was back in Balhuish and his parents to find out about the shit he was in, so he asked if I could ring for him and tell Vinnie it was for an American tourist who was willing to pay a huge whack of cash for the ride."

"And you went along with this?"

"I believed him, yes. Why wouldn't I?"

"You didn't ask yourself what this 'thing' was, the loan shark wanted your friend to do?"

"Of course, I speculated. I thought it was maybe drugs or stolen goods, something like that. I wasn't happy about it, but Fergus was in a desperate situation and, you know, we go back a long way and all that." He dropped his head into his hands. "I just wasn't thinking."

"No, you weren't. What happened next?"

"I booked the boat in for him with Vinnie, and that was that. But then on the night of the storm, Fergus called me again, before the lines went down. He was off his head, shouting and swearing, saying everything had gone wrong and people were hurt.

"And still you didn't ask what it was all about?"

"I did, but he still wouldn't say. I told him the weather was too rough and dangerous to sail over and he'd need to stay put until the storm blew out, but he went ballistic, screaming at me. And then he hung up."

"Sorry, but this isn't making sense. Why then, did you agree to take me over to the island the next morning?"

"I panicked. I thought he was probably still stuck there and I might be able to help him somehow."

"Help him get away, you mean. Is that why you smashed the radio?"

"I didn't realise someone had been killed until we got there," Kilpatrick replied.

"So you faked your assault."

"Aye, and it fucking hurt."

"To allow your friend to escape?"

Kilpatrick nodded.

"Where did he go?"

"To hide out at his parents' farm."

"How did you know where he was?"

"I didn't, but I thought where else would he go to stay alive in this cold?"

"So they knew all about it?"

"I don't know." Kilpatrick sank into his chair, as though the weight of the secret pressing down on his shoulders had lifted.

"Please wait here, Mr Kilpatrick," Bone said. "Interview paused at—"

"What's going on?" Kilpatrick interrupted. "Are you going to arrest me?"

He turned off the recording and leapt back up the stairs. "Do you have a spare PC to watch the interviewee in room one?"

"Are you serious?" the desk sergeant said. "We have two, and both are out at the farmer's market, probably stocking up at the Easter holiday shop."

"Could you keep an eye on him for me?"

"You don't fancy asking DCI Harris to help you, then?" the desk sergeant joked and followed Bone downstairs.

THIRTY-ONE

Jock Dulhoon waited a few hours until he was sure the police had gone. In the bedroom, he removed a shoebox hidden at the back of the wardrobe, opened the lid, and took out a bulging envelope. With a quick look inside, he sealed it and rushed out to his car before his wife returned.

When he reached the Raphorse estate, he had to check Google Maps to find Craig Sneddon's property. Turning into his cul-de-sac, he was stopped by two thugs.

"Here to see Mr Sneddon," the old farmer said nervously.

"What about?"

"I'm Fergus Dulhoon's father."

"So! Who's he?" Thug One shrugged.

"My son has some business with your boss, and I want to sort it out."

"And how are you going to do that?" Thug Two asked, leaning in through the window.

"My business," Dulhoon said.

"Park up there and get out," Thug One said.

Dulhoon obliged, then climbed out of the car. Thug One grabbed Dulhoon and manhandled him over to the wall of the nearest house, spun him around, and frisked him.

"What's that?" he asked, fumbling with the envelope in Jock's jacket pocket.

"It's what he owes," Dulhoon said.

"Follow me," Thug One barked.

"Will I come with you or wait here?" Thug Two asked.

"Oh aye, why don't you come with us and let the Finniestons surround the street, ya numpty."

"Just wondered, that's all." Thug Two huffed.

"Well, fucking don't." Thug One nodded at Dulhoon to proceed, and followed him up to the steel gate.

The thug pressed the buzzer. "What's your name again?"

"Dulhoon."

"Mr Dulhoon to see Mr Sneddon. He wants to pay off his bill."

The door clacked and swung open. The two men stepped in. Another tank on legs approached and frisked Dulhoon again and marched him into the house.

Sneddon was in his office at the top of the house. A fourth goon was standing guard at the door. As Dulhoon approached, the guard knocked, went in, and closed it behind him.

"Wait here," Dulhoon's chaperone said, and went back downstairs.

Dulhoon glanced up the hallway. At the end, there was an imposing framed print of Dali's *Christ of Saint John of the Cross* that reached from floor to ceiling and loomed ominously towards him. He wondered if it was the real thing and Sneddon had nicked it from Glasgow's Kelvingrove Art Gallery. The door flew open, the guard gestured, and Dulhoon went in.

Sneddon was behind a smoked glass-and-steel desk at the far side of a gloomy room. He was leaning under an Anglepoise lamp, tapping vigorously at a calculator.

"Sit," he ordered and continued to stab aggressively at the buttons. Dulhoon sat on the upright chair directly in front of the desk. The goon moved in close behind. Dulhoon turned, and the goon moved closer.

"Mr Sneddon, I've—" he began.

"Cease," Sneddon cut back and carried on working.

Dulhoon glanced around the office. One side of the room was racked up with a line of tall filing cabinets, and on the other side, there was a pool table and a 70s-style drinks cabinet, loaded up with various spirits, complete with a mahogany body and smoked-glass front and top that matched the loan shark's desk.

Sneddon finally stopped tapping, slowly closed what looked like a ledger, and turned his stare on Dulhoon.

"I see the likeness. He's inherited the same loser looks. What do you want?"

"I want this to stop and for you to leave my boy alone."

"Sure, no problem. For you, anything. Anything else? Would you like me to bail out your farm before it goes to auction? I can do that as well, no charge." He sneered.

"I have this," Dulhoon said and reached into his coat pocket.

The goon grabbed his arms.

"Let him be, Perry," Sneddon said.

The thug released him and stepped back.

Dulhoon removed the envelope and pushed it onto Sneddon's desk.

"What's that?" Sneddon stared at the bundle.

"It's fifteen thousand. It's what he owes with five thousand interest."

Sneddon picked up the envelope, slid his finger along the seal, peeked inside, and then sniffed the contents. "Ah, the sweet smell of success." He sniffed again.

"I want you to leave my boy and us alone now," Dulhoon said.

"It's very touching, and to be honest, I'm quite moved. My dad would have rather killed me himself than pay my debts. Oh, but then again, I never had debts because I'm not a fucking loser like your son."

"Take the money, please."

"Oh, I'll take the money, no problem with that."

"And you'll leave us alone?"

"Here was me thinking it was an early birthday present."

"It's all I have. I'm begging you."

"Like a doggy?" Sneddon stood and moved around the desk. "Woof, woof!" He approached the chair.

Dulhoon leaned back.

"Okay then, beg. Go on."

"I'm not begging," Dulhoon said.

"Hear that, Perry? The man says he's begging then doesn't beg. I'd say that's what I call a disobedient doggy that needs to be house-trained." He leaned into Dulhoon's face.

"On your knees and beg. Woof, woof!" he spat in his face.

With shaking limbs, Dulhoon slid from the chair onto the floor.

"That's it, good boy, now beg your master."

Dulhoon straightened up into a kneeling position and raised his arms.

"So cute, isn't he? We should give him a doggy biscuit, or some food. Go get a tin." He smiled.

The guard chuckled and left the room. Dulhoon glanced around and in a quick move reached down to his sock and pulled a knife from a scabbard taped to the inside of his ankle. He plunged the blade into Sneddon's thigh. The loan shark staggered backwards into the desk.

Dulhoon jumped up and went for him, but Sneddon swung out, his fist connecting with the side of Dulhoon's head. Jock tumbled forward onto the floor, and Sneddon leapt on him. In a quick manoeuvre, he reached behind his back, whipped out an even bigger knife and, yanking Dulhoon's head back by the hair, he ran the blade across Dulhoon's throat.

"You see, size does fucking matter, you waste of fucking air!" He dropped Dulhoon's quivering body onto the floor, and a thick lake of blood spread out across the polished oak.

The guard returned clutching a tin of dog food.

"Get something to wipe this fuck's fucking shit up off my fucking floor."

"You want this?" the gormless guard asked.

"What do you think? Come on. Look at it. Go get a fucking mop!" He stepped back.

Dulhoon's body stopped moving.

Sneddon glanced down at the knife still protruding from his thigh.

"Fucking ruined my joggers, you fud."

With a wince, he yanked it out and dropped it on the floor next to Dulhoon's prostrate body. He returned to his desk and from a drawer, he found a leather belt and tightened it around the top of his leg. He sat and emptied Dulhoon's cash onto the desk, counting it. "Two for the price of one. What fucking losers."

THIRTY-TWO

The second interview room turned out to be a converted holding cell, complete with bars on a narrow high window and a stainless-steel loo. Walker and Buchan were perched at a table, opposite Fergus Dulhoon, who was busy chewing frantically on some gum.

"A word, DI Walker," Bone said, interrupting the interview.

Walker put her iPad down.

Buchan checked in the time on the tape machine.

Dulhoon stopped fidgeting.

"What's up?" Walker asked Bone once outside.

"Lonnie has just admitted that he helped Fergus organise his trip over to Balhuish Island," Bone spoke quietly. "He set up the boat hire for Fergus with Trough on the morning of the attacks."

"Result."

"There's more. He also told me that Fergus was up to his neck in debt with an as-yet-unnamed loan shark, though we can probably guess who that is. This loan shark promised to write off his debts on completion of a 'thing,' as Kilpatrick described it."

"What's *the thing*?" Walker said.

"He insisted he didn't know, but he also said that the loan shark was threatening Fergus's family if he didn't go through with whatever it was."

"Serious then?"

"I'd say deadly serious. Then Fergus called Lonnie late that night to say everything had gone wrong, people were hurt."

"God, he really was purging, wasn't he?"

"Looks like we've got the bastard then," the desk sergeant said, leaning over from in front of the next room.

The two detectives turned.

"Sorry," the sergeant replied. "Difficult not to nosey in."

"Would you like me to do the honours?" Walker asked.

Bone shook his head and mouthed, "No chance."

They went back in, and Bone pulled the only remaining chair over to the table. Fergus looked up in surprise, his eyes widening when he saw Bone.

"Mr Dulhoon. I'm DCI Bone for the RCU, Kilwinnoch. I've just been next door interviewing your friend, Lonnie Kilpatrick, and I've come in to inform you that Mr Kilpatrick has volunteered significant and substantive information regarding the crimes committed on Balhuish Island on April 3rd, and your involvement."

"No," Dulhoon replied, and continued to gnaw at the gum.

"I'm afraid that's a yes. He's confessed to everything, how you told him about your spiralling debts and your run-in with a loan shark. The favour he wanted you to do, the threats he made to your family. Shall I go on?"

"I don't know where this dross is coming from. Has he lost his mind?"

"How he helped sort out your ride to Balhuish Island with Vincent Trough, now tragically deceased, and then your phone call to him on the night of the attacks describing how things on the island had gone terribly wrong and people were hurt—"

"Stop."

"There's plenty more." Bone smiled.

"He's lying," Dulhoon protested.

"Quite an in-depth and detailed fabrication he's spun, if that's the case. And why exactly would he do that?" Bone asked.

"I don't know. Maybe he's involved and trying to cover his own arse."

"By framing you?"

"Maybe. I don't know."

"That's not a very nice thing to say about your best friend, now is it? Someone you've known your entire life, like a brother," Buchan interrupted.

"I can't explain it. He's lying." He flicked his tongue.

"Is that Juicy Fruit you're chewing?" Bone said.

"Are you going to arrest me for eating as well now?"

"I'm just curious, as the smell of it was bugging me."

"Aye, so what?" Dulhoon huffed.

"I didn't even think you could still buy it these days."

"Do you want a bit? Is that it?"

"No, thanks. It's just that I found a Juicy Fruit wrapper on Balhuish island and I was thinking to myself, wow, that's a coincidence. Two sticks of Juicy Fruit in the space of a few days."

"I'm not the only person that buys it, you know."

Bone leaned into the tape machine. "For the DIR, DCI Bone confirms that Fergus Dulhoon is chewing Juicy Fruit gum."

"Fuck's sake," Dulhoon mumbled.

"Anyway, back to your best friend's apparent lies. You see, I don't think that's right because when I left him he was sitting in there shaking and crying because he's terrified of going to jail for a long time. And that's where you are both going unless you start cooperating."

"No comment," Dulhoon said, and folded his arms.

"He's also furious with you. I'd say your selfish behaviour has obliterated your friendship. All those bonds and loyalties, gone forever just because of your gambling addiction, and yes, he told us about that as well."

Dulhoon rubbed his brow.

"Mr Dulhoon, you have one last chance here to do what's best for your friend, save him from a painful jail term, and tell us the truth."

Dulhoon stared at the table for a moment or two.

"Do the right thing, Fergus," Walker added. "You're not a bad person."

"Please don't hang any of this on him," he said finally. "This is all me."

"This?"

"I never wanted any of it. He forced me to do it. I had no choice."

"Who?"

"I'm frightened. I can't tell you. I'm frightened for my mum and dad. He even threatened my sister, who lives in London. I don't know how he even knew anything about her."

"I promise we'll do everything we can to protect you and your family." Bone leaned in. "Just give me a name."

"My debts were spiralling out of control. I couldn't get any more money from anywhere. Not to pay for bets, but to make interest payments. I was desperate, so I went to a loan shark in Stirling."

"We need a name," Bone pressed.

"A lowlife called Craig Sneddon."

Bone glanced over at the cassette machine whirring in the background. "How much did you borrow from him?"

"Ten K." He looked up. "I know it's a lot, but it wasn't all just gambling. He promised me that the interest and payments would be reasonable."

"They always do," Walker said.

"But within days, he started racking up the interest until it was impossible to pay him back."

"And that's when he came up with this proposition?" Bone asked.

"Not at first. He threatened to kneecap me, then kill me, then he'd move on to my family. At that point I was so desperate, I told him I'd do anything for him, run drugs or whatever he wanted me to do to get him out of my life."

"What did he ask you to do?"

"He told me to—" He stopped and wiped his dry lips against the back of his hand. "He told me I needed to take care of an individual, and once I'd completed this job, he'd wipe my slate and leave me and my family alone."

"Take care of?"

"Hit, kill."

"How did you feel about that?" Walker asked.

"Sick to my stomach, but he said it was a member of a rival gang, total fucking scum who deserved to die. I said no at first, but he ramped up the threats, and he even sent one of his men round to the farm to cause some damage and steal a few things, just so I knew he was serious."

"And you agreed."

"Yes, but he'd cornered me. It was either that or all of us would be killed. I convinced myself that if these criminals were as bad as him, then I'd be doing you guys a service. I know it's mad, but I was terrified."

"Okay, so you got to the island…?"

"I picked up the boat at Trough's yard early, about seven, to give me a chance to set up over there and get myself mentally ready."

"Wasn't Trough surprised to see you?"

"Yeah, but I told him I was planning a practical joke on a few uni friends who were heading over there later."

"How did you plan to kill him?"

"With a butcher's knife. I read up on which part of the body to strike so that it was quick."

"Were you not worried that this was taking place so close to your home?"

"I fucking freaked out about that, but Sneddon told me that the guy was expecting a pickup there."

"What sort of pickup?"

"I didn't ask, but assumed it was some sort of drug cartel thing."

"You hid out in the old war bunker, is that right?"

"Seven fucking hours in the freezing cold. But then they arrived, and that's when everything went tits up."

"Explain."

"I was expecting some goon, but when I saw the couple in their wedding gear, I thought it was a mistake. I backed off, but the guy spotted me holding the knife and lunged at me. He took me down, grabbed the knife, and made me tell him what I was doing. But when I tried to explain, the girl must have misunderstood me.

"To be honest, I wasn't making much sense at that point. She just exploded, accusing the guy of setting the whole thing up. And then she went for him like a banshee. They grappled on the ground, and I ran to the trees. But then she had blood all over her wedding dress." He stopped and sighed, his breath shallow. "She collapsed. He ran at me again. We fought, and that's when I stuck the knife." His shoulders shook. "It was self-defence. He was going to kill me."

"Did you kill him?"

"I don't know. I ran off, but by then the storm had moved in, and I hid for a while in the bunker again, hoping it would blow over, but it didn't."

"And that's when you called Lonnie Kilpatrick for help?"

"Yes, I thought he might help me work out what to do, but he didn't answer me, so I went back out into the blizzard to check on them. They were both together in the graveyard. I didn't get close. I thought they were alive, so I took Vinnie's boat across to the mainland."

"You hit the rocks?"

"I almost drowned. It was horrendous. I just made it to shore."

"And what did you do then?"

"I went to the farm."

"Your father's farm? So they knew what had happened?"

"No, I swear. When you found me there, that was the first my dad knew I was there. I hid out in one of the hay barns until I could work out what to do next. But then you arrived, so I nicked the quad."

"And then later you nicked the boat from Loch Gillan?"

"Aye, Lonnie helped me get back, but I never told him what had happened and he never asked. He's completely innocent."

"So you're saying that when it came to the crunch, you bottled it, and the fatality and injuries were all an accident?"

"That's right. I just wanted to run. I couldn't do it."

"That doesn't explain why Mr and Mrs McDermid had multiple stab wounds and severe lacerations. To me, that looks more like a frenzied assault."

"There was a big fight. The injuries must have happened during that." Dulhoon chewed frantically on the gum.

"But you revisited the victims while I was at the boat raising the alarm."

"I wanted to check they were still alive."

"Or finish them off?"

"No!" Dulhoon protested.

"And if nerves or conscience got the better of you, how does that explain what you did to Mr Trough? Was that a big fight as well?"

"I didn't kill him. That wasn't me."

"Who was it, then?"

"I don't know, maybe Sneddon, trying to cover his tracks. Maybe I'm next, and Lonnie, then my mum and dad, my sister. He told me that if I breathed a word of it to anyone, he'd—"

"Yes, kill you and your family. We've got it now."

"He needs to be stopped."

"But the storm had cut off all access to and from Balhuish," Buchan interrupted. "If this was the work of one of Sneddon's men, then how did they get in and out of the village?"

"Look, all I know is I did not kill Vinnie. I've known him my whole life. He's like an uncle to me. I couldn't do that."

"There's a lot you say you couldn't do, Mr Dulhoon," Walker said.

"I'm telling you, it wasn't me."

"You know that if you admit to everything, we can plea bargain your sentence and help protect you from Sneddon's gang, but if you insist on this charade, then you'll be on your own."

"Please, don't do that." Dulhoon held up his hands. "I need to be protected from this thug and I'm so scared what he might do to my family."

"One more admission, that's all it takes," Bone insisted. "And we'll see what we can do."

"I'm not going to admit to something I didn't do. I've told you everything, but Vinnie Trough's death was not my doing. I'm sorry that an innocent man died and his wife was so badly hurt, but that was an accident. I bottled it, and that's when this McDermid guy went for me."

"Fergus Dulhoon, I'm arresting you on conspiracy to commit murder against Laurence McDermid and

Vincent Trough, and grievous bodily harm on Clare McDermid—"

"It was an accident! I didn't go through with it!" Dulhoon tried to climb out from behind the desk.

Buchan and Walker restrained him while Bone persevered with the arrest. When they'd concluded, Buchan and the desk sergeant transferred him to a holding cell. Then they repeated the process with Kilpatrick, who also wailed like a giant hairy baby and collapsed off his seat onto the interview room floor.

When Bone informed DCI Harris, he jumped up from his desk and did a weird shuffling dance in front of him. "You lot are good, aren't you? I mean, we've not had this much excitement at Lomond station since The Krankies opened the extension in 77." He roared with laughter.

"I think we have more than enough on tape to charge them, but you'll need to sign off on that one," Bone said, ignoring, as best he could, Harris' remark.

"I hope you didn't tape over one of my teenage playlists," he joked.

But Bone was way past even a curt response. "Are you okay to sort that?"

"Of course, thank you. Does that mean the case is now closed?"

"No, we might have the monkey and the organ grinder, but we still don't know who the ringmaster is," Bone replied.

"What?" Harris crossed his eyes in mock confusion.

"The person who ordered the hit on Balhuish Island."

"Ah, gotcha! Or should that be *not quite* gotcha!" He sniggered.

"I'll get a copy of the reports sent over to you asap so that you're completely up to speed. It is officially your investigation, after all," Bone reminded him.

"Indeed, indeed. Thank you."

"We'll get out of your hair now, but please keep the two downstairs apart. Last thing we need is cross-contamination of statements. And they'll probably need solicitors."

"You're teaching me how to suck eggs, Inspector Bone."

"Sorry, force of habit," Bone replied. "It was—"

"Okay, now eff off back to effing Kilwinnoch. That's enough excitement for one effing police career, thank you very much." Harris chuckled.

On their way out, Walker stopped in the car park. "I thought we had decided the groom had hired Sneddon to hit his new wife. He did have the motive of getting his hands on her money now that they were married."

"But you heard what Dulhoon said in there. Sneddon ordered him to kill both of them. Why would McDermid pay for his own murder?"

"Maybe Dulhoon got it wrong, or he doesn't want to admit he was supposed to kill her, as it sounds worse in his mind?" Buchan suggested.

"No. I'm not buying that. Sadly, there's still a glaring hole in this, and the procurator fiscal's office will be the first to spot it."

"And the Trough murder is also still hanging. Forensics found nothing at the scene."

"That's more likely to be Dulhoon gunning for a manslaughter charge, and he's hoping we don't have anything on him for that."

"Which we don't," Walker interrupted.

"Not yet, but what we do have is enough to finally nail Sneddon."

"Who do we call first?"

"Okay, you start with SCU and get an armed response unit over to that scumbag's fortress asap. I'll ring Gallacher, but I think we need to re-interview the parents and McDermid's brother."

Walker's phone rang.

"Hold up, it's Sheila." She answered and a few moments later hung up. "James Willerby's story checks out. His client, Gavin Barraclough, from Brookdale Close, Raploch, was on bail and due to appear at the Sheriff Court in Stirling on the 4th of April."

"Don't tell me, he absconded?"

"Yup."

"Oh, Jeez." Bone rubbed at his temple. "It's likely these two will be remanded into custody and sent up to Stirling. I think it's time to get ourselves back to Kilwinnoch, regroup, and try and sort out this bloody mess once and for all."

He looked over at Buchan. "I'm sure I can request for you to join us. You're part of this nightmare as well." He smiled.

"Thanks, sir, but it's probably better I keep an eye on things here, what with our current staffing issues and all that." She rolled her eyes.

"Say cheerio, though, before we go," Walker said.

"I'll pop over when I sort everything here. You carry on," Buchan said, and with a deep sigh, she went upstairs to find Harris.

THIRTY-THREE

Willerby lingered a little longer in the office than he should have, and instead of driving straight back to the hospital as he'd promised his wife, the rising nausea in his throat forced him to turn around and head for his house.

Upstairs in his bedroom, he dug out a sports holdall from the back of the wardrobe and, opening drawers, he snatched up clothes and rammed them into the bag. Dashing through to the en suite, he collected his shaver, toothbrush, and paste and dropped them into the bag.

A loud thump came from downstairs, and he stopped. He held his breath and listened. Someone was moving around down there. *Police?* He edged to the bedroom door and pushed his head around. All was quiet. He put the bag down and crept downstairs.

At the bottom, he stopped and peered along the hallway, through the open door into the living room, but couldn't see anyone.

"Lynda?" he said, moving slowly down the hall. But there was no response. At the living room door, he leaned in, but the room was in semi-darkness, the bay window curtains still pulled from days before.

"Is there anyone there? Inspector Bone?" He reached for the light, but before he could turn it on, his phone rang. "Shit!"

He fumbled it out of his pocket. It was his wife. He was about to answer, but someone grabbed his arms from behind, and his screeching mobile fell onto the carpet. His hands were quickly bound and before he could cry out for help, his mouth was taped over and a hood forced over his head. He tried to wriggle free, but the grip around his torso was too strong. He was yanked backwards, his heels scraping along the parquet flooring. A second set of arms grabbed his feet, and he kicked out, but they were forced together and tied so tight it cut off the circulation.

The mobile stopped ringing.

He was hoisted aloft and carried outside and into the front garden, where gravel crunched as his assailants manhandled him down the drive. He tried to yell again, but the gag muted his scream. The sound of doors opening met him, then he was inside the terrifying echo chamber of his assailants' vehicle. He was dropped with force onto a cold metal floor, and pain shot across his chest. The doors slammed shut, and a low-pitched growl filled his ears. He tried to scramble away from the unseen threat, but a voice near his ear shouted, "Shut it!" and the growl ceased.

An engine coughed to life and his captors' vehicle accelerated. His prostrate body bounced and banged wildly from side to side, his head slamming against steel walls. Many minutes later, the violent movements suddenly stopped, and with a loud clunk, hands were on his legs once again, freeing them, but before he could kick out at his assailants, he was dragged out and dumped on his feet.

Strong arms held him fast, as the hood was removed, and the sharp, dazzling sunlight seared his eyes. He squinted to try and make out where he was and who had abducted him. Straight ahead, two blurred shapes emerged from the glare. He raised his bound hands and tried to rub his eyes to see. The abstract shapes slowly sharpened. Two rottweilers were poised a few metres in front of him, their teeth bared, saliva oozing from their jaws. A masked man was standing between the two of them, his arm raised.

Willerby tried to shout for help, but the gag suffocated his desperate cry. The man slowly lowered his arm.

"*No!*" Willerby tried to scream, and the giant black beasts surged towards him.

He tried to turn, but stumbled over his own feet and fell forward. The first dog jumped on top of his back, and with the same low-pitched growl, sank its teeth into his shoulder, its long incisors piercing his suit jacket like a straw through tissue paper. He lashed out to try and shake it off, but the second dog rammed into his face and bit down on his cheek, ripping his gag from his mouth.

"Stop!" he screamed in agony, but the dogs frenzied on their first taste of blood.

The first dog jumped from his back and battered against Willerby's side, ramming its snout under him. The second forced Willerby's head back, and it clamped its jaws around his throat, blocking Willerby's airway. With one final attempt to dislodge them, he kicked out, but the first dog leapt on his legs and ripped its teeth into his thigh. Searing pain surged through his body, and with a final blood-gurgling breath, he lost consciousness.

THIRTY-FOUR

After the team had packed up, they reconvened in the hotel lobby. Urquhart came out of the bar to greet them. "Is that you away, then?"

"For now anyway, but I'm afraid you haven't got rid of me. I'll probably be back at the weekend," Bone replied.

"Well, it's been emotional," Urquhart joked.

The hotel's chef appeared from the dining room.

Bone shook his hand. "Thanks for not poisoning us, Ross."

"I was tempted," Ross joked and handed Bone a package.

"What's this?"

"A wee gift from the kitchen."

Bone opened it up. "Oh, Jesus. You know where you can stick that." He handed the chef back a packet of frozen mackerel.

"Make sure you send that bill in, Gordon."

"Already emailed. It took me days to type in all those noughts." Urquhart grinned.

"No sign of your American guests, or Junior? I wanted to thank him again."

"Guests have gone. Off to Edinburgh for some peace and quiet. Junior's playing golf this afternoon."

"Golf? Where the hell is that?" Bone asked.

"He's up on the cairn with a bag of balls and a driver, practising his swing. Every time the Open comes to Scotland, he thinks he'll make the wild card and win the bloody thing."

"The man is a living legend," Walker said.

"Living bloody nightmare, more like."

"Right, let's go," Bone said. He glanced around. "Where's Will?"

Harper appeared from through the back.

"Have you decided to stay? Where's your bag?" Bone asked.

"Sir, I just checked my email, and one's come in from Castle Internet Café. Where the email cancelling the photographer's booking came from."

"Aye?" Bone replied.

"You remember when I contacted them before, they said their CCTV footage refreshed every couple of days? Well, a member of staff has managed to retrieve the deleted files. Apparently, they were stored on—"

"Keep going, Will," Bone interrupted.

"Sorry, aye, so the footage from the day the email was sent is on a temp file, but they can't send it over."

"Right, Walker, come on. You stay here, Will, and keep us updated."

"Are you going or not?" Urquhart asked.

"You've got us for a bit longer, I'm afraid, Gordon."

"Bloody hell. If I'd known that, I wouldn't have been so nice to you." He went back into the bar.

Bone checked out the front. "Press is still there. Let's go round the back. Look after my bag, Will."

"Oh aye, no bother," he grumbled.

"And ring the internet café and let them know we're on our way."

"Sir," he replied and lumbered his colleagues' bags back to the now-recommissioned conference room.

***

The Castle Internet Café was located on a side street just off Stirling's main shopping area. A pasty-faced young woman greeted them when they arrived.

"It's on the office computer out the back," she said.

They went through the café with terminals lined up on either side of the narrow space. A few teenagers were slouched over screens playing video games.

The musty office was piled high with hard drives, screens, and boxes of tangled cables. The woman squeezed through the mess to a desk in the corner.

Isle of the Dead

"When my colleague mentioned you were looking for the CCTV recordings, I had a dig around the memory. It was a bit of a challenge to find it, which I'm always up for, but I knew the recordings would still be there." She looked across at the detectives, who were stranded on the other side of the chaos. "Sorry, I'll move these."

She pushed a tower of boxes out of the way, and they joined her at the desk. She tapped at the keyboard, and the screen filled with lines of code.

"Just a sec." She continued. The screen blacked out, and a grainy grey image appeared. "Bingo. Your colleague mentioned that the 30th of March, at 2:32 p.m. was the day and time you wanted to see?"

"That's correct, yes," Bone replied.

The image flickered and disappeared. "It's okay, don't panic." She continued to type, and the footage returned. "This is fifteen minutes before. Let me—" The footage leapt forward, then slowed again. "And now six minutes. See the timer, top right?"

A figure with their back to the camera appeared bottom left. They walked across the room and stopped to speak to a second figure.

"Who's that?" Bone said.

"That's my manager, Jimmy," the woman said.

"No, the customer," Bone replied.

The video continued, and the pair went over to one of the computer terminals. They stopped, and the figure turned for a moment, then sat.

"Can you rewind that and pause when the customer shows their face?" Bone asked.

"Sure." The woman replayed the section and hit the button as the figure turned.

Bone shot a look at Walker. "Thank you for your help. Is there any way you can save this footage and make sure it isn't deleted?"

"As long as it's on here it's safe."

"Okay, this is evidence, so please don't let anyone touch it until our recovery team gets here."

"Oh God, yeah, no problem. I'll tell the manager when he gets back."

Bone and Walker dashed out.

"I'll ring Sheila and tell her to dispatch officers to the Willerbys' house and his workplace. We're going to need the ARU on standby as well," Bone said.

They jumped in the car, and he dialled through.

"Hospital?" Walker asked.

Bone nodded.

THIRTY-FIVE

When they reached the outskirts of Stirling, she was about to take the exit for the hospital when Bone's phone rang.

"Brody?"

"Sir, about thirty minutes ago, a couple of hillwalkers dialled nine-nine-nine to report finding a man badly beaten and barely breathing up at Ochil Forest Park. The caller found ID on the victim and identified him as James Willerby."

"Oh, Jesus Christ," Bone said. "He's alive?"

"I believe so, yes. He's been airlifted to Stirling Royal."

"Conscious?"

"I don't know."

"Anything else comes in, ring me."

He turned back to Walker. "Willerby's been assaulted and dumped in the woods in Ochil Forest Park."

"What?"

"Sounds like Mr Sneddon's thugs got to him first. He's been airlifted to Stirling Royal, to join his daughter. What a bloody mess." He redialled Baxter. "Have officers been sent to the hospital yet?"

"On their way, sir."

"Okay, we're nearly there." He hung up again. "If Sneddon had a purge to protect himself, then Clare and her mum could be in serious, bloody danger."

Walker put her foot down and turned on the siren.

Screeching into the car park, they parked up at the A & E entrance and ran into the reception.

"You go and check on the wife and daughter, and I'll find out where he's been taken," Bone said.

Walker carried on, and Bone dashed over to the desk.

"DCI Bone, Kilwinnoch Police Station." He flashed his badge.

An inebriated man with a bandaged and bloodied head, who'd been leaning over the counter, stepped back and sang the theme tune from *The Sweeney*.

"Thank you, Mr Drysdale. If you'd like to take a seat, please," the receptionist said sternly.

"You saying I can take one hame wae me and this polis officer won't arrest me?" He erupted in laughter, and a string of thick saliva swung down from his lower lip.

"An injured man, found in Ochil Forest Park has just come in," Bone shouted over the din.

"Sorry, sir, hold on," she said to Bone and raised her arm.

The security guard who'd been watching from the entrance rushed over and manhandled the drunk away from the desk.

"You were saying?" she asked.

"An injured man, airlifted from Ochil Forest Park, where is he?" Bone repeated.

She checked her computer and shook her head. "Sorry, the system is really slow at the moment.

"It's police business, so hurry, please."

"I can only go as fast as the system will allow, Inspector." She glanced up with a disapproving look. "Okay, got him. A Mr James Willerby, dog attack."

"A what?"

"That's what it says. He's up in the Serious Injury Unit, third floor, follow the signs."

He ran across the waiting area and took the stairs three at a time, and at the top he checked left and right and spotted the sign to the department. He raced along the winding corridor, swerving past patients and doctors until he came to a door that led straight into the SIU. There were two PCs already in the reception and a paramedic on his way out.

"Where is he?" Bone asked one of the PCs.

"He's through there." The officer pointed at the ward door.

Bone pulled at it, but it was locked.

"Where are you going?" a nurse said, emerging from a back room.

"DCI Bone. I need to speak to James Willerby."

"I'm afraid doctors are attending to his injuries at the moment."

"Do you know what happened?"

"He was brought in about half an hour ago with severe lacerations to his face and body and substantial blood loss. Lucky for him, one of the hillwalkers who found him was a doctor and most certainly saved his life. And speak of the devil." She pointed to a man in full walking gear coming out of a loo on the far side of the foyer.

Bone approached.

"I'm Inspector Bone from Kilwinnoch Police Station. You found the victim, is that correct?"

"Yes, we'd just come down off the hill and were taking a shortcut through Forest Park when we saw these two huge rottweilers attacking a man. There was a van parked up nearby, and two guys were just standing there, watching it happen. We ran over, shouting at them to stop, and they called off the dogs, jumped in the van, and drove off, leaving the poor sod flat out. Thankfully, he was still alive, though unconscious at that point, with some horrendous facial injuries, but I managed to stem the blood loss as best I could until the paramedics arrived. I'm a GP."

"Is he conscious now, do you know?"

"He was awake, but by no means lucid."

"Did you get a look at the men who had set the dogs on him?"

"No, we were too far away. And to be honest, if we'd been nearer, they might have turned them on us."

The ward door opened, and a doctor appeared.

"We're going to need a statement. Can you pass your details to the officers?" Bone said to the walker.

"Of course, yes."

The doctor approached. "Are you family?"

"No, police. DCI Bone. How is he?"

"He's alive and stable," the doctor said. "He lost a lot of blood, but very lucky. One of the bites narrowly missed an artery. The GP who found him did a fantastic job, and once we got him back, we managed to get him stabilised and out of the woods, so to speak. We're just waiting for the consultant surgeon to arrive to assess his facial and body injuries. Unfortunately, he's going to need quite a few operations to sort out the mess those dogs have made of his face."

"Is he conscious?"

"He's very groggy."

"It's vital I speak to him."

"He's had quite a lot of pain relief, so I wouldn't expect much sense out of him. A few minutes, okay?" He held door the open. "Third cubicle down."

Bone went through and peeked between the curtains. Willerby was half propped up, his head almost completely covered in bandages and tape. A nurse was by his side, gently adjusting one of the bandages that had slipped down over his left eye. Willerby groaned as she tugged at the edge.

"Would you like a little more pain relief, James?" the nurse asked.

Willerby slowly nodded.

"Mr Willerby," Bone said.

The nurse turned.

"You shouldn't be in here," she said, looking alarmed.

"It's okay, I'm DCI Bone for Kilwinnoch station." He held up his warrant card.

Willerby moaned again.

"I need to speak to Mr Willerby in private, if that's okay?"

"He's really too weak to talk. He's had a lot of morphine and other sedatives. I'll be back again shortly, James." She pulled the curtain closed behind him.

Bone drew nearer.

"Did Sneddon do this to you?"

"I tried—" Willerby rasped.

"What was that?" Bone leaned in.

"To stop it. The day before. But it was too late. He just wouldn't ... stop."

"Sneddon?"

Willerby nodded. "Lynda doesn't know."

"Doesn't know what?"

"I wanted him dead. But it just all went wrong. I tried to— I'm so sorry." He sobbed.

"James Willerby, I am arresting you—"

The curtain flew back.

"Sir, Clare Willerby has gone." Walker panted.

Willerby tried to raise his arm, but it fell by his side.

"When I got there, officers and nurses were searching the ward and neighbouring corridors."

"Save her," Willerby wheezed.

Bone followed Walker back out into reception. "Where's the mother?"

"She's not there either."

"How long ago?"

"Ten minutes, tops. The nurse said she wanted her mother to help her get to the toilet."

"And they let her? What were the officers doing, who were supposed to be watching them? It doesn't matter." Bone turned to the PC standing by the ward entrance. "Watch him. Don't let anyone in or out."

They dashed out.

"Have you checked the loos?" Bone asked.

"Yes, three sets, no sign."

"They must be doing a runner. Car park. The daughter's in no fit state to walk, so they can't have got far in ten minutes."

They raced back through the warren of corridors to the A& E Department and rushed out the front.

"You go left and I'll go right." He set off.

"Hold up." Walker stopped him and pointed. "Yellow Mini hatchback heading onto the main road, right there."

"Shit, that's them."

They ran to the Land Rover sandwiched between two ambulances. A security van was parked adjacent, and a guard was clocking the number plate.

"Police, get your van out of the way," Bone said, jumping in.

The man hurried around his van, reversed, and Walker hit the pedal and accelerated across the car park to the exit.

At the hospital entrance, Bone scanned the main road ahead. "Where did they go?"

"It's one way, so they had to go right," Walker said. She turned on the siren and ran the red light.

They raced to the next roundabout and screeched to a halt.

"Which way now?" Walker asked.

"Don't know. Bridge of Allan?"

"Their house?"

"Maybe to pick stuff up so they can disappear?"

"Okay." Walker took a sharp right and sped on towards the city centre.

They drove through and over mini roundabouts and junctions, and then onto the ring road. But as they approached the city centre, cars started to slow. She weaved in and out as best she could while Bone hollered at drivers to get out of the way. Another mile on, and the traffic came to a standstill.

Bone looked up at the moonroof. "How do you open that?"

Walker searched the dashboard, found the button, and the skylight opened. He unbuckled, stood, stuck his head through the top, and searched the two lines of cars backed up at the lights ahead.

"We're moving," Walker said, and turned the sirens on again.

She veered left into a gap, and Bone was thrown sideways. He caught a flash of yellow right towards the centre. He tumbled back down into his seat.

"Go right at the lights. They're heading for the centre."

"Now you bloody tell me," Walker said and cut in front of a lorry.

A couple of cars ahead swerved over onto a narrow strip of hard shoulder, and Walker squeezed the pool car through the gap.

"Hold on," she said and took the junction in third, the Land Rover almost toppling.

"Let me get my seatbelt back on before you bloody kill us," Bone said, grappling with the lock.

"Where now?" Walker said.

"Left at the clock tower," Bone said.

"Got her." She veered off the main road.

They carried on through rows of more houses, and the road narrowed.

"There it is, going up the hill, heading for the castle," Bone said.

She took a right and headed up the steep incline. "Any sign of backup?"

Bone turned around. "Not yet."

"Shit." Walker slammed the car into third to take the incline.

The Mini was a few hundred yards away. It took another right onto a cobbled street lined with ancient stone buildings. Walker edged closer, but then it accelerated away. They roared on past ruined fortress gates, the noise of the siren bouncing off buildings that squeezed in around them. Finally, they reached the top of the road and the car park, with the castle looming directly ahead.

The Mini had stopped on the far side by the castle entrance, its engine still running as though it were out of breath from the frantic chase.

Walker switched off the siren, rolled the car into the entrance, and stopped. She was about to jump out when Bone grabbed her arm.

"Wait. They must have heard us. Why are they not getting out?"

"I don't like this." Walker glanced over her shoulder. "Where's the bloody support unit?"

They held off a moment longer, and then Bone opened the door and slowly stepped out.

"Where are you going?" Walker asked.

"To stop whatever is going on over there."

"Shouldn't we wait for backup?"

"I don't think we can."

Walker followed him out.

"I'm going over," Bone said. "When they arrive, keep them away until I give the word."

"Are you sure about this?"

"Nope," he said, and set off towards the car.

Halfway there, the driver's door opened, and Bone stopped.

"Mrs Willerby," he called out. "You need to bring your daughter back to the hospital."

Mrs Willerby glanced over, then back at the car.

The sound of sirens filled the air again, and three squad cars and a police van screeched into the car park. Walker rushed over, waving her arms. They stopped and an armed officer in full protective gear jumped out of the van.

"Turn off your sirens," Walker ordered, and silence returned.

"Stand by. There's an unarmed mother and daughter in the vehicle. We don't want to spook them," Bone said.

The officer turned to his team, who had already lined up along the bottom of the car park and gestured for them to stay back.

The passenger door swung open, and Clare McDermid stumbled out, clutching her side.

"Clare!" Bone cried out.

She ignored him, shuffled around to the driver's side, and produced a knife from her dressing gown pocket.

Bone spun around, gestured to the officers to hold their line, then turned back to the distraught bride.

"Clare, you need to put that down." He edged closer. "Put that down."

"Tell him!" Clare shouted at her mother.

Mrs Willerby shook her head and continued to sob.

"Tell him!" Clare ordered again and brandished the knife.

"Stand down," Bone hollered back to the officers.

"We only wanted the very best for you, my darling." Mrs Willerby held out her arms.

"Don't you fucking *darling* me," Clare retorted. "Tell him, or I swear I'll end all of this right now."

"It all went so wrong. We just wanted him out of your life once and for all."

"My life, Mother. My fucking life. My choices, that you've destroyed forever."

"He was never going to make you happy."

Mrs Willerby turned to Bone. "We just wanted to scare him off, but when we realised how stupid it all was, we tried to stop it, but that monster wouldn't back down."

"Sneddon?" Bone asked.

"He's an animal!" she howled, and her words echoed across the car park.

"You killed him, Mother. You! No one else!"

"That was never what we wanted. We just wanted you to have a happy life. But he was going to ruin everything we wanted for you."

"No one is ever good enough for you. The perfect couple. The perfect life. Well, it's a fucking lie. You've controlled me my entire life. Laurence wasn't the monster, Mother, you are. You and Dad. You did this. You are despicable. You make me —" Clare staggered sideways and grabbed her side. "You—"

She tumbled to the ground, and her mother caught her before she hit the tarmac. Bone rushed forward and dragged Mrs Willerby away. Two ARU officers appeared from behind and cuffed her. Bone returned to Clare, who was slumped over on the ground.

"Let me die," Clare cried.

Bone looked down, and the knife was embedded in her stomach, her hand still tightly gripped around the handle.

"Medical assistance!" he yelled.

Two paramedics crossed the ARU line, their bulky equipment bouncing on their backs. Bone held her in his arms until they reached her, and he let them take over.

The ARU officers hoisted Mrs Willerby onto her feet. She tried to break free, but they restrained her.

"Please forgive us!" she pleaded with her daughter. "Please!" she screamed again.

"Get her out of here!" Bone ordered.

The ARUs manhandled the hysterical mother back to the arrest van.

Walker ran over. "Are you okay?" She pointed at the blood on Bone's shirt.

Bone glanced down. "Not mine."

The ARU officer in charge approached. "Just so you know, a second tactical unit dispatched to Craig Sneddon's property, has reported finding the body of a man in Sneddon's basement, and a car parked up outside registered to a Mr John Dulhoon."

"Oh Christ." Walker sighed.

"We've finally nailed the bastard." The officer smiled.

"Yea, but at what cost?" Bone replied and walked off towards the castle's ramparts, the daughter's desperate, tragic plea to die still ringing in his ears.

THIRTY-SIX

In stark contrast to the last time Bone had been on the island, the midsummer sunshine was beating down on the tiny jetty, tipping the temperature over thirty degrees. He helped Clare McDermid alight from the boat, and the rest of the guests followed behind. She was clutching a funeral wreath of white and cream lilies and carnations.

Clare stopped and stared up the path into the woods ahead.

"You okay?" Bone asked.

She glanced over. "Can I take your arm?"

"Of course," he said.

They set off together at the front of the funeral party, with Walker, Harper, Buchan, and Matheson following slowly behind.

Once through the woods, Clare stopped again when she caught sight of the tiny graveyard. She looked back as though she'd changed her mind.

"We don't have to do this," Bone said.

She shook her head and carried on, weaving slowly through the gravestones until they reached the two weatherworn Celtic crosses sitting side by side, where her husband had lost his life and she'd almost lost hers. She paused again and took a deep, shaky breath. Then, letting go of Bone, she moved forward alone and knelt by the first monument, cleared a few leaves, and placed the wreath by its base. She stared at the flowers for a moment, her eyes welling with tears, and she wept in silent pain.

The officers formed a semi-circle a few feet away and bowed their heads in respect. Clare placed her palm on the cross, mouthed a few breathless words, and tried to stand up, but almost toppled back over. Bone rushed over and helped her to her feet. They stood together for a few minutes longer, then she turned and took Bone's arm again. They walked back to the path and down to the beach and the boat waiting to take them back to Loch Gillan.

Back in the village, Clare stopped at the squad car Bone had arranged to collect and return her to Stirling.

"Would you like me to go back with you, or perhaps DI Walker?" he asked.

"No, I'll be okay. I need to be alone now. But thank you for all your kindness over the last few months. I don't think I would have made it without your support, Inspector Bone, and that of your counsellors."

"We have an outstanding team who got me through some very tough times." He helped her into the back of the car. "Are you sure you don't want to stay for something to eat before you go?"

"I think that's long enough here," she said and pulled the door shut. She wound down the window. "And please, thank your team for coming today. You are all in my heart."

The PC by the driver's door glanced over at Bone, who nodded, and he jumped in.

"Remember, you can ring me anytime," Bone said, and the car drove off.

He returned to the team waiting in front of the hotel.

"She's a very brave woman," Walker said.

"Mental demons like that don't just vanish into thin air. She has a long way to go, but hopefully, today will help with some closure at least." Bone sighed.

"I can't believe that vicious thug, Sneddon, is still denying all knowledge," Harper said.

"It doesn't really matter, though, as the SCU has more than sufficient evidence, including Jock Dulhoon's murder, to put him away for a long time. I doubt he'll see the light of day before he dies."

"But if he never pipes up, I suppose we'll never know if the parents did try to stop it. For Clare McDermid's sake, wouldn't that help her?" Buchan chipped in.

"I don't think it would make any difference. In her mind, her mother and father killed the love of her life, and there's no coming back from that, and she has a point, to be honest."

"Blood's thicker than water?" Harper suggested.

"In so many more ways than one." Bone ran his forefinger along the scar on his temple.

"At least we got a confession out of that poor hapless sod, Fergus, and his accomplice, and Dulhoon dropped his ridiculous voluntary manslaughter plea." Harper continued.

"But still no admission that he murdered Trough." Walker added.

Bone sighed. "That's still hanging over the investigation. The truth will come out in the end, though. It's a waiting game."

Walker turned to the others. "Right, that's that then. I think we'll get out of your hair, sir, and head back home."

Alice and Michael appeared from around the side of the hotel. "Not so fast," Alice ordered. "There's about a dozen burgers on a barbecue back at the cabin, and we're never going to plough through that lot on our own."

"Aww, who's that handsome young man on your arm there, Alice?" Walker smiled.

"Him? No idea," Alice pulled a face.

"Michael?" Harper asked.

Michael ran over and kicked his shin.

"Ouch," Harper yelled, grabbing the boy in a headlock, and rubbing at the top of his head until he screamed to stop.

"That's very kind of you, Alice, is it?" Buchan said. "Lovely to finally meet Mrs Bone."

"Likewise," Alice replied, "and this is our son, the one with the new giant haystack hairstyle."

Michael blushed and flattened down his ruffled mop.

"I'm sure you all must be hungry after all that, but if you'd prefer to drive back to Kilwinnoch for a deep-fried bridie?" Alice joked.

"Come on," Bone said.

They all headed over to the cabin.

On the way, Walker caught up with Alice. "I thought we'd be the last people you wanted hanging about here after we held him captive for so long."

"I thought, if it means I see him a little more, then I suppose I'll just have to put up with his groupies."

"Ha, aye right." Walker laughed.

"No, you're always welcome here, Rhona. Maddie and Erin, too."

Walker put her arm around Michael's shoulders, and he head-butted her side gently.

"That's some view you've got there," Buchan said, stepping onto the decking out the front of the cabin.

"Aye, I've seen worse," Bone agreed.

"Oh Jesus, the burgers are burning." Alice jumped down onto the narrow beach and marched over to the barbecue that was belching enough smoke to fill a herring factory.

"Smells good, though," Harper said. "It's such a shame Mark's missing out. He'll be so bloody furious when he finds out."

"Finds out what?" Mullens emerged from the cabin.

"Bloody hell, when did you get here?" Bone asked in surprise.

"About half an hour ago, and before you ask, no, I haven't touched any of the burgers or your fridge, or your drinks cabinet."

Bone shook his hand. "Thanks for coming, mate. You're looking good."

"Apparently, death does warm up after all," Mullens replied.

"You kept that quiet," Walker said.

"I know. It almost gave me an ulcer keeping my mouth shut. I'd love to have seen your ugly smacked-arse faces when you thought you had to go straight back to the concrete cancer that is our beloved station," Mullens said.

"Panic over, all is fine," Alice called up from the sizzling griddle.

Bone glanced into the cabin. "Did Sheila not come with you, then?"

"Ahem," Baxter interrupted, standing by the French doors.

"Don't tell me, quick ciggie?"

"Something like that." Baxter pushed her lighter into her handbag.

"Okay, so now we are all here, I just wanted to say thank you to every single one of you for the over and above effort you made during what was one of the toughest investigations we've had to deal with."

"Understatement," Harper said.

"At least you had a decent mattress," Walker interrupted.

"You're never going to drop that, are you?"

"Nope."

Bone thumped the decking balustrade. "Okay, everyone. I just wanted to say that today has been traumatic and tragic, with so many lives lost or almost destroyed. But we have to remember that our hard work has solved the most serious of crimes, but also we've helped to finally put one of Scotland's most notorious criminals behind bars and facilitate the dismantling of his entire operation. It's been a tough week, so I wanted to thank you most sincerely indeed. So let's stuff our faces and forget all about it for a wee while." He turned to Mullens. "Except you, of course. We've got some hay for you to chew on."

Mullens gave him the finger.

They all jumped down onto the beach, but Bone stopped Harper.

"I want to show you something."

Michael joined them, and they went back into the cabin.

"Nice in here," Harper said, admiring the juxtaposition of rustic living space and ultra-modern kitchen.

"This way," Bone replied.

They went into Michael's room.

"Thought you might like to see this," Bone said. "Tell him what you're working on, Michael."

"It's Luke Skywalker's T-65B X-wing starfighter," Michael said, sitting on a stool next to an arm-sized Airfix model.

"Oh my God!" Harper said, his jaw almost touching the floor. "It's magnificent."

"Thought you might appreciate it," Bone said. "I wanted to build a Galleon, but Michael had other ideas. Have you seen his Death Star?" He pointed to a black globe the size of a football dangling from the ceiling over Michael's bed.

"Oh my God," Harper repeated, and went over for a closer look.

Michael giggled.

"Didn't I tell you?" Bone nudged his son. "Worse than you."

"It even glows in the dark, like it's just about to explode," Michael enthused.

While Harper was distracted, Bone slipped out, and a few moments later, returned.

"This starfighter is so amazing. It's even got all the filthy burn marks along the side," Harper said, his eyes wide as saucers.

"Yes, it came with transfers that stick on but it looks real, don't you think?"

"It's bloody fantastic." He stopped. "Sorry, did I swear?"

"Haha, you're under arrest."

"Ahem," Bone said, at the door.

Harper turned.

"Sorry to disturb your geek party, but you have a promise to fulfil." Bone was holding up a pair of swimming shorts.

"What?"

"You thought I'd forgotten, but you've promised, more than once I might add, to try wild swimming with me."

"It was only a rhetorical statement, like maybe one day. I didn't actually mean it."

"Well, I do. Get these on and meet me on the jetty out front in five minutes."

"I'm not going now."

"I could have ordered you to do it in April. It's practically a bath out there now. Five minutes."

Michael slapped his hands together. "Chop-chop!"

"Not you as well," Harper complained. "Where's the bathroom?"

"Just there on the right. Five minutes!" Michael repeated.

Harper finally emerged from the cabin, his towel wrapped around his shoulders to cover his embarrassment as best he could.

Everyone cheered, and Bone jumped up onto the deck, already undressed for his swim.

"Follow me," Bone said.

Their audience cheered and whooped again, and Harper reluctantly complied.

"I'm really not sure about this," he said.

"Ah, get on with it, ya wee moose," Mullens bellowed and eyed up his trunks.

At the jetty, they both stopped.

"Now, the best way to do this is to lower yourself very slowly into the water to allow your body to adjust to the freezing cold water," Bone said.

"Ball freezing," Mullens shouted.

"Just stop it," Harper complained.

"Okay, so drop your towel," Bone said.

With more cat whistles, Harper shed his protective shield.

"Get yourself onto the top step of the jetty ladder."

Harper nervously shuffled forward and lowered himself down. "Here?"

"Yes, that's just about—"

Bone shoved him, and he toppled backwards into the water with a huge splash. The party erupted in laughter, and Bone dived in after him.

"Jesus Christ, Jesus Christ." Harper emerged, scrambling to get back to the deck.

Bone swam around him. "Count to five, Will, and swim gently."

"It's fucking freezing," he chattered.

"One, two, three, keep swimming, that's it, four and five."

Harper swam erratically alongside the jetty. "It's not so—" He continued to swim.

"It's bloody roasting," Bone said.

"Hardly," Alice shouted to him.

"How are you now, Will?"

Harper turned away from the jetty and headed towards the open loch. "It's getting easier," he called out.

"There you go. See, I told you." Bone looked back at his colleagues lined up along the deck. "Even if it is the height of the summer and warm enough for babies to swim in."

A roar of laughter filled the bay, and Harper continued to swim out towards the point.

"It's fabulous!" Harper shouted again.

"Hold on, that's too far." Bone swam after him, fearing a passing basking shark would mistake his pale-skinned colleague for a colony of trunk-wearing, peely-wally plankton.

THE END

T G Reid

DCI BONE RETURNS IN...

Night Comes Falling

*A DCI Bone Scottish Crime Thriller
(Book 6)*

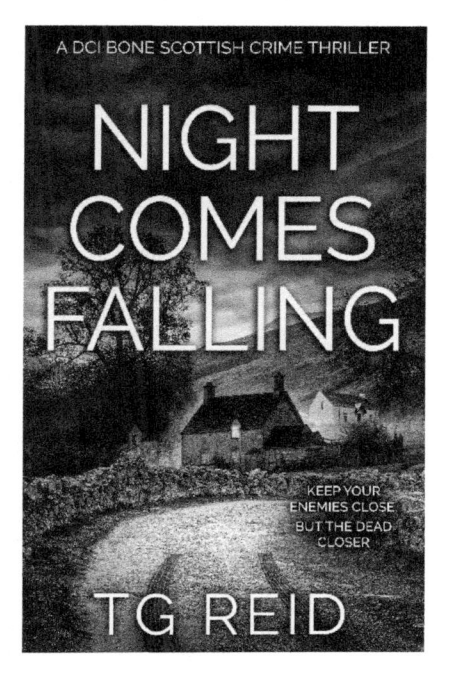

Pre-order Now on Amazon

T G Reid

JOIN MY DCI BONE VIP CLUB

AND RECEIVE YOUR *FREE* DCI Bone novel

T G REID

WHAT HIDES BENEATH

Secrets Always Surface

Scotland's hottest summer on record is already too much for DCI Duncan Bone. As if the water shortage wasn't enough, a body turning up at the bottom of Kilwinnoch's dried up reservoir sends Bone to boiling point.

With three suspects on the loose and time running out, the Rural Crime Unit needs to find the smoking gun and nail the killer before another victim is slain.

Visit tgreid.com to sign up and download for FREE.

ACKNOWLEDGEMENTS

Quite frankly, I would be up s**t creek without the love, support, patience and occasional /essential big stick form the following wondrous human beings.

Andrew Dobell, Emmy Ellis, Hanna Elizabeth, John Farnan, Diana Hopkins, Hannah Jane, Meg Jolly, Dylan Jones, Kath Middleton, Terri O' Brien, Jeni Reid, Gordon Robertson, Shakey Shakespeare

My majestic ARC Team – The Mighty Boners!

My dear friends, bloggers, reviewers and crime champions: Lynda Checkley,

Deb Day, Donna Morfett, Kelly Lacey.

To the magnificent Mr. Steve Worsley (the voice of DCI Bone) for his outstanding narration of the series.

Also, massive thanks once again to the splendiferous admin teams and readers at UK Crime Book Club and Crime Fiction Addict Facebook groups.

And last but never least

I wish to thank all Bone fans around the world who continue to buy, download, read, review, comment and message me with kind words of support and often accidental euphemisms that even I hadn't thought of.

Printed in Great Britain
by Amazon